spy school BRITISH INVASION

Also by Stuart Gibbs

The FunJungle series
Belly Up
Poached
Big Game
Panda-monium
Lion Down
Tyrannosaurus Wrecks

The Spy School series
Spy School
Spy Camp
Evil Spy School
Spy Ski School
Spy School Secret Service
Spy School Goes South
Spy School British Invasion

The Moon Base Alpha series
Space Case
Spaced Out
Waste of Space

Charlie Thorne and the Last Equation
The Last Musketeer

STUART GIBBS

spy school  BRITISH INVASION

A spy school NOVEL

Simon & Schuster Books for Young Readers

New York   London   Toronto   Sydney   New Delhi

SIMON & SCHUSTER BOOKS FOR YOUNG READERS
An imprint of Simon & Schuster Children's Publishing Division
1230 Avenue of the Americas, New York, New York 10020
This book is a work of fiction. Any references to historical events, real people, or real places are used fictitiously. Other names, characters, places, and events are products of the author's imagination, and any resemblance to actual events or places or persons, living or dead, is entirely coincidental.
Text copyright © 2019 by Stuart Gibbs
Cover design and principal illustration by Lucy Ruth Cummins,
copyright © 2019 Simon and Schuster, Inc.
British flag illustration copyright © 2019 by Thinkstock.com
Map art by Ryan Thompson
All rights reserved, including the right of reproduction in whole or in part in any form.
SIMON & SCHUSTER BOOKS FOR YOUNG READERS
is a trademark of Simon & Schuster, Inc.
For information about special discounts for bulk purchases, please contact
Simon & Schuster Special Sales at 1-866-506-1949 or business@simonandschuster.com.
The Simon & Schuster Speakers Bureau can bring authors to your live event.
For more information or to book an event, contact the Simon & Schuster Speakers
Bureau at 1-866-248-3049 or visit our website at www.simonspeakers.com.
Also available in a Simon & Schuster Books for Young Readers hardcover edition
Book design by Lucy Ruth Cummins
The text for this book was set in Adobe Garamond Pro.
Manufactured in the United States of America 0320 OFF
10 9 8 7 6 5 4 3 2 1
The Library of Congress has cataloged the hardcover edition as follows:
Names: Gibbs, Stuart, 1969– author.
Title: Spy School British invasion / Stuart Gibbs.
Other titles: British invasion
Description: First edition. | New York : Simon & Schuster Books for Young Readers,
[2019] | "A Spy School Novel." | Summary: "Follows the spies-in-training on a hunt to find the leader of the evil organization SPYDER and take them down once and for all"—
Provided by publisher.
Identifiers: LCCN 2018025412| ISBN 9781534424708 (hardcover) |
ISBN 9781534424715 (pbk) | ISBN 9781534424722 (eBook)
Subjects: | CYAC: Spies—Fiction. | Adventure and adventurers—Fiction. | Friendship—
Fiction. | Schools—Fiction. | England—Fiction.
Classification: LCC PZ7.G339236 Sn 2019 | DDC [Fic]—dc23
LC record available at https://lccn.loc.gov/2018025412

In memory of my uncle Alvin and my cousin Andy,
who always looked out for me

THE BRITISH MUSEUM

London,
England

TO THE
COTSWOLDS

RIVER THAMES

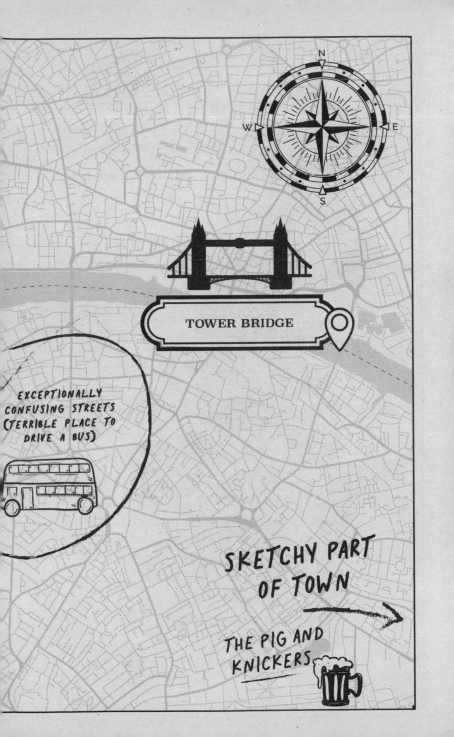

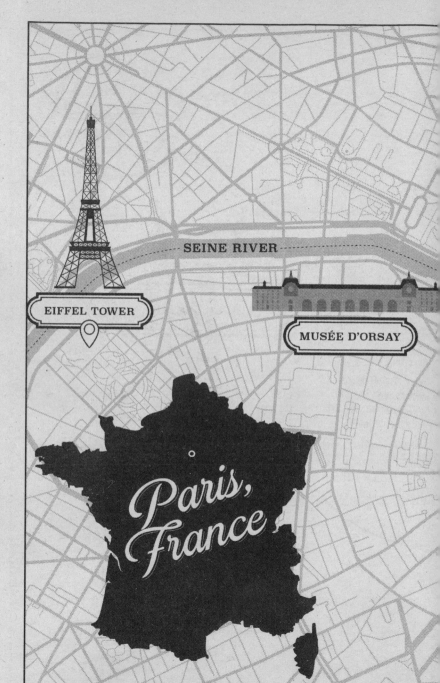

SEINE RIVER

EIFFEL TOWER

MUSÉE D'ORSAY

Paris, France

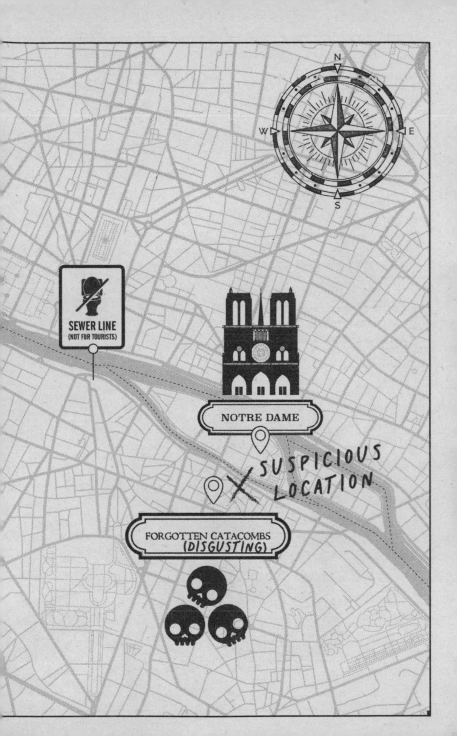

Contents

spy school BRITISH INVASION

To: All Members of Operation Screaming Vengeance
From: ████████████

Just a reminder that Screaming Vengeance is getting underway at 1200 hours today.
To reiterate what is at stake here:

We have a chance to take down SPYDER once and for all. This is the best opportunity we have ever had to bring this evil organization to its knees and finally end their wicked plans to cause worldwide chaos and mayhem once and for all.

However, this mission will certainly be dangerous. SPYDER is probably aware that we are coming for them and will do whatever they can to stop us. Which probably involves death. We're not dealing with the Boy Scouts here.

We will be going it alone. Since SPYDER has already corrupted untold numbers of agents at the CIA, we cannot trust anyone at our own agency. However, there are still hundreds of good CIA agents (we just don't know who they are), and they won't look kindly upon a rogue mission. Should anything go wrong—and I'm not going to sugarcoat the truth here; there's a very good chance that will happen—the CIA will disavow your status as agents-in-training.

Given this, I do not expect you to make your decision lightly. If you do not show up at 1200 hours to participate in the mission, I will understand. I won't be pleased with your cowardice, but that is your decision to make.

The meeting will take place in the penthouse suite at Aquarius, which I have commandeered from SPYDER. The elevators are secured, so when you arrive, call me on the intercom and give the password "Golden Eagle."

A light lunch will be served.

INTERROGATION

Aquarius Family Resort and Spa

Quintana Roo, Mexico

March 30

1300 hours

The key to defeating SPYDER, the most dangerous consortium of evildoers on earth, sat in the middle of the dining room table of the penthouse·suite.

It was an actual key, as well as a metaphorical one. A small, old-fashioned silver key, like the kind that would open a jewelry box. There was a tiny 1206 stamped on it.

Until that very morning, SPYDER had been plotting to melt half of Antarctica with several hundred tons of illegally obtained nuclear weapons and flood every coastal city on earth. Luckily, my friends from spy school and I had thwarted them. But while we had captured ten members of the organization, the leaders had managed to escape. Still, thanks to our actions, SPYDER was almost bankrupt, the leaders were on the run, and we had it on good authority that the key could help us finally defeat them once and for all.

The only problem was we had no idea how to do that.

Which was why I had been tasked with grilling Murray Hill about it. We were seated across from each other at the dining room table, wearing garish T-shirts and Bermuda shorts that we had bought at the resort gift shop. The outfits we had been wearing previously were soiled with mud and sweat, and all the rest of our clothes had sunk in a lake when our plane had crashed into it a few days earlier. Unfortunately, the resort gift shop had been our only option for new outfits.

"What does the key open?" I asked Murray, trying to sound as professional as possible.

"A lock, obviously," he replied. "It's a key. Duh."

"I know that. I meant *which* lock?"

"Oh. Sorry. You should have been more specific." Murray grinned broadly, then said, "I don't know."

I fought the urge to leap across the table and forcibly wipe that grin off Murray's face. Despite having been at the Academy of Espionage for a little more than a year, I wasn't very skilled at physical combat, but I was pretty sure that I could defeat Murray. Murray wasn't much of a fighter either. Like me, his strength was his brains.

At fourteen, Murray was only a year older than me, but he had already been a part of several devious plots with SPYDER. He had originally been a spy school student like me, lasting only a year before SPYDER corrupted him with the lure of easy money and power. Over the next fourteen months, he had become my nemesis, cropping up in one evil plan after another. However, SPYDER had recently betrayed him, trying to kill him along with me on our flight to Mexico. Now he wanted to destroy them; he was the one who had brought the key to our attention in the first place.

Unfortunately, Murray wasn't the slightest bit trustworthy. Despite how upset he was at SPYDER for double-crossing him, he had double-crossed me plenty of times. I was quite sure that no matter how much he claimed to want to bring SPYDER down, he was really only looking out for himself. He had spent the last few hours negotiating his own freedom in exchange for helping us—and now he appeared to have no actual help to give.

In the seat beside me, Zoe Zibbell tensed in anger. A fellow second-year student like myself—and one of my closest friends at the academy—she had even less patience for Murray than I did. "There must be two billion locks in the world," she said. "And you're telling us you don't have any idea which one this key opens?"

"Nope," Murray said pleasantly. "But Joshua Hallal probably does. After all, it was *his* key."

"Joshua is unconscious," I reminded Murray.

"I'm sure he'll come around sooner or later. It's not like he's in a coma or anything," Murray said, then thought to ask, "Is he?"

I looked to Zoe, unsure what the answer to this was myself. She shrugged in return.

Joshua Hallal was currently in the infirmary at the Aquarius Family Resort and Spa, a sprawling beachside hotel complex on the eastern edge of the Yucatán Peninsula in Mexico. At seventeen, he was even more devious and evil than Murray and had thus been the youngest member of SPYDER's elite leadership. Like Murray, he had also started as a spy school student before switching sides; unlike Murray, he had been an extremely good spy school student, regarded as one of the best in his class. His defection had been a great shock. Unfortunately for Joshua, being evil hadn't been as lucrative as he'd hoped—due to my friends and me thwarting SPYDER's evil schemes—and it had taken a serious toll on his body; in a previous battle with us, Joshua had lost an arm, a leg, and an eye. His limbs had been replaced with extremely high-tech robotic versions, while the missing eye was covered with a patch, all of which left him looking like a cyborg pirate.

Things had gotten even worse for Joshua that morning. The other leaders of SPYDER had left him behind when they fled, and in the process of trying to escape us, Joshua had fallen into a very large sinkhole and shattered his remaining arm and leg. The resulting pain had been so severe that he had lost consciousness, and he had remained that way through the ensuing hours while he had been rescued and doctors had placed his remaining limbs in casts.

Cyrus Hale, the expert spy who was our mission leader, was standing guard over Joshua in the infirmary, ready to interrogate him the moment he woke up.

"All right," I said to Murray. "Let's forget about what the key opens for now. This morning you said you would explain how to defeat SPYDER with it. So why don't you do that?"

"Do you mind if we order something to eat first?" Murray asked. "I'm famished."

"You're not getting anything to eat until you talk," Zoe said, with surprising menace for a girl who was less than five feet tall. Zoe didn't look dangerous, but she had excelled in her self-defense classes lately.

"Starving people is torture," Murray told her. "And torture is against the Geneva convention."

"You're not starving," Zoe informed him. "It's been ten minutes since you last ate. You cleaned out the entire mini-bar!"

"I get hungry when I'm stressed," Murray replied. "And turning in evidence on an organization like SPYDER is extremely stressful. They'll want me dead for this."

"They already want you dead," I told him.

"Oh. Right. Maybe *that's* why I'm so stressed." Murray searched the folds of his shirt, as though hoping to find an overlooked morsel of food in them. To my surprise—and his delight—he did. "Hey! Look at this! A rogue Skittle!" He popped it in his mouth.

For most of the time I had known him, Murray had the least healthy eating habits of anyone I had ever met. More than half of his diet had been bacon. However, over the previous month, he had been incarcerated at spy school and forced to eat nothing but health food, and he had become impressively lean and fit as a result. That had all gone out the window since our arrival in Mexico. Murray had quickly reverted back to his old diet. In the last hour alone, he had eaten at least a pound of Skittles, fourteen other assorted candy bars, six bags of chips, eight cans of soda, and a plate of leftover room service nachos. Even though the nachos were at least two days old and the cheese on them had congealed so badly it appeared to be bulletproof.

Thus Murray's recently toned body was decaying at a startling rate. His posture was slumped, he had sprouted a second chin, and his belly now bulged pregnantly.

"Come on, Murray," I said. "The sooner you open up, the sooner you can eat. We'll order anything you want from room service. I hear their BLT is incredible." I waved a room service menu tauntingly in front of his eyes.

This was a lie of my own. The resort wasn't about to send any room service at all to the penthouse suite. The management was very angry at us for destroying a good portion of the penthouse and the resort's water park while in pursuit of the SPYDER agents and was demanding several million dollars in damages and unpaid bills. Cyrus Hale had argued that the resort itself was at fault for renting out its penthouse to an evil organization in the first place and that he had half a mind to arrest the entire management team. That hadn't gone over very well, and now the Mexican police were trying to sort everything out. In the meantime, all room service and maid service had been canceled.

But Murray didn't know that. So he cracked. "Okay," he said. "But you have to understand, I only have a guess as to what the key does. I'm not one hundred percent sure."

"Spill it," Zoe said.

"As I'm sure you know, SPYDER is a tricky organization to work for," Murray explained. "There's no honor among thieves, and everyone is always worried about someone else stabbing them in the back. Literally. Even Mr. E, the head of the whole shebang, is worried about it. That's why he keeps his identity such a secret. Almost no one there has ever even seen him. I certainly haven't."

"The members of SPYDER don't even know who their own boss is?" I asked, incredulous.

"Nope. He always wears a mask—if he shows up for the meetings at all. Most of the time, he talks to us on the phone—and when he does that, he uses a voice modulator. No one knows squat about the guy: who he is, where he lives, where he came from . . . with one exception." Murray leaned across the table, excited by his own story. "There were always rumors that Joshua Hallal had figured this stuff out—that he had the real skinny on Mr. E—and that he was using it as leverage in the organization."

"You mean he was blackmailing his own boss?" Zoe asked.

"In a sense. If you think about it, it does explain some things. Like how someone as young as Joshua got to be in charge of so much. Yeah, he was evil and all, but there are people who were a lot more evil than him who didn't get promoted nearly as fast. Like the one guy who tried to blow up his own friend in an attempt to assassinate the president of the United States *and* get control of the entire US nuclear arsenal."

"That was you," I said.

"I know!" Murray exclaimed. "That was exceptionally evil! You think Joshua Hallal could have come up with something that exquisitely wicked? No way. So did *I* get a promotion for it? No. I got a price on my head."

"I'm also not your friend," I pointed out.

"You were once." Murray checked the folds of his shirt, hoping to find more escaped Skittles, but came up dry. "Anyhow, point is, everyone at SPYDER figured Joshua must have some serious dirt on Mr. E. Now, if *I* had access to that kind of information, I'd put it somewhere safe. Somewhere I knew Mr. E wouldn't be able to find it—and yet somewhere others could still access it with my permission. And then I'd set up some sort of fail-safe system. Like a computer program that will disseminate the information unless I enter a code every day. Then I'd say to Mr. E, 'If you ever kill me, then I'll fail to enter that code. And when that happens, e-mails will go out to the heads of every spy and law enforcement agency on earth, directing them to the exact location where I've stored all the info on you, and within twenty-four hours, you and your entire organization will be destroyed.'"

"So you think that's what Joshua set up?" Zoe asked. "You think this key provides access to all the information we need to bring SPYDER down?"

"Yes. That's exactly what I think." Murray was a

consummate liar, but because of this I had a very good sense of when he was telling the truth. He appeared to be doing that now.

Even so, I wanted confirmation. I leaned close to Zoe and whispered, "What do you think?"

"I think this is legit," she whispered back. Her big round eyes were alive with excitement.

She had showered after our slog through the jungle in pursuit of Joshua Hallal that morning. In our close proximity, she smelled wonderfully of lemon verbena hotel shampoo.

The thought occurred to me—as it had quite often lately—that Zoe was much more attractive than I had realized. I pulled away from her quickly, before I did anything awkward, and then realized that pulling away from her quickly was awkward itself. "We should tell the others," I said.

"Why don't you do that?" Zoe picked the silver key up off the table and scrutinized it closely. "Maybe I can find some clues as to where this goes." She then shifted her gaze to Murray. "Plus, I'm not letting this weasel out of my sight."

"You can just admit you have a crush on me," Murray taunted. "You don't have to make excuses."

"Ick." Zoe looked physically ill at the thought of having a crush on Murray. "It's because I don't trust you, you slimeball."

I got up and left the dining room, heading through the

penthouse suite in search of the rest of my team.

There were only seven of us on Operation Screaming Vengeance, and four of us hadn't even graduated from spy school yet. It was a woefully small force to be going up against an organization like SPYDER, which was so powerful and secretive, we really didn't even know how big it was. And yet we had little choice: SPYDER had turned so many agents inside the CIA, we couldn't trust our own agency anymore.

Despite this, at least one of the spies-to-be on our team was as talented and gifted as any adult in the CIA. Erica Hale was only two years older than me, but she was a legacy in the spy game: Her family could trace its lineage back all the way to Nathan Hale in the American Revolution, and her grandfather was Cyrus, the man in charge of our operation. Cyrus had been training Erica to be a spy since she was a toddler, and she had excelled under his tutelage. If Erica hadn't been my partner on all our missions, I would have died several times over.

So I went to see her first. Partly this was because I trusted her the most, and partly it was because I wanted to impress her with what I had learned from Murray. Erica and I had a complicated relationship; I knew she liked me, but she had been taught from an early age that friendships were liabilities in the spy game. And thus, romances were simply a very bad idea. I was trying to convince her that friendships could be assets—and that romance might be even better—with mixed results. In the midst of a mission, Erica tended to be as business oriented and emotionless as a filing cabinet, but I desperately wanted affirmation from her anyhow.

Erica was a few doors down from the dining room, in the master bedroom, interrogating another spy my age.

This was Ashley Sparks, a SPYDER agent-in-training. Ashley had once been a promising young gymnast for the United States, but after missing the cut for the Olympic team by a hundredth of a point (and a questionable call by a judge) she had turned to evil. Ashley had a habit of combining two words into one, like "swawesome" (sweet plus awesome) or "jidiot" (jerk plus idiot)—which was the one she used to describe me and my team the most.

"I'm not telling you jidiots anything," I heard her say through the bedroom door. "I don't care what you do to me."

"Really?" Erica responded. "Let's put that to the test."

I figured Erica was bluffing, but I wasn't completely sure, so I hurriedly entered the room without knocking.

Ashley was seated in a chair with her wrists bound behind her back. She wore her usual outfit, a spangled gymnastics leotard, and had on glittery eye shadow. Except for the scowl on her face, she didn't look like someone who worked for the most evil organization on earth.

Erica stood before her, wearing her usual outfit as well, a

sleek and stylish black unitard with a white utility belt. She was holding a small blowtorch.

"Erica!" I exclaimed. "We're not supposed to torture the prisoners."

Erica frowned at me like I had just told her Christmas had been canceled. "She just said she didn't care what I do to her."

"I think that was a figure of speech." I turned to Ashley and said, "Hi." Even though she was evil, it seemed like the polite thing to do.

"Get bent, ferd," Ashley said.

I looked to Erica, confused. "Failure plus nerd?"

"Freak plus nerd, you jidiot," Ashley said.

"Watch the attitude," Erica warned her, "or I'll charbroil your kneecaps."

"There's no torturing!" I said again. "It's against the law."

"We're in Mexico, not America," Erica pointed out. "US law doesn't apply here." She stepped toward Ashley and fired up the blowtorch. A lick of blue flame burst from the tip.

Ashley's bravado faded slightly. Beads of sweat formed on her upper lip.

"I know what the key does!" I said quickly, before Erica could fricassee any parts of Ashley's body. "You don't have to use that!"

Erica flipped off the blowtorch, looking disappointed.

We stepped to the side, and I relayed what Murray had told me. As I spoke, her annoyance faded and she became more and more intrigued.

"Very interesting," she said when I was done. "Of course, we still need to know where the key goes."

"Joshua's the one who would know that. Maybe we should check in with your grandfather."

"Good idea." Erica set the blowtorch down and looked to Ashley. "We're not done here," she warned, then led me out of the bedroom.

"You were only bluffing with that, right?" I asked, once we were out of range for Ashley to hear us.

"You think she'd hesitate to use that if the tables were turned?" Erica asked.

"You didn't answer my question," I said.

"You didn't answer mine, either."

I frowned, unsure what I believed Ashley would do. She and I had once been friends, back when I had been sent to infiltrate SPYDER's evil spy school. When Ashley learned I was working for the good guys, she felt I'd betrayed her, and she'd hated me ever since.

We passed another bedroom. Inside, I could hear another interrogation going on. Mike Brezinski, my closest friend from growing up and the newest recruit to spy school, was trying to get information from Warren Reeves, the newest recruit to SPYDER. Warren had defected from spy school, where he had been exceptional at camouflage and minimally talented at everything else.

"Stop playing dumb with me," Mike warned. "Tell me everything you know about the leaders of SPYDER."

"I don't know anything," Warren said defiantly. "Ask anyone. My mind is completely empty." It took a moment for what he'd said to sink in. "Wait a minute. That's not what I meant. . . ."

We passed two more bedrooms, the doors of which had been hastily modified so that they could be locked from the outside, turning the rooms into makeshift prison cells. Paul Lee and Vladimir Gorsky, two of the world's most successful illegal arms dealers, were in those rooms. No one had gotten around to interrogating either of them yet.

"Did Ashley give you any information about the leaders of SPYDER?" I asked.

Erica shook her head. "She says she never met them."

"But she and Warren went to their yacht and were there for hours. . . ."

"The leaders were on a different deck. Ashley and Warren weren't allowed to access it. They only communicated through written notes, which were all burned afterward. Mr. E doesn't communicate electronically. No e-mail. No texts. No cell phone calls. So all messages are completely untraceable."

We passed through the kitchen, which had taken a beating. Erica had fought off four of SPYDER's henchmen in it a few nights before, using every appliance at her disposal. Erica was a formidable opponent. Most of the pans had skull-size dents in them, and a waffle iron was still embedded in the wall.

Three of the henchmen were now out on the deck, bound to patio chairs; the fourth, Dane Brammage, the biggest and most dangerous, was also in the infirmary. He had suffered a severe concussion when a waterslide had collapsed on his head while he was pursuing us earlier that morning.

Erica's parents were in charge of questioning the henchmen. However, that's not what they appeared to be doing.

Erica's father (and Cyrus's son) was Alexander Hale, who until recently had been regarded as one of the finest spies at the CIA. Then it had been revealed that his entire career was built on lies. Alexander was really only good at two things: making himself sound good and taking credit for other people's work. Despite lacking competence, though, he still meant well and tried his best.

Erica's mother was Catherine Hale, who would have been regarded as one of the finest spies at Britain's MI6, except for the fact that almost no one on earth knew she was actually a spy. She was that good. Most people thought she was simply an exceptionally enthusiastic museum curator—including Alexander Hale, until that very morning.

The Hales had been divorced for a few years, but Alexander had still been very upset to discover that his wife had been lying to him about what she did for their entire lives—even though, as a fellow spy, he should have been lying to her about what he did as well. He hadn't been able to let go of this all morning.

"I can't believe you weren't honest with me!" he exclaimed. Alexander was wearing a bespoke three-piece suit, and he would have looked impressive in it anywhere but the tropics. In the scorching heat and humidity, he was soaked in sweat.

"Oh, for Pete's sake, Alexander," Catherine said. Even though she was obviously exasperated, her melodious British accent made her sound happy and cheerful. "When were you ever honest with me?"

"That was different!" Alexander protested. "When I lied to you, it was for the good of the United States."

"Well, when I lied to you, it was for the sake of England."

"That's not as important as lying for the United States. America is more important than England."

Catherine wheeled on Alexander, fire in her eyes. "Do not make this argument about which country is better," she warned. "If you do, I will crush you."

The three henchmen looked to Erica and me helplessly. It appeared that they would have all been happier being tortured than listening to Alexander and Catherine bicker any longer.

Erica didn't seem to want to hear it anymore either, because she quickly interrupted. "Ben got some information about what the key goes to."

Catherine and Alexander turned to her, looking embarrassed about being caught in midargument. Catherine's anger immediately dissipated. "That's wonderful, Benjamin!" she trilled. "What did you learn?"

Before I could launch into the explanation again, Erica's phone sounded an alarm. Erica immediately grew worried—which was of great concern to me, because Erica almost *never* looked worried. Anything that could shake her was most likely extremely bad news.

"That's Grandpa's emergency signal!" she exclaimed, then spun on her heel and raced back the way we had come. I followed her, as did Catherine. Alexander attempted to follow us, but he first tried to dramatically slap a clip of ammunition into his gun and dropped it. The bullets scattered all over the rooftop patio, and Alexander promptly slipped on them and landed flat on his back, groaning in pain.

The Hale women and I left him behind. After several missions with Alexander, I knew we were probably better off without him. We raced back through the penthouse suite, then down the emergency staircase. Erica and Catherine were both in exceptionally good shape. It took everything I had to keep up, while neither of them seemed the slightest bit out of breath.

The whole way, Erica kept trying to call her grandfather, but there was no answer. This worried Erica more, which made me worried as well.

We finally reached the ground floor and charged out of the stairwell and into the main building at the resort. The infirmary was a small room just off the lobby. There wasn't much to it: two examination tables, a closet full of medication, and a few chairs. The doctors at the resort mostly treated minor tourist issues like sunburn and traveler's gastrointestinal distress.

The Hales and I froze in shock at the sight that greeted us.

A great struggle had obviously taken place. The furniture had all been overturned and broken. The pharmacy had been looted. Three people lay unconscious on the floor: the doctor, a nurse—and Cyrus Hale. Cyrus's phone was clutched in his hand. Sending the alarm code to Erica had probably been his last act before passing out.

Joshua Hallal and Dane Brammage were gone.

TYPOGRAPHY

Aquarius Family Resort and Spa

Quintana Roo, Mexico

March 30

1330 hours

Catherine immediately ordered Erica and me to make sure that Cyrus was all right, then ran off in the direction she figured Joshua and Dane would have gone. To my surprise, Erica listened to her. The only thing that could stop her from chasing down enemy agents, it seemed, was concern for her grandfather.

She immediately dropped to his side, placed her fingers against the carotid artery in his neck, then heaved a sigh of relief. "He's alive. He has a pulse, but it's weak."

I checked the doctor and the nurse the same way and found they were still alive as well. Both had syringes jabbed into their rear ends with the plungers depressed, indicating that they had been sedated. Meanwhile, Cyrus had been rendered unconscious the old-fashioned way: He'd been clocked on the head. There was a welt the size of an apricot just above his right eye, while a metal bedpan lay close by, severely dented from the impact with his skull.

Erica removed some smelling salts from one of the many pouches on her utility belt and waved them under her grandfather's nose, but he remained stubbornly inert.

There was a gurney folded up against the wall, most likely the same one Joshua had been brought in on. Erica leapt to her feet and unfolded it. "C'mon. Let's get him back to the penthouse."

"You're sure it's safe to move him?" I asked.

"Safer than leaving him here. For all we know, SPYDER might still have operatives on the loose." Erica ducked into the pharmacy closet to grab some of the remaining bandages and painkillers. "Might as well stock up on these while we're here. Given that lump on his head, he'll need them."

Cyrus was heavier than he looked; for an older man, he was almost pure muscle. It took us a while to get him onto the gurney.

Catherine returned as we wheeled Cyrus out of the

infirmary, a frown etched on her face. "They're long gone. They stole a car from the valet at the front of the hotel and sped off a good five minutes before I got there. I never could have caught up to them."

"Did you tell the police?" I asked.

"Of course, but I doubt it will do any good," Catherine replied. "Joshua and Dane are probably lying low already."

"Lying low?" I repeated, surprised. "Joshua has two fake limbs and the other two are in casts, while Dane is the largest human being I've ever met in my life. How could those two possibly not get noticed?"

"You'd be surprised," Catherine said.

Cyrus remained unconscious while we wheeled him from the infirmary to the private elevator for the penthouse suite and then rode it up to the top. Alexander happened to be passing by when the doors pinged open. He shrieked upon seeing the state of his father.

"What happened?" he gasped.

"Joshua and Dane got the jump on him somehow," Erica said.

Alexander looked as though he couldn't make sense of this. "That's not possible. No one's ever gotten the jump on Dad before."

Catherine put a hand on his arm and spoke in a surprisingly caring tone, a hint of what their lives might have been like long ago. "Cyrus is getting on in years. And he was retired until recently. Maybe he's a little off his game."

Alexander nodded understanding, but the news that his father was getting old only seemed to make him feel worse. He followed behind us morosely as we wheeled Cyrus into the one room that didn't have a SPYDER agent incarcerated in it.

This was the room that Dane Brammage had been using. The bed had buckled under his bulk, as though a hippopotamus had been sleeping in it.

Cyrus stirred slightly on the gurney and murmured something softly.

"Dad?" Alexander asked, rushing to his side. "Can you hear me?"

Cyrus's eyes flew open. "The enemy is getting away!" he exclaimed. "We need to stop them!"

"He's conscious!" Alexander exclaimed.

"The redcoats have fled from their positions on the Delaware!" Cyrus went on. "Let's rout them and end the British scourge once and for all!"

"He's conscious, all right," Erica said sadly. "Unfortunately, his mind's in the wrong century."

Cyrus glared at all of us. "Don't just sit there!" he shouted. "Go tell General Washington I need more troops! The fate of the Continental Army hangs in the balance!"

"Take it easy, Cyrus," Catherine said. "You've had a nasty bonk on the noggin."

Cyrus's eyes went wide at the sound of her accent. "She's British!" he shouted to us. "There's a spy in our midst! Seize her and I'll have her tarred and feathered!" He lunged for her, but his legs went out on him and he collapsed to the floor, unconscious again.

Catherine looked to Alexander, concerned. "I haven't seen Cyrus much in the past few years, but I'm assuming that's an atypical episode?"

"Yes," Alexander agreed. "Although once, when I was quite young, he got a bad concussion and thought he was a member of the Mongol Horde for a week." He knelt down, hooked his hands under Cyrus's arms, and hoisted him into the bed.

Cyrus started singing "Yankee Doodle" in his sleep.

"I'm afraid this takes him out of commission," Catherine said. "We can't have our leader thinking he's still fighting the American Revolution. We'll have to proceed with Operation Screaming Vengeance without him."

"Couldn't we wait a bit to see if he comes around?" I asked hopefully. Cyrus was crotchety and gruff, but he was still a good spy with a great deal of experience. I didn't like the idea of our team shrinking even smaller than it was.

"It's too dangerous for him," Erica said. "Another good whack on the head could send him into a coma. And it'd be dangerous for us as well. We need every member of our team to have their full mental faculties, or this mission will be a failure."

"This mission's *already* a failure," I pointed out. "All we have is a key—and the only person who knows where to find the lock it fits just escaped with his favorite hit man."

"It might not be quite that bad," someone said behind me.

We all turned around to find Zoe emerging from the dining room, clutching the key in one hand and dragging Murray behind her with the other. "I think I have a lead," Zoe announced.

"That's a relief," Mike said, exiting the room where he'd been interrogating Warren. "Because I'm getting nowhere with this guy. The doorknobs in this place know more about what SPYDER is up to than he does."

"What do you have?" I asked Zoe expectantly.

Zoe held up the key triumphantly. "There's a number printed on this—1206."

"Yes," Erica said dismissively. "Probably denoting the number of the safe-deposit box or whatever it goes to. Unfortunately, that doesn't do us any good if we don't know where the box is."

"The number isn't important," Zoe said. "At the moment, I mean. But what *is* important is that it's printed in Tottenham font."

The rest of us stared at Zoe blankly. Except Mike, who

gaped at Zoe in amazement. "Holy cow," he said. "You're into typography?"

Zoe turned to him, her eyes flashing with excitement. "Into it? I *love* it."

"Me too!" Mike exclaimed. "How has this not come up before?"

"I don't know!" Zoe said. "I was going to try to start a typography club at school last month, but then Ben got wrongfully accused of trying to assassinate the president, and that kind of sucked up all my spare time. . . ."

"Whoa," I said. "Hold on. What's typography?"

"The art and technique of arranging and designing type to make written language and numbers more legible, readable, and appealing," Mike said. "People who study it are called typophiles—although I prefer the term 'font-natic.'"

"Font-natic!" Zoe giggled. "That's great! I love it!"

I looked at Mike, shocked that he had an interest I didn't even know about—and a bit jealous that he and Zoe were bonding over it so quickly. "How come you never told me you were into this?"

"I thought you'd think it was lame," Mike replied.

"It *is* lame," Murray said. "Liking fonts is even lamer than collecting posters with kittens on them. . . . Waaaugh!" He suddenly tripped and went crashing painfully to the floor.

It didn't appear that Erica had moved at all, and yet I was

quite sure she was the one who had tripped him. After all, Erica had a secret affinity for posters with kittens on them. They were all over the walls of her dormitory room, along with a surprising array of gingham throw pillows. I had sworn never to reveal any of this under penalty of death.

"So tell us, Zoe," Catherine said, ignoring the fact that Murray had just face-planted into the tile floor at her feet. "Is there a way forensic typography can tell us where this key might go?"

"I think it can at least point us in the right direction," Zoe said eagerly. "Tottenham is an extremely rare font. It was created during the 1850s by an amateur typographer in London named Samuel Hewes, but it was rarely used." She pointed to the numbers on the edge of the key. "As you can see, the font is a bit too narrow, and so all the letters and numbers blur together a bit."

Mike cringed in disgust. "Ooh. That is a terrible font. It's almost as bad as Durkin."

"Ugh," Zoe agreed. "Do not get me started on Durkin. Worst. Font. Ever."

"You have a least favorite font?" I asked Zoe, unable to help myself.

"Doesn't everyone?" Mike asked.

"No," Murray replied, peeling himself off the floor again.

"Mine's Ipswitch," Mike said.

"Ipswitch!" Zoe groaned. "That one's awful!"

"I kind of like Ipswitch," Alexander said.

"Really?" Zoe asked. She and Mike shared a look and laughed, like Alexander had just showed up at a high school football practice and announced that he was captain of the chess team.

Erica said, "I realize you two are having a lovely time bonding here, but we're getting off track. What does all this font stuff mean?"

Zoe said, "Due to its shortcomings, Tottenham wasn't used by very many people *except* for Samuel Hewes. And Hewes wasn't a typographer by trade. He only dabbled in it. His *real* job was as a silversmith."

"So," Erica said, "the chances are, Samuel Hewes made that key some time during the 1850s in London."

"Exactly!" Zoe exclaimed.

"Sorry," Alexander said. "I'm completely lost here."

"It's really quite brilliant." Catherine was pacing the kitchen now, her eyes alive with excitement. "All we have to do is find out what large commissions Samuel Hewes received around that time and that ought to narrow down where the key is from."

"Why large commissions?" Alexander asked.

"Because the number on the key is 1206," I guessed, putting things together myself. "Meaning that there were more than twelve hundred locks being created."

"Correct," Catherine agreed. "And while banks must routinely commission that many safe-deposit boxes these days, back in the 1850s it was a much less common occurrence. In fact, I'd surmise that it would be extremely rare indeed. Especially someone asking for the type of craftsmanship evident in this key. Samuel Hewes might not have been much of a typographer, but given the quality of this, he was an expert silversmith. In fact . . ." Catherine paused by Zoe's side to take a look at the key again. "This is really quite exquisite. A small bank probably wouldn't be able to afford quality like this on such a large scale. You'd be talking about only a handful of larger banks, or . . . Oh my." Her mouth made a perfect little O of surprise as a thought struck her.

"What is it, Mom?" Erica asked.

"I think I know where that key goes: the vaults in the British Museum."

"Which one?" Alexander asked blankly. "There must be hundreds of museums in Britain."

"No. *The* British Museum," Catherine corrected. "That's what it's called. It's one of the largest archaeological museums in the world. Home of the Rosetta Stone and the Parthenon Marbles and a dozen mummies and thousands of other objects from antiquity."

"Mummies?" Murray asked, paling a bit. "Mummies give me the creeps."

"I'm sure the mummies feel the same way about you," Erica said, then turned to her mother. "You're sure about this?"

"No," Catherine admitted. "But it makes sense. The vaults of the museum were commissioned in the 1850s to store everything the museum was collecting from around the world. I've been down there. It's an enormous space. There must be at least five thousand storage units of various sizes." Catherine ran her fingers through her hair. "I'm such a fool. I should have thought of it the moment I saw that key. Come, children. Gather your things right away." She spun and headed back down the hall.

The rest of us followed her. "You really think Joshua Hallal stored this stuff in a museum rather than in a bank?" I asked.

"The British Museum's vault is as secure as any bank," Catherine told me. "Perhaps more. After all, it hasn't been robbed in more than a hundred and fifty years."

"If it's so secure, how are we going to get into it?" Mike asked.

"That's no problem at all," Catherine replied. "My cover is a museum curator! I already have the credentials. Now, where did I leave my passport?" She ducked around the corner, already working on her packing list.

Mike flashed the rest of us an excited grin. "Looks like we're going to London!" he exclaimed.

TRANSIT

En route to London

March 31

0600 hours

Normally, getting to London on the spur of the moment would have been difficult.

For starters, it should have been expensive. Until only a few months before, I hadn't even been on an airplane, due to the costs. My parents both worked at a grocery store; we lived in the farthest fringes of the suburbs of Washington, DC, and the only vacation we had ever taken was to Virginia Beach. The only way I could afford spy school was because it was free; the CIA paid for the program. (Meanwhile, my parents thought I had an all-expenses paid scholarship to

St. Smithen's Science Academy for Boys and Girls, which was a front for spy school. The entire junior spy training program—and my participation in it—was top secret. Erica was the only student whose parents knew what she was really doing.)

Luckily, Catherine Hale had our travel taken care of. She had flown one of MI6's jets to Tulum, parking it at a private airfield close to Aquarius that catered to wealthy clients and foreign governments. We didn't have to pay a thing for our flight. The fuel was pricey, but MI6 had an expense account at the airport. (Apparently, it was common for British spies to head to Mexico and the Caribbean on "fact-finding" missions.)

The second potential problem was that none of us had brought passports. When we had set out a few days earlier, we hadn't even known we would be leaving the country. I didn't even own a passport—or so I had thought.

It turned out Cyrus had procured one for me. Once he had learned I was in Mexico—along with Mike and Zoe—he had called in a dozen favors at the State Department to have passports made for us right away, then brought them down. He hadn't known that we'd end up heading to England, but we would have needed the passports anyhow to get back to the United States.

Erica had been carrying her passport all along, tucked

into a secret pocket in her utility belt, as Erica was always prepared for emergencies. Or adventure.

Murray Hill had his passport too. He was always prepared for fleeing the country at a moment's notice.

Given that, we wasted no time getting out of Mexico. Joshua Hallal was on the loose and certainly knew where we were going—it was *his* secret location, after all—so he would be trying to beat us there. Our only hope was that Joshua, being an easily recognizable fugitive with his broken limbs, wouldn't be able to arrange transportation to London as quickly as we could.

We still had the rest of SPYDER to worry about too. We didn't know if they were aware of Joshua's potential evidence against them, but we figured there was a good chance they'd be heading that way as well.

There was no choice but to leave Cyrus behind. The last time I had been on a small plane for a mission—only three days before—I had nearly been killed in a missile attack. We all hoped we wouldn't have anything like that happen to us again, but if we did, there was no way Cyrus could have handled it in his addled state. His friends in the Mexican police promised to take care of him—as well as keep an eye on the other SPYDER agents we had apprehended. The rest of us headed to the airstrip.

The jet was nicer than the one I had come to Mexico on,

but that wasn't saying much. Then again, we didn't plan to do much except sleep. I'd had very little rest over the past few days, and even though it was early afternoon when we took off, I was exhausted. This was the case for my fellow agents-in-training as well. Despite being eager to explore their newfound mutual love of fonts and typesetting, Mike and Zoe quickly passed out in their seats; Murray, who had the metabolism of a house cat, was asleep soon afterward. Even Erica was tired; she had probably slept far less than the rest of us and had certainly fought more bad guys. Normally, she prided herself on her vigilance, but with her mother on board, she allowed herself the luxury of legitimately relaxing for once.

After Catherine had the jet in the air, she engaged the automatic pilot and dozed herself.

So I let myself nod off as well. The seats on the jet were much bigger than the ones on a regular passenger plane, allowing me to curl up in mine. It wasn't the best sleep I'd ever had, as my fears about SPYDER kept clawing their way into my dreams, but I still managed to get enough to recharge my batteries.

I woke somewhere over the North Atlantic.

Everyone else was still asleep, save for Alexander Hale. He was seated in the chair across the aisle from me, fidgeting anxiously in the darkness. When I had first met Alexander, he had been the epitome of the suave, debonair gentleman spy, always cool, calm, and collected. The ensuing years had not been kind to him. His fraudulent nature had been exposed, and he had fallen from grace. Now he was sullen and morose. He still looked awfully good in a suit, though.

"Are you all right?" I asked.

Alexander shrieked in fright and tried to leap from his seat, but his seat belt held him down. It took him a few moments to gather his wits. "Sorry about that, Benjamin. You caught me by surprise. I thought you were still asleep."

"Have you slept at all?"

"Me? Er, no. When you're up against a foe as crafty as SPYDER, there's no time for sleep. You have to train yourself to go without it. Why, once, when I was on a mission in the Punjab, I went twelve entire days without so much as a nap."

"I don't think that's true, Agent Hale."

Alexander frowned, disappointed I had caught him in a lie. Back when we'd first met, he had regaled me with dozens of similar stories, and I'd believed every last one of them . . . for a while. "Of course. I was merely testing your mental acuity. Keeping you on your toes. The truth is, I . . . well . . ." Alexander seemed to be trying to come up with a plausible lie, but couldn't do it and gave up. "The truth is . . . I'm too nervous to sleep."

"Really?" I couldn't hide my surprise. I had known Alexander to be many things—foolish, egotistical, incompetent—but never nervous. If anything, his over-blown image of himself often gave him delusions that he could handle things he had no business handling.

"Yes," Alexander replied. Then he leaned across the aisle and whispered to me, even though everyone else on the plane was asleep. "This may come as a shock to you, but . . . I'm not quite as good a spy as I appear to be."

"That's not a shock," I told him. "I'm well aware that you're a bad spy."

"Oh," Alexander said. "I don't know if 'bad' is the right word. . . ."

"You're right," I agreed. "I should have said 'terrible.'"

Alexander lowered his eyes. "Is it that obvious?"

The correct answer to that was "yes." But instead, I said, "Erica told me a lot about you."

"Yes. She's the good spy in the family. I should have known I couldn't put anything past her." Alexander sighed heavily. "I never had a choice about being a spy, the way you did, Benjamin. This is the family business. I was expected to do it, no questions asked. No matter how many times I told my father I didn't want to."

"I always thought you *liked* being a spy."

"I liked the *image* of it. And I'm pretty good at that part: looking suave, being charming. But as for the actual spy-ing part—the dangerous missions and defusing bombs and nearly getting killed on a regular basis—I'm not a fan. I was never good at any of that stuff, to be honest, no matter how much my father tried to teach me. I only got into the academy because I was a legacy, and I nearly flunked out my first year, which would have upset my father even more. No Hale had ever flunked out of spy school. But then I discovered what I *was* good at: cheating."

I sat up slightly, not surprised by the revelation, but by the fact that Alexander had admitted it. Now that the truth was coming out, however, it seemed as though he'd been desperate to tell someone for a long time. "Really?"

"That's right. I cheated my way through spy school. I stole test answers. I came up with ingenious ways to copy the work of my fellow students. I took credit for things other people had done. I admit, it was loathsome and despicable— but it was also exceptionally good training for being a spy. In this business, it often doesn't matter how you get the job done, so long as it gets done. In fact, in my senior year, I was busted for cheating on my final exam in Advanced Deception. My professor was so impressed by my methods, though, that she gave me an A-plus. It was the best grade I ever got. In fact, I would have done worse if I'd actually studied for the exam and taken it the right way.

"The problem was, once I got started along that path, I didn't know how to stop. I kept using the same techniques that had gotten me through spy school, and they kept serving me well. I moved up in the ranks. People respected me. Everyone wanted to have me to parties. Eventually, I suppose, I started to believe my own lies. I started to think I was truly a good spy, even though I wasn't good in the slightest." Alexander shook his head in shame. "I mean, I was *married* to a secret agent for years and I never had an inkling. She must have thought I was the world's biggest idiot."

"Maybe," I said. When Alexander cringed in response, I quickly added, "But I know she was really in love with you. That wasn't a lie."

Alexander managed a weak smile. "The point is, I might have pulled the wool over my own eyes for years, but now I've pulled it back off. I *know* I'm the weak link on this mission. Even worse than those of you who have only been in school for a few months. But this isn't a normal mission. In the past, if I screwed up, it didn't really matter to me who got hurt. This time it does. Catherine and Erica are on this mission, and if I mess up, something bad could happen to them."

"Maybe not. They're two of the most competent spies I've ever met."

"It's also possible that something bad could happen to *you*. And though you're not my son, Benjamin, I feel somewhat paternal where you're concerned." Alexander's smile broadened.

I smiled as well. My own feelings about Alexander had changed over the past year: I had at first been in awe of him, then disdainful, then downright disgusted, but I realized that I'd now developed a sort of begrudging friendship with him. "Catherine and Erica will look out for me."

"I'm sure they will. But that doesn't mean they'll be able to protect you." Alexander's face grew grave. "I know you've gone up against SPYDER before, and I know that it has been dangerous. But this time you're going to face down the leaders of the organization, who are as devious and malicious a group of scoundrels as there has ever been."

I swallowed hard. Nothing Alexander had said was a surprise to me, and yet I had been so eager to bring down SPYDER, I had buried my concerns. Now, hearing that Alexander had those same concerns—and that he was actually worried himself—brought everything to the surface again. SPYDER was an incredibly cunning and deceitful organization, which had corrupted the CIA—the very agency tasked with bringing it down. The idea that my friends and I could defeat such a formidable enemy seemed almost impossible.

And yet we had thwarted SPYDER before. Several times.

"This time is different," I said, doing my best to convince myself that it was true. "We're not going up against SPYDER directly this time. We're merely chasing down a way to destroy them."

"When is a tiger most likely to attack you?" Alexander asked me. "When you're trying to take away something it wants—or when you're trying to hurt it?"

"Um . . . ," I said. "It seems like both of those situations would be dangerous."

"Really?" Alexander asked. "Hmm. Maybe that wasn't the best analogy. Would it work better if I used a polar bear?"

"Not really."

"How about a rattlesnake? Ooh! Or a tarantula? That would be better because a tarantula's a spider. So spider/SPYDER. It works on multiple levels."

"That's all right. I understand what you're trying to say. SPYDER will be even more dangerous than usual this time around."

"Exactly! The leaders know we're coming for them, and they will do *anything* to protect themselves. Are you prepared for that?"

"Not really," I said. "But I'm willing to do what's expected of me anyhow."

Alexander smiled. For a moment I saw a hint of the old, rakish superspy who had come to recruit me. "I appreciate your honesty, Benjamin. As well as your determination. I could stand to be more like you. I, too, am willing to do what's expected of me, to the best of my abilities."

"It's about time," said someone else.

Alexander and I turned to see that Erica was sitting awake in her seat behind us.

"How much of that did you hear?" Alexander asked, reddening around the ears.

"Enough. Do me a favor, though?"

"What is it, Pumpkin?"

"Okay, do me two favors. One: Don't ever call me 'Pumpkin' again. Two: Try not to do what's expected of you to the best of *your* abilities. Try to do even better than that. Because the best of your abilities, so far, hasn't been that good."

Even though what Erica was saying wasn't particularly nice, her tone wasn't as icy as usual. There was actually a tiny bit of warmth to it, indicating that she was trying to give her father advice rather than simply dismissing him.

Alexander picked up on this too. His smile spread wider across his face. "It's a deal, Buttercup."

"Ugh. Don't call me that, either." Erica unbuckled her seat belt and started for the cockpit.

After she had passed, Alexander leaned across the aisle and whispered to me conspiratorially. "She used to love being called that when she was a child."

"Buttercup?" I asked, surprised.

"*Princess* Buttercup. She used to wear a pink dress and a tiara and everything."

"That was a disguise," Erica said. "I was only pretending

to be a secret agent going undercover as British royalty." She shook Zoe awake gently, then roused Murray with a smack to the face.

"Hey!" he said, coming to. "What was that for?"

"A couple thousand things," Erica replied. "But it's time to get up anyhow."

As she said this, the plane dipped downward slightly. I lifted the shade over my window. Broad daylight spilled into the body of the plane.

Below us, I could see long green tracts of land, the curve of a wide river, and in the near distance a large city.

"Is that London?" I asked.

"That's right," Erica replied. "It's time to get to work."

CULTURAL APPRECIATION

The British Museum
London, England
March 31
0800 hours

One of the biggest drawbacks to being a spy is that you don't get to do much sightseeing.

Technically, I saw a good amount of the Yucatán Province in Mexico, but not in the fun, relaxing way that most tourists would. My visit to an archaeological site was at the tail end of a death march through a hostile wilderness; the only time I got to ride any of the waterslides at our hotel was when I was fleeing for my life down one; and instead of having an enjoyable ATV tour led by a knowledgeable guide, my ATV experience had been a hair-raising chase through the jungle with the fate of the world hanging in the balance.

My visit to London looked like it would be more of the same. My whole life, I had dreamed of visiting that city; I had a long list of places I wanted to see there. But we had no time for tourism. True, I was heading to the British Museum, which was a major tourist attraction, but I was only going there to acquire Joshua Hallal's secret cache of information. In the meantime, I merely got brief glimpses of Parliament, Buckingham Palace, and the London Eye as we sped past them in a taxi from the private airstrip.

All seven of us were crammed into one small van. MI6 had not been alerted to our arrival; Catherine feared that her own agency, just like the CIA, was corrupted by double agents for SPYDER. The weather was stereotypically British: cold, gray, and rainy.

My fellow spies-in-training and I were all dressed for the wrong climate. We only had our tropical resort wear, and there wasn't time to stop to get properly attired. Catherine had promised to take us to a decent haberdasher later in the day, but for the time being we had the heat in the cab cranked to eleven.

The adults were better off. Alexander's suit, which had been horribly out of place in the tropics, now looked quite fashionable, save for a few splatters of mud. Since Catherine had just come from England, she had the right kind of clothes to return in: an extremely stylish dress, boots, and a raincoat.

Meanwhile, my parents had no idea that I was in England at all. Or that I had been in Mexico the previous few days. They thought I was spending my spring break working on a big thesis project at St. Smithen's. Not that I could have alerted them to the fact that I was in London anyhow. The mission was top secret, and we were all banned from any non-mission communication. We couldn't even use our phones, as the GPS would allow us to be tracked and pinpointed by our enemies. (Catherine, Alexander, and Erica had special CIA phones that were immune to tracking, but the rest of us hadn't been issued those yet. Not that it would have mattered; my phone, along with Murray's, Zoe's, and Mike's, had been destroyed when we'd fallen into a cenote a few days earlier.)

Erica watched the scenery slide past the window, though I doubted she was looking for landmarks like I was; knowing Erica, she was plotting potential escape routes should we have to flee for our lives. Murray was grumbling about how hungry he was and asking if we could stop to get some food every three minutes. Mike was still catching up on his sleep, having wakened only long enough to shuffle across the tarmac from the jet to the taxi. But Zoe, crammed into the seat beside me, seemed equally bummed that we couldn't visit any of the places we were passing.

"Are we near the Tower of London?" she asked hopefully as we wormed our way through the city. "I've always wanted to see that."

"I'm afraid we're heading the opposite direction from it right now," Catherine informed her.

"How about Harrods? Or Covent Garden? Or Claridge's? Oh! I've always wanted to get tea at Claridge's."

"Don't bother," Erica told her. "All they do is charge you eight pounds for a cucumber sandwich with the crusts cut off."

"Erica, don't be a wet blanket," Catherine said, then told Zoe, "Tea at Claridge's is simply delightful. Perhaps, after we take care of SPYDER, we could visit there."

"That'd be great!" Zoe exclaimed.

"At this point I'd pay eight pounds for a three-day-old tuna sandwich," Murray groused. "I'm starving."

"How is that possible?" I asked him. "You ate all the snacks on the plane."

"They were *healthy* snacks," Murray grumbled. "With wheat germ and fiber and other stuff that hamsters eat. There was barely any fat in them at all."

"I promise you, we will get more food—and clothing— soon," Catherine told all of us. "But as it is there is no time to waste. For all we know, Joshua Hallal is already here. You'll just have to be hungry—and chilly—a bit longer."

"That's easy for her to say," Murray muttered under his breath. "She has a raincoat and a slow metabolism."

"It shouldn't be too much longer," Catherine said. "We're here."

The British Museum was at the top of my list of places to see in London, but once again it looked like my visit would be very different from that of the standard tourist. We weren't even coming in through the main entrance. Instead, we had pulled up to a security gate around the back. Rather than facing the museum's famous neoclassical facade, with its rows of Greek columns, we were facing a drab employee parking lot and three overflowing dumpsters. Catherine flashed her official curator ID to the bored guard on duty, informed him that she was leading a small field trip there for her daughter's school, and handed over our new passports. The guard gave them all a cursory glance and then waved us through.

I shook Mike awake. "Hey," he said drowsily, prying his eyes open. "Is this the museum?"

"Yes," I told him.

Mike stared out the window at the closest dumpster. Two rats the size of Chihuahuas were fighting to the death over a soggy pizza crust. "Doesn't look that impressive," Mike observed.

We all hopped out of the cab and hurried through a light drizzle to the employee entrance. There was a small foyer where another guard was on duty, controlling a second set of secure, alarmed doors. The guard observed the arrival of our wet, improperly dressed group with concern until Catherine breezed through the door. Then her face lit up as though she were a small child who had just found Santa Claus coming down the chimney. "My stars, Mrs. Hale! It's been far too long since you've graced this entrance."

"It certainly has, Lizette," Catherine agreed. "My work in the States has taken much longer than I expected. You're looking well, though."

Lizette started to make more small talk, but then flushed as Alexander came through the door. If Alexander was still nervous about our mission, he wasn't showing it. Instead, he was displaying his usual calm and collected guise. Lizette was obviously attracted to him—as most women seemed to be. "Mr. Hale! You're here too?" Lizette exclaimed, then looked to Catherine. "Are you two back together?"

Catherine reddened a bit. "He's . . . just here for a visit."

"Oh, I hope it's more than that." Lizette leaned forward and whispered conspiratorially to Catherine. "He's a fine piece of man, that one. And the two of you always looked smashing together, if I might say."

Catherine handed our passports to Lizette, seeming like

she was in a hurry to change the subject. "We've brought some friends from the States as well today. I thought I'd give them a bit of a behind-the-scenes tour, show them the spots that regular tourists don't get to see."

"That sounds like fun." Lizette leafed through the passports, freezing when she got to Erica's. She then looked up in shock at Erica herself. "My stars. Is this Princess Buttercup, all grown up?"

Erica went rigid. "I don't know what you're talking about."

"It *is* you!" Lizette exclaimed. "I can't believe it! It's been more than a decade since I last saw you! Oh, you were always so adorable in your dresses and your crowns."

"Dresses?" Murray asked, on the verge of cracking up. "Crowns?"

"Oh my, yes," Lizette went on. "And she was always lugging around a little princess doll as well. What was her name? Fifi Frimsy-Popp?"

"You had a doll?" Zoe asked Erica, astonished.

"I was pretending to be a secret agent undercover as British royalty," Erica said through gritted teeth. "The doll was part of the costume."

"Sure it was, Princess Buttercup," Murray taunted.

"Call me that one more time and I will forcibly remove your head from the rest of your body, then cram it up your rear end," Erica threatened, then looked to her mother. "Can we please go? Time is wasting."

"Of course," Catherine said, then turned to Lizette. "You don't mind if we hurry along, do you? There's so much to see."

"By all means!" Lizette pressed a button under her desk, which allowed the secure doors to click open. "Come on in, folks. Have a good time!"

There was a security booth with a metal scanner and an X-ray machine, but Lizette trusted the Hale family so much, she didn't even ask us to pass through it. We were allowed direct access to the museum. Which was good, because I was relatively sure Catherine was packing a weapon or two.

We passed through the security door quickly, nodding our thanks to Lizette. Alexander flashed her a warm smile, and she fluttered her eyelashes at him in return.

"This way," Catherine told us, leading the way through the secure doors. Now that she didn't have to make friendly small talk with Lizette, she was all business.

I had been hoping our path through the museum might lead us past some of the famous artifacts that were stored there, so that I could at least get to see them, even if only for a few seconds. Sadly, that wasn't the case. Instead, Catherine immediately guided us down a set of stairs and into the basement level of the museum, which looked like the basement level of pretty much every other building I had ever been in. It was drably painted, dingily lit, and—because it was in London—slightly damp. Since we had arrived early, no other employees were there yet, or at least we didn't see any. The subterranean hallways were eerily empty.

Catherine obviously knew her way around; she moved quickly through the maze of halls, never bothering to check a map, the same way that Erica was always able to navigate through the secret tunnels under spy school.

Zoe was equally upset that this was the only part of the museum we were seeing. "Catherine," she asked. "If we actually find what we're looking for, is there any chance we might be able to see some of the museum? Even for just a minute or two?"

"Ugh," Murray said. "All that's up there is a bunch of old rocks. You're like the only person on earth who would think that's interesting."

"Me and the five million people a year who visit the museum," Zoe pointed out.

Catherine said, "It would be a tragedy to bring you here and not let you see any of the collection. If we're right about the key, I'd love to show you the head of Pazuzu, but then, I've always had a soft spot for the Babylonian empire. Ah! Here we are!"

We arrived at a set of double doors that didn't look much different from any of the other doors we had passed, except that there was more security around them. Wires snaked away from them, indicating they were alarmed, security cameras were mounted overhead, and there was a card reader on the wall. Luckily, Catherine's ID worked in it. She swiped the card through and the doors clicked open.

We passed into a small glass-enclosed anteroom with another secure door on the other side. "This is for climate and pest control," Catherine explained. "Many of the objects stored down here are extremely delicate. We don't want them getting moldy or eaten by bookworms." She slid her card through a second reader, and the next set of doors clicked open too.

We entered the vault. It was almost the size of a soccer field—so big it was hard to make out the far end of it. Every once in a while there was a massive column shoring up the floor above. As opposed to the dingy hallways we had just come through, the vault was beautiful. The walls were almost entirely taken up with lockboxes, but they were all fronted with polished wood, rather than being dull metal. There were thousands of them, stretching off into the far recesses of the room.

Instead of drab industrial flooring, there was stylish carpeting, although paths had been worn in it over the decades of use. The middle of the room was filled with dozens of long wooden tables, but there were also several spots with large, plush leather chairs. Due to the climate control, it was much warmer and drier than the rest of the basement. Every now and then there was an ancient artifact on display, simply for the people lucky enough to visit: a few gorgeous ink drawings from Asia were framed on the walls, while intricate sculptures sat atop pedestals throughout the room. A few curators had come in early; two were perusing a large ancient map on one of the tables, while others were reading ancient texts or carefully examining small artifacts. They all looked up curiously as we entered, then immediately returned to their work. It was like being in a library, although one that was kept secret from most of the world.

"Wow," Zoe gasped, echoing my thoughts. "This is amazing."

"Of course you'd say that," Murray taunted. "Books, art, and scientists. It's nerd heaven down here."

The lockboxes along the walls varied greatly in size. There were long, flat ones that I figured held maps and paintings, thicker ones that probably held texts, and larger ones for bulkier artifacts. Each had a number on a tiny brass plate. The ones closest to our left started at 1 and then continued clockwise throughout the room.

Zoe and Mike both gasped with excitement when they saw the font the numbers were etched in. "Tottenham!" they exclaimed at once, then beamed at each other proudly in a way that made me feel slightly jealous.

"Looks like we're on the right track, thanks to you font-natics," Catherine said, impressed. Then she fished the silver key from her pocket and ordered, "Let's find number 1206."

Although the lockboxes were numbered sequentially, the fastest way to find the right one was still to fan out to different points of the room and see who ended up the closest to it rather than circumnavigating the whole place in a clump. (We had all learned this in a "Time Optimization" seminar a few weeks before.) I headed toward the farthest side, though I kept a close eye on Murray. Despite his claims to be against SPYDER, I still didn't trust him. I wouldn't have been surprised if he'd concocted this entire plan to get us into the vault so that he could steal something.

If Murray was up to no good, though, he didn't play his hand. Instead, he went directly to another part of the wall and diligently began searching for the right box.

"I've got it!" Mike yelled from across the room.

All the other curators immediately shushed him.

The rest of us hurried over.

Box 1206 was the size of a loaf of bread, surrounded by other boxes of about the same size. A stunning Japanese watercolor print hung on the wall above it.

Erica ran her hand along the edge of the boxes around it, then displayed a residue of dust her fingers had picked up. "A lot of these haven't been opened in years," she observed, then pointed to 1206, which was dust-free. "But not this one. It's been opened more recently."

"How recently?" Alexander asked.

"I don't know," Erica admitted. "But sometime in the last few months, I'd guess."

There was a small keyhole at the edge of the wooden door. It looked like it was the right size for Joshua's key, but there was only one way to tell for sure.

We all looked to Catherine expectantly.

"Here goes nothing," she said, sounding slightly nervous that this might have all been a mistake. She inserted the key in the lock and turned.

It worked.

There was a *click*, and the wooden door swung open, revealing . . .

"It's empty," Mike said.

Indeed, there was nothing inside except shadows. A sense of gloom immediately descended on everyone. Catherine made a squeak of dismay.

"That's just great," Zoe muttered.

"Hold on," Erica said. "Sometimes there's more than meets the eye." She reached through the tiny door. The lockbox went farther back than we had realized, far enough to almost swallow her entire arm. Erica felt around inside, then broke into a sudden smile. Then she triumphantly withdrew her hand.

She was holding a single flash drive.

"That's it?" Alexander asked. "That's all there is?"

"This is plenty," Erica replied. "This single drive can hold more information than all the books in most libraries. Let's get out of here before anyone else comes looking for it." She closed the door to the lockbox, turned the key, then put it in her pocket.

We all headed for the door. The other curators were so intent on their work, they barely seemed to notice us.

I kept an eye on them, however. I'd been caught off guard by SPYDER enough times that I didn't trust anyone. Even the elderly, harmless-looking woman scrutinizing jade trinkets might have been a double agent.

She wasn't, though. She didn't try to kill us as we left the vault, and neither did anyone else.

I breathed a sigh of relief as we returned to the basement hall and found ourselves without anyone else around once again. Catherine led us back through the maze.

Erica removed her smartphone and a connecting cable from her utility belt, then jacked the flash drive into the phone.

"What's on there?" Zoe asked eagerly.

"Give me a moment," Erica said. "It'll take a little while to load."

"In that case," Mike said, then turned to Catherine, "is there a men's room around here anywhere? I really need to go."

"There's a water closet right around the corner ahead," Catherine replied.

Mike looked confused. "Why do you keep water in a closet? And am I supposed to pee in it?"

Catherine tittered. "No, you silly goose. In the British Isles, we call a bathroom a water closet."

"Ah," said Mike. "Well, I need to stop there. I've had to go for a while, but I didn't want to hold up the investigation."

"I could stand to pop in there myself," Alexander said.

I was thinking it might not be a bad idea to make a pit stop when Murray said, "Do any of you smell something strange?"

"Besides you?" Zoe asked.

"Ha ha." Murray sneered. "I'm serious. There's a strange smell down here. It's familiar, but I can't quite place it."

Catherine stopped, concerned, and sniffed the air. "A sort of floral scent?"

Alexander inhaled. "I believe that's *Eau de Luxuré*. It's a very expensive French perfume. One of my main contacts in France wears it all the time."

"I know that perfume too," Murray said, suddenly growing worried. "Jenny Lake wore it."

"Your evil ex-girlfriend?" I asked him.

The same thought occurred to everyone at once. "Take cover!" Erica yelled, but we were all doing it anyhow.

Which was a good thing, because at that very moment, Jenny and seven other heavily armed enemy agents stepped around the corner ahead and opened fire on us.

ESCAPE PLANNING

The British Museum
London, England
March 31
0845 hours

One of the things I had become very good at as a spy-in-training was taking cover.

This was a talent I had already possessed upon arriving at spy school, honed by years of eluding the bullies, creeps, and other assorted miscreants at my middle school. But now, after a year of being suddenly attacked, ambushed, waylaid, and blindsided—both in class and on missions—I truly excelled at fleeing at the first sign of trouble. If taking cover had been an Olympic event, I would have been a serious contender for the gold.

The moment the enemy force began rounding the corner, I turned tail and fled for my life. By the time anyone managed to get a shot off, I was diving around a corner. Thankfully, my fellow spies were doing the same thing, even Murray, who generally had the reflexes of a sloth in a coma. If nothing else, he had an exceptional sense of self-preservation and stayed right on my heels as I ran.

Our flight wasn't sheer cowardliness. One of the early things we had learned at spy school was Prybil's First Law of Self-Preservation: The best way to avoid being shot is to not be in the path of a bullet. Though it seemed glamorous to stand one's ground, whip out a gun, and fire back, this usually kept you in the very place that the bad guys were aiming. Besides, most of us didn't have weapons to whip out and fire back with anyhow.

So we all dashed around the corner as bullets tore up the hallway behind us. Although I had started out slightly ahead of the others, Catherine quickly flew past me. (Perhaps I would only win silver in Olympic Cover-Taking, being edged out by Britain.) "Follow me!" she ordered, then led the way around yet another corner.

Mike was right beside me as we ran, a slightly pained look on his face. "They couldn't have waited until *after* I got to the bathroom?" he moaned.

We could hear the pounding of enemy footsteps behind us. Jenny was our age, but the rest of her team were adults: powerful, intimidating men and women. "You can run, Murray!" Jenny Lake shouted. "But you can't hide! I'll find you soon enough!"

"You picked a real winner there," Zoe told Murray. "Is she working for SPYDER now?"

"I'm not sure," Murray said. "She's extremely fiendish and immoral. There's a lot of evil organizations that would want to hire her."

"What did you even see in her?" I asked.

"*I'm* extremely fiendish and immoral," Murray replied. "You need to have common interests to make a relationship work."

"This way!" Catherine shouted, shoving through a doorway. We all piled through it behind her just as a fresh fusillade of bullets ripped through the air.

We were in a stairwell, which we quickly ascended to the floor above.

As we did, alarms began to sound. Klaxons echoed through the museum and red lights flashed.

We emerged into an enormous gallery filled with breathtaking Egyptian sculptures. There were giant sphinxes, towering pharaohs, and a granite orb the size of a refrigerator delicately balanced on the point of a squat stone obelisk. At the far end was an entire temple that had been uprooted from the Nile and rebuilt inside the museum. The gallery was the sort of place I would have been thrilled to visit had I not been running for my life. Zoe must have felt the same way, because I heard her gasp in awe despite our dire circumstances.

Sadly, we couldn't even pause for a moment to take in the spectacle. Not only did we have people chasing us, but the alarms had triggered an emergency lockdown. Huge steel plates were quickly descending in the doorways. They were dropping like the portcullises in old castles—only, instead of keeping intruders out, these were designed to lock people *in*.

"Run!" Catherine shouted—as though that hadn't occurred to any of us—but we were too late. The steel plates came down with ominous *thud*s, cutting off our escape.

There was only one place to take shelter: the Egyptian temple. We blatantly ignored the signs that told us to stay off the antiquities, jumped over the protective railing, and ran up the steps, slipping behind the ancient columns of the entrance just as Jenny and her cohort of fellow evildoers emerged from the stairwell.

Although we needed to stay quiet, Alexander couldn't help himself. He was freaking out about the security system. "Why on earth are there steel doors on the exits?" he gibbered. "What possible reason could there be for a security system like that?"

"It's to deter thieves," Catherine said, calmly removing a small, stylish handgun from a holster on her ankle. "The idea is, if they trip the alarm, they won't be able to escape from here with anything."

"But we aren't thieves!" Alexander said desperately. "And now we're trapped in here with the enemy!"

"Yes. I don't think the security system was designed with this scenario in mind." Catherine tossed a second gun to Erica. "Use that wisely, dear. There are only six sedation darts in it."

Erica frowned. "Sedation darts? You didn't bring a *real* gun?"

"You know I don't like killing people," Catherine said sharply.

"I doubt those guys feel the same way," Zoe pointed out.

"They're *evil*," Catherine reminded her. "We should do our best not to sink to their level. Plus, with bullets, if we miss one of them, we could damage one of the artifacts in this room, and I would really be dismayed if I did that."

"You're worried about the *artifacts?*" Alexander whined. "If we don't take out these people, we're going to be *dead*. Did you bring a gun for me?"

"Of course not," Catherine replied. "The last time you had a sedation gun, you shot yourself in the foot and slept through your entire mission."

"You know about Budapest?" Alexander asked, surprised.

"I know about everything," Catherine replied.

Meanwhile, Mike was crouched behind the column closest to me, his legs crossed tightly over his privates. "Could you guys just take care of these people quickly?" he asked. "I *really* need to go."

I peered out from behind my column. This was the first time I'd had a decent look at our pursuers. For a brief moment, I was struck by the absurdity of the fact that I was hiding in a six-thousand-year-old temple *inside* a whole other building, but I forced myself to focus on the issue at hand.

There were eight of them, including Jenny. They were dressed for action rather than style, with protective Kevlar vests and running shoes, and they were moving deliberately through the gallery toward us, slipping from the cover of one statue to the next, trying to stay protected from any weapons we might have. All wore helmets with mirrored visors, so I couldn't see much of their faces except their mouths, which made it hard to tell them apart. Jenny was recognizable only because she was talking the most.

"There's no escape," she taunted. "We know you're in the temple. You might as well just give yourselves up."

"Jenny!" Murray shouted. "I know things ended badly between us, but do you think you could find it in your heart to not kill me?"

Jenny said, "I'd be happy to let all of you go free if you'll just hand over what you found today."

"Really?" Murray asked excitedly. "Well, if that's the case, I'll bring it right out." He turned to Erica and said, "Hand it over."

Erica didn't take her eyes off the approaching enemies. "No way. She's bluffing, you pinhead. Ben, figure out how to get out of here, *fast*."

"*Really* fast," Mike corrected. "Or I'm going to wet myself."

"I'm working on it," I told them. Which was true. In addition to checking out the approaching enemy, I had also been casing the room. There were four entrances blocked by the steel doors. There were no windows and the walls all appeared to be a good foot thick. The only other exit was the door to the stairwell, which was now on the opposite side of the gallery and had eight enemy agents cutting off access to it.

The agents were now halfway across the room, fanning out to approach us from all sides, still moving from the cover of artifact to artifact. Jenny peeked out from behind the obelisk that held the giant granite orb and yelled, "Are you guys handing over the goods or not?"

"We'd be happy to!" Erica yelled back, doing a bit of bluffing herself. "Just drop your weapons, and we'll hand it right over."

"I'm afraid that's not an option," Jenny said. "You see, we have to . . . Ow!" She reeled backward as Catherine plugged her in the neck with a sedation dart, then called to her team, "They've got sedatives and they're really fast acting. . . . Unnngghhhh." She collapsed to the floor.

"One down, seven to go," Catherine noted.

Erica looked at me expectantly. "Well? What's the escape plan?"

"Er . . . ," I said. "I don't quite have one yet."

"You don't have a single idea?" Erica asked, annoyed.

"Well, I have *one*," I said. "You could sedate all the bad guys and then we could just wait for the police to come."

"That's the best you've got?" Erica snapped.

"It could work, couldn't it?" I asked.

"I don't think that's very likely," Catherine told me. "They're more heavily armed than we are, and they're going to be far more cautious now that I've taken out Murray's girlfriend."

"Ex-girlfriend," Murray corrected. "She had issues."

One of the seven remaining enemy agents dashed from behind a sphinx, racing to the cover of a sarcophagus. Erica and Catherine both fired at him, but the agent ducked away just in time and they missed.

"See what I mean?" Catherine asked, sounding upset with herself.

That meant we were down to nine darts for seven bad guys. And at the rate they were moving, the bad guys would have us surrounded within minutes.

I cased the room again, desperately trying to come up with something.

"Erica," Zoe said, surprisingly calm given the circumstances. "While you're busy fending off the bad guys, why don't you let me look at your phone? I can see what's on Joshua's flash drive."

Erica didn't say anything, but she must have thought the idea was all right, because she removed her phone and slid it across the floor of the temple to Zoe.

I noticed Mike sneaking back into the far recesses of the temple. Unfortunately, Catherine noticed him too. "Michael," she said sternly, "please tell me you're not heading off to relieve yourself in the temple."

Mike froze, obviously caught in the act. "I'm checking to see if there are any secret passages out of here," he lied.

Catherine sighed heavily. "I understand that this is a dire situation, but I will not have my agents urinating on the antiquities."

"The bad guys are *shooting* the antiquities!" Mike exclaimed. "I'm just going to pee on them! I'll bet thousands of ancient Egyptian boys peed on this temple! Maybe it's really a giant ancient water closet!"

"Michael," Catherine said. "Please show some decorum."

"I need to go so badly, my eyes are turning yellow," Mike said desperately. "If I don't get out of here soon, I'm going to burst!"

The moment he said this, an idea seemed to strike him. He turned to me, so excited that he appeared to have momentarily forgotten his urgent need to pee. "Ben! I have an idea about how we can get out of here!"

I looked to him expectantly. "What?"

"Remember when my brother accidentally backed the car through the garage door?" he asked, then pointed across the gallery.

I considered what he was pointing at, grasped what he meant, then looked to Catherine. "Do you have any idea how thick those steel plates are?"

"About an inch, I think," she replied.

I made some estimates about mass and inertia, then quickly did some calculations in my head. "I think that would work."

"What would work?" Catherine asked, sounding slightly worried.

I didn't answer her, though, because I knew she wouldn't like what I had in mind.

An enemy agent bolted from his hiding place behind a stone elephant. Erica fired two shots at him. The first bounced off his Kevlar vest, but the second caught him in the arm. He yelped in pain, then angrily opened fire on us as he collapsed into unconsciousness. Bullets pocked the hieroglyphics on the opposite side of my pillar.

"You heathen!" Catherine shouted at him as he passed out. "These are priceless relics!"

Meanwhile, Zoe didn't seem much happier as she examined Erica's phone. "Um, Erica. It looks like this flash drive was booby-trapped. When you jacked in, it activated a worm and fried your phone."

Erica cursed under her breath. She sounded more annoyed about this than she did about the approaching bad guys.

"Is that bad?" Alexander asked.

"Yes," Erica said with a sigh. "I should have predicted that. Now we still don't know what's on that drive, and I've sacrificed my phone." She looked at me. "What's the plan for getting out of here?"

"I'm going to need a laser pointer, a good-size rock, and a way to throw it hard," I told her.

"Benjamin," Catherine said. "Is this escape plan going to do damage to any of these priceless artifacts?"

"Possibly," I replied. "But on the positive side, it will keep the bad guys from doing damage to any of us."

"I don't approve," Catherine said.

"Mother," Erica said, "we don't have a choice."

"Where are we supposed to get a rock?" Murray asked. "We're in a museum, not a quarry."

Erica considered that for a moment, then ran from her pillar to mine. I couldn't be quite sure, but it appeared that she moved a fraction of a second slower than she was capable of, giving the enemy agents the tiniest bit more time to react.

Three of them sprang from their hiding places and opened fire. Bullets tore into the pillar as Erica dove behind it.

Catherine hit one of the enemy in the arm with a dart. She collapsed with a groan, thwacking her head on a caryatid.

Five agents left. Six darts.

A few large chunks of pillar, loosened by the bullets, tumbled to the ground.

Erica picked one up and showed it to me. "Big enough?"

"Yes," I said, impressed.

"Good," Erica said, then tossed her gun to Mike. "You're on guard duty. I'll get the other supplies."

"You trust him with a gun but not me?" Alexander asked, hurt.

"Yes." Erica removed a small black device from her utility belt and slapped it into my hand. "Laser pointer." Then she reached under the top of her sleek black outfit.

"Erica!" her mother gasped, horrified. "What are you doing?"

"We need a way to throw this stone hard," Erica said. "I'm getting a sling." With that, she deftly removed her bra.

I averted my eyes.

"Please," Erica said. "It's just underwear. Now, let me know where you need me to throw this." She dropped the stone into one of her bra cups and began to whirl it around.

I aimed the laser at the exact point I had calculated the stone needed to hit. I wouldn't have trusted anyone else to make the shot, but I was quite sure Erica could handle it. She was the student-body champion in every single marksmanship competition. Whereas I was lucky to ever come within eight feet of the target.

Catherine, who was already upset that her daughter was using her underwear as a weapon, now paled when she saw where I was aiming. "Oh no. I don't like any of this one bit."

Erica leapt from behind the pillar once again, whipping the stone around in her bra.

The enemy agents made a sudden, coordinated attack, all leaping from their hiding places at once and opening fire.

Erica let go of her bra and tumbled across the floor to the cover of another pillar. The stone sailed through the hail of bullets, flew across the room—and nailed the giant granite orb at the exact spot I had marked.

The orb rocked slightly, but that was all it needed to dislodge from its delicate perch on the top of the obelisk. There was a crack like a gunshot as it broke free, and then it crashed to the floor and began rolling across the gallery.

The noise caught the enemy agents by surprise. They reflexively looked that way, which allowed Catherine and Mike to shoot two more of them.

The remaining agents found, to their dismay, that they were directly in the path of the giant orb. While they scrambled out of the way, we raced from the temple and fell into line behind the ball, keeping it between us and our enemies as it rolled through the gallery.

One of the enemy clambered up onto a sarcophagus to avoid being flattened, leaving her rear end the perfect target, Catherine pegged her hard, and she collapsed, snoring atop the effigy of Thutmose II.

There were now only two agents left.

Despite this small victory, Catherine looked sick to her stomach as the orb careened along like an enormous bowling ball. It didn't hit anything big, but it did glance off a rack full of Byzantine pottery, which toppled, shattering the priceless artifacts all over the floor.

The two enemy agents left made a desperate attempt to regroup and mount another attack, but we had the jump on them. Well, Erica did. She grabbed an ancient metal shield off a stand and laid out one agent with it, then chucked it like a Frisbee at the last, bonging it off his skull before he could open fire. Both bad guys collapsed to the floor, writhing in pain.

Which should have meant that there were no enemy agents left. But before we could even breathe a sigh of relief, a group of emergency-backup bad guys blasted through the same door we had entered the gallery from, armed to the teeth.

Thankfully, they were all the way across the gallery, which offered us a few seconds of reprieve. I crossed my fingers and hoped Mike's plan would work and that my calculations were right.

The orb was gaining speed as it rolled through the gallery. It still wasn't moving *fast*, but there was plenty of force behind its mass. It slammed into one of the steel plates, which crumpled like tinfoil and tore free from the doorway, creating an escape route for us.

We funneled through the hole behind it and found ourselves in the main foyer of the museum. At one point, it had been outdoors, between the two main wings of the museum, but in the year 2000 a glass ceiling had been installed over everything. Now the foyer was a large expanse of white marble floor with a café and a gift shop. Normally, at that time, it would have been full of tourists excited to get into the museum, but due to the alarms, the only people there were a few museum security guards, who had all been gathered around the steel door. Now they scattered like extras in a Godzilla movie as the orb rolled through like a juggernaut and plowed into the gift shop.

We took advantage of the chaos and raced for the main doors.

"I am dreadfully sorry about all this," Catherine said apologetically as we ran past the guards. "Please do forgive our mess. It was a life-or-death situation."

We charged through the remains of the flattened gift shop and barged out the exit into the plaza in front of the building. A large crowd of tourists was gathered there, unaware of what had been happening inside, impatiently waiting to get into the museum. Most seemed annoyed that it was several minutes past opening time. We quickly wound our way through them all and then fled through the streets of London. We jagged left and right through alleys and main routes until we felt convinced that we had shaken the bad guys—if they had even attempted to follow us out in public in the first place. We melted into the crowd of commuters and tourists in the theater district, then found a coffee shop that finally allowed Mike to go to the water closet. The rest of us all went too, as per Hogarth's Theory of Fear-Based Urination.

It was only then that my heart finally stopped thumping and I felt a sense of relief. It wasn't quite as big a sense of relief as Mike's, but it was sizable. We had tracked down

Joshua Hallal's flash drive and eluded a horde of bad guys. True, we still had to find out what was on the drive itself and we had destroyed some ancient relics, but at least we were all alive and had scored the first strike against SPYDER.

Then I emerged from the bathroom and saw all our faces on a TV screen. The British police had just accused us of attempted art theft, declared us public enemy number one, and issued warrants for our arrest.

Suddenly, I didn't feel relieved anymore.

My friends all showed similar reactions as they emerged from the restrooms and discovered the news.

"We need to find somewhere to lie low," Alexander proclaimed. "And fast."

"I know just the place," Catherine replied.

SANCTUARY

Top level

Tower Bridge

March 31

1000 hours

"You have to be kidding me," Mike said.

"It makes sense," I told him.

"No, it doesn't," Zoe replied. "There's no way this place was designed for British security. It's a national landmark, for Pete's sake."

"You'd be surprised how often that turns out to be the case with national landmarks," I said.

The national landmark in this case was the Tower Bridge of London. We were in a secret room tucked into the very highest peak of the northern tower, peering east through the windows at the city of London.

The rain had let up, but the sky was still a low ceiling of slate-gray clouds, casting the city in somber tones. On the riverbank to our left, the Shard, a pointy glass skyscraper that was the tallest building in Europe, stabbed upward, while the Tower of London squatted on the bank to our right, a thousand years older than the Shard, more or less. Several stories beneath us, the Thames River flowed sluggishly toward the North Sea.

According to Catherine Hale, the unique design of the bridge, with its twin towers and double-decker spans over the river, had nothing to do with alleviating traffic. While history books and tour guides all claimed that the purpose of the additional second span was to allow pedestrians to cross the Thames while the lower bridge was open to let boats through, Catherine insisted that was all smoke and mirrors to distract the public from the bridge's true purpose: surveillance.

"It was commissioned in 1874," she'd explained while carefully leading us there via a shadowy network of back alleys and decommissioned subway tunnels. "At the time, airplanes were science fiction. The true power of every nation—including London—was its navy. So if there was ever going to be an attack on this city, it would be coming up the Thames. The towers were built in order to give us a view out toward the ocean. If anyone dared to attack—most likely the French—we would have advance warning of their arrival. And we'd be able to rain bombs down on them from above."

I was surprised by how blasé my own response to all this was. In the past year, I had been just as shocked as Mike and Zoe to discover that the Washington Monument and the Statue of Liberty were both secretly built for national security reasons in the United States. Now it made perfect sense to me that the British had done the same thing, however bizarre it might be.

"Think about it," Murray said to my friends. He was slouched on a stool in the corner, eating a Cadbury chocolate bar he'd bought from a vending machine down at street level. "The whole idea that the second level of this bridge is for pedestrians is crazy. Exactly how much time would it save anyone to schlep all the way up ten flights of stairs, cross the bridge, and schlep back down again? By the time they did all that, they could have just waited for the bridge to close and saved themselves all the effort."

Mike and Zoe considered that. "That's actually a good point," Zoe admitted.

"The British government couldn't even keep selling that malarkey," Murray went on. "They shut the upper level down in 1910 because no pedestrians were dumb enough to use it." He wadded up a pamphlet he'd been reading and tossed it to us.

I caught it and unfolded it. It was a tourist brochure about the bridge. According to it, the upper levels of the towers had been unused until 1982, when the bridge was opened as a tourist attraction. We had seen the tourists queued up as we had snuck into a secret entrance in the base of the bridge along the bank of the Thames. The brochure showed several glossy photos of the upper span of the bridge, where there was now a glass floor that allowed tourists to look straight down at the road and the river below.

The part of the bridge that we were in appeared to have been forgotten. We had taken a hidden staircase up to it, and the steps had been thick with dust and ancient rat droppings. Now we were inside the large pyramid that topped the northern tower of the bridge, and the furnishings around us also looked as though they hadn't been disturbed in years, if not decades. Piles of codebooks from World War II were stacked in a corner, a map pinned to the wall showed countries that hadn't existed since 1945, and in an old ashtray there was a stubbed-out cigar that looked as though it might have been smoked by Winston Churchill.

I had asked Catherine how she'd known about this place when no one else at MI6 seemed to. She had simply given me a sly wink and said, "Alexander's not the only one whose family business has been espionage."

There were actually two separate rooms inside the pyramid: the crow's nest at the very top, where we were at the moment, with its windows that allowed us to see the surrounding area for miles; and a larger room below, which had served as a command center for British Intelligence. That was where Erica, Catherine, and Alexander were. Erica and Catherine were trying to figure out how to crack the information on Joshua Hallal's flash drive. Alexander was pestering both of them about having kept Catherine's true identity a secret from him for so long.

"Relationships are supposed to be built on trust," we heard him saying through the floor.

"Please, Dad," Erica said with a sigh. "This is not the time. We have a major crisis to deal with."

"We do," Alexander agreed. "It's a crisis that our entire relationship was founded on lies."

"I meant the fact that we're all fugitives," Erica said.

We had been trying to piece together what had happened by tracking the news on Alexander's and Catherine's phones. All the reports claimed that we had made an attempt to steal several historically significant objects at the British Museum that morning—including the Rosetta Stone—but had triggered the alarm and then destroyed some priceless artifacts during our escape. But there was no mention of our attackers or of the gunfight at all. Either Jenny Lake and her team had managed to escape unnoticed and quickly cover up every bit of evidence that they'd been there, or someone was manipulating the media. Perhaps the bad guys had moles within British Museum security—which would explain how they'd gotten into the museum in the first place. Or maybe the British Museum security was so embarrassed that they were hiding the true story themselves.

Whatever the case, we were in trouble. The British were very fond of their antiquities, and the idea that we had launched the first attempted robbery of their beloved museum in decades—and damaged many artifacts in the process—had the entire country up in arms. Every single person the news interviewed wanted us thrown in jail. A few had suggested bringing back the death penalty.

Zoe stood next to Mike at the window, looking out at the city, and said, "That was a pretty great idea you came up with to get us through the steel wall at the museum."

"Thanks." Mike turned to her and gave her a shy smile. "Although Ben's really the one who worked out all the math for it. . . ."

"But *you* were the one who came up with the plan in the first place," Zoe said. "We were all expecting Ben to do that, but it was you. How'd you think of it?"

"Because I had to pee so badly," Mike replied. "I was thinking about my bladder bursting, like a dam collapsing, and that triggered this flashback to the time when my brother backed my dad's car through the garage door. So I figured maybe we could do the same thing with that giant rock. It's a good thing I had all those sodas on the plane. Otherwise, I might never have thought of it."

"I'm sure you would have thought of it anyhow," Zoe said.

I wasn't sure, but it seemed like she might have fluttered her eyelashes at him as she said this.

I went to the other side of the attic room and looked out to the windows to the east, feeling jealous.

Murray joined me there. "Looks like your buddy Mike's moving in on Zoe," he observed. "And she's giving him the all clear. Are you cool with that?"

"Sure," I said sullenly. "I'm happy for them."

"Really?" Murray licked the remnants of his chocolate bar off his fingers. "It doesn't look like you're happy at all. Which is weird, because I thought you had the hots for Erica, not Zoe."

"I don't have the hots for anyone," I lied, staring off at the horizon.

"Oh. Well, I guess that's good then. Because those two are doing some serious bonding. First there's the whole weird nerdy love of typesetting. And now they're in major flirtation mode over this escape thing." Murray performed an over-the-top imitation of Zoe, fluttering his eyelashes wildly. "Oh, Mike, you were *sooo* smart back there. I used to think Ben was the brains of this team, but now I see it's you. . . . Ow!" A well-aimed shoe nailed Murray in the head, and he dropped to the floor.

"You think I can't hear you mocking me?" Zoe asked angrily. Her other shoe was in her hand, ready to be thrown at the slightest provocation. "I'm only ten feet away, you idiot."

"I wasn't mocking you," Murray lied, staggering back to his feet. The tread from Zoe's shoe was imprinted on his forehead, right between his eyes, making it look like someone had stepped on his head. "I was only practicing a fake voice, just in case."

"How stupid do you think I am?" Zoe asked.

"Not stupid at all," Murray said quickly, hoping to avoid another shoe to the face. "You're the total opposite of stupid. Brilliant, even."

"That's right." Zoe stormed across the room, grabbed the shoe she'd thrown off the floor, then slipped it back on her foot while she glared at Murray. "And since I'm so darn brilliant, I don't trust you one bit. I know you're pretending to be on the same team as us for right now, but I've got my eye on you. If you keep stirring the pot, the next shoe goes where the sun doesn't shine."

Murray gulped, aware that wasn't an idle threat.

Zoe stormed back to the window by Mike, though she was no longer in the mood for flirting. Murray had destroyed the moment.

I didn't trust Murray either. I suspected the same thing that Zoe did—that his comments to me had less to do with any friendly concern for me than they did with fomenting dissent between me and my friends. Most likely, Murray was trying to drive a wedge between all of us, diverting our attention from him until he saw an opportunity to get the jump on us or to flee.

But that didn't mean he hadn't struck a nerve with me.

As crazy as it was, I didn't like the idea that Mike and Zoe were hitting it off at all. Only a few weeks before, I had been completely focused on Erica and upset that maybe Mike was going to steal her attention from me. (Mike was cool and handsome and had a way of winning over girls.) Then I had discovered that Zoe had liked me—and ever since I'd been increasingly confused about what to do. I was certainly still hung up on Erica—even though she'd told me there could never be anything between us, as that would jeopardize our missions. But I also found myself drawn to Zoe, realizing that she was amazing and clever and pretty. A few nights before, during our mission in Mexico, she had told me she wasn't going to wait around forever for me to make up my mind. Now it appeared that she had already shifted her attention to Mike, which I didn't like one bit.

It was all driving me a little crazy, distracting my attention from the mission. I wondered if that was why I hadn't been able to figure a way out of the Egyptian gallery. Then again, maybe I simply hadn't been thinking well under pressure. Or maybe I just wasn't the guy who could always be counted on to come up with a solution in the midst of a crisis.

Whatever the case, I had failed while Mike had succeeded, and now Zoe's interest in him was stronger than it had been before.

There was a sudden, piercing wail from the floor below us. We all shared a look, fearing the worst, then bolted down the rickety staircase to see what had happened. Even Murray was concerned enough to follow us.

We came down into the command center. The room was a warren of outdated spy equipment, some of which appeared to date to the days before electricity. There were dusty computers that still used vacuum tubes and an actual telegraph in one corner. The security system was only a few decades out of date, however: Some ancient monitors the size of filing cabinets displayed flickering black-and-white camera feeds from the stairwell we had come up.

Catherine Hale was sitting at a desk, staring at her phone in shock. Up until that point, Erica's mother had only been incredibly calm and collected in front of me, unflappable even in the midst of beating up several enemy agents. Now, however, she was a wreck, her hair disheveled, her clothes mussed, her eyes rimmed with red.

"What's wrong?" Mike asked.

"The *queen* is angry at me," Catherine said, on the edge of tears. "She issued a statement about the British Museum and said I was a traitor to the country! *Me!* My whole life I've fought to serve England, and now I'm a stain on our history!" She broke down, sobbing into her hands.

Erica moved to her side quickly and spoke to her with a tenderness I didn't know she was capable of. "You're not a stain. We just need to prove our innocence. . . ."

"And how are we supposed to do that?" Catherine wailed. "I've been disavowed as an agent! My own colleagues have turned on me! I'm public enemy number one, destroyer of priceless artifacts, the shame of my country. Every MI6 agent, policeman, and meter maid is hunting for us. If I hadn't known about this hideout from my grandfather, we'd all be locked up in Newgate Prison by now."

Erica slapped Joshua Hallal's flash drive on the table in front of her. "We decode this, and then we find SPYDER and bring them down. Once we reveal what they've done, it will clear your name. And all of ours."

Catherine blew her nose into a monogrammed handkerchief. "That's a Sisyphean task and you know it. We don't even know that SPYDER is behind this."

"Of course they are," Erica said confidently. "Who else would want the information on that flash drive so badly?"

"A rival criminal organization looking to take SPYDER down," Zoe suggested. "If all of SPYDER's most important secrets are on that drive, their enemies could destroy them with that information." She looked to Murray. "I assume a scumbucket like you knows a few groups it could be."

Murray nodded knowingly. "CRUSH and SKORPION have never liked SPYDER much, though I'd put my money on ITGA. They're about as evil as people get."

"ITGA?" Alexander asked curiously.

"Yes. The International Tulip Growers Association."

"Um . . . ," Mike said. "That doesn't sound very evil."

"That's the whole point," Murray said. "It's a front. If they called themselves the International Association of Evil People Who Commit Crimes for a Living, the good guys would have caught on right away."

Alexander gasped in shock. "Are you telling me that every tulip grower in the world is part of an international criminal consortium?"

"No," Murray explained patiently. "The legit growers are part of ITFA, the International Tulip Farming Association. From what I understand, they're a lovely group of people, mostly Dutch. Although I wouldn't mess with the International Daisy Farmers Association if I were you."

"Are they also a front for evil?" I asked.

"No," Murray said. "Daisy farmers are just jerks."

"The point is," Zoe said, before Murray could go on, "maybe your ex-girlfriend Jenny has joined up with one of those groups. And they're looking to get their hands on that drive before SPYDER can get it. It's possible that SPYDER might not even know that drive exists."

"SPYDER knows everything," Erica said dismissively. "They're definitely the ones who attacked us today. What other organization would have the ability to launch an assault on us in the British Museum and then manipulate the police and the media to make them think we were behind it?"

"It doesn't matter who's behind it," Catherine said bitterly. "The sad fact is, they've hung us out to dry. We can't crack that flash drive: there's a level-seventeen trapdoor retrovirus built into it that fries any device we try to access it with, and no doubt, even if we *could* access it, the information will be encrypted. It'd take an entire team of cryptographers to break that, and I'm sure the gang at MI6 doesn't feel like helping me right now."

"Then we find someone else who can break it," Erica said calmly. "A world-class hacker. There's ten million people in this city. Surely there must be *someone* who can deal with this. Possibly even the person who encoded it in the first place. I know Joshua doesn't have the skills to build an encryption system like this. So he must have outsourced it to someone."

Erica's surprisingly caring demeanor seemed to make Catherine feel a little better. Catherine pulled herself together, picked up the flash drive, and examined it closely. "There *is* someone here in England. I suppose this could even be his handiwork. He goes by the name Orion. But there's no way we could get him to look at this."

"Why not?" I asked.

Before Catherine could answer me, an alarm went off. It was a very old alarm, and it hadn't sounded in so long that the equipment had decayed badly. Instead of sounding like a warning Klaxon, it sounded more like an inebriated goose.

We all turned our attention to the security monitors. A phalanx of British agents in riot gear was charging up the stairs.

"Oh, nuts," I said sadly.

MI6 had tracked us down.

DEFENSIVE DRIVING

Tower Bridge

London, England

March 31

1030 hours

"Follow me!" Catherine Hale pocketed the flash drive and leapt to her feet.

Instead of heading down the staircase that we had come up to get to the secret rooms—which would have led us straight into the horde of MI6 officers—she twisted a coat hook on the wall. There was the pained groan of neglected machinery, and then the room shuddered so hard that a shelf full of dusty codebooks collapsed. A section of the wall popped open with a gasp of musty air, revealing a secret exit.

We threw all the locks on the door to the stairwell, then filed out the secret exit behind Catherine. This led us down a rusty maintenance staircase and into a large room for tourists that gave the history of the bridge—minus the espionage angle. While the tourists had accessed this level via a relatively new bank of elevators, there was also an official stairwell. Zoe, Mike, and I headed toward it, but Catherine cut us off.

"Not that way," she warned. "MI6 will have men stationed at the base. We'll need to use the emergency escape." With that, she led the way onto the pedestrian bridge toward the tower on the far side of the river.

There were actually two parallel bridges at this level, each with a glass floor. Bridge museum officials staggered the entrance times to each to alleviate crowds; the line to the right was cordoned off at the moment, meaning there were significantly fewer people in it, save for a small group of teenagers in school uniforms on a field trip at the far end. We tossed aside the cordon, ignoring the protests of the pasty young museum guide who worked there, and charged across the river. The guide chased after us, yelling, "Hey! No cutting the queue! Get back here and behave like decent humans!"

If we hadn't been fleeing for our freedom, it probably would have been fun to stop and look down through our feet. The schoolkids at the far end of the passage certainly seemed to be enjoying themselves, gasping and giggling at the vertiginous view. As it was, I had time for only a fleeting glance, allowing me to note that the pedestrian bridge we were on was actually spread wider than the traffic bridge below. If you were on one side, cars and double-decker buses were passing beneath us, but on the other, it was a ten-story drop down into the turbid river below.

We were halfway across the bridge when the schoolkids stopped gawking at the scenery, snapped guns from holsters concealed beneath their Eton jackets, and aimed them our way. "Stop right there!" the girl in the lead shouted.

We all froze in our tracks. The guide who had been chasing after us turned even paler than the standard British native. "You know what?" he asked. "The queue jumping's not such a bother. I'll just return to my post." He raced back the way we had all come.

The rest of us couldn't do that. There were seven British students and each had a gun trained directly on one of us.

Now that we'd stopped running, I had time to focus on the schoolgirl in the lead and realized I knew her. In the nine months since I had last seen her, she had grown two inches and dyed her hair platinum blond, but it was definitely Claire Hutchins. Claire was a student at the MI6 version of spy school. We had first met at spy camp the previous summer, when she had come on an exchange program with several fellow students—some of whom were also aiming guns at us at the moment. Claire and I hadn't hit it off well at first, but she had ended up helping out on a mission and even dated Hank Schacter, a spy school student a couple of years above me (although that hadn't ended well).

"Claire!" I exclaimed, before I could think things through. "It's me! Ben Ripley!"

"I bloody well know who you are," Claire snapped. "I'm not daft, you idiot. You're all under arrest."

"You know we weren't behind what happened at the museum," said Erica, who'd been on the mission with Claire as well. "We were fighting SPYDER there, not working with them."

Claire narrowed her eyes suspiciously at Murray. "If you're not working with SPYDER, why's this tosser with you? He's one of them. I remember from West Virginia. The mole from your spy school."

"I flipped sides," Murray explained helpfully. "To the good guys this time. I've seen the light. By the way, I love what you've done with your hair. It really brings out your eyes."

"Thanks." Claire smiled, flattered, before catching herself and getting angry again. "There'll be no sweet-talking your way out of this. Right now we have piles of evidence against all of you. So put your hands where I can see them. MI6 will be here shortly."

I looked to Catherine Hale for guidance, expecting that she, being a member of MI6 herself, might try to explain to Claire and her fellow students what was going on. Instead, she obediently raised her hands.

However, as she did, a few coins clattered to the glass floor, as though they had dropped from her pockets. They rolled across the glass and toppled noisily in a few random spots. "Oh dear," Catherine said. "Looks like my change purse has a hole in it." She looked to all of us. "Children, step to the right, please."

Though her tone was sweet, there was an edge to it that said we should simply obey her and not ask questions. So we all shifted a few steps to the right, keeping our hands held high.

Claire instantly grew suspicious. She glanced at the coin that had rolled the closest to her, then warily took a few steps back, so that she was now on the regular floor, rather than the glass.

"Catherine," Alexander said warily. "What have you done?"

"I told you we were heading to the emergency escape," she said calmly. "Well, this is it. Children, don't be alarmed, but we're in for a bit of a drop."

I looked down at the coin that was closest to me. Although it looked very much like a real coin, I now realized it was a fake. A few things tipped me off: It was the tiniest bit thicker than a real coin; the color was slightly off, indicating it was made from a different type of metal; and, while I was staring at it, it emitted a burst of high-frequency energy that shattered the glass floor beneath my feet.

The windows to our sides shattered as well, and the concussive force knocked Claire and her fellow students onto their rear ends, but the disintegration of the floor was the part that really concerned me, as I was standing on it.

To my side, I heard Zoe and Mike both gasp, "Uh-oh."

And then we were falling.

Since we had all followed Catherine's orders and stepped to the right side of the floor, we were all heading for the river and were not about to splatter on the road, but ten stories was still a very long way to drop. I had time to see Claire staring at us in shock through the brand-new hole in the walkway as we fell away from her. I had time to start shivering from the sudden shift into the cold air outside and the wind whistling around me. I had time to hear that someone was screaming in abject terror—and then to realize that it was me.

In my defense, I wasn't the only one screaming. Screaming turned out to be a rather normal response to falling through the floor of a famous landmark and plunging to your possible death. Zoe and Mike were also screaming.

Alexander wasn't, but that was only because he appeared too terrified to make a sound. Meanwhile, Murray was screaming enough for an entire crowd of people.

Only Catherine and Erica appeared calm about the whole thing. Erica actually seemed to be enjoying herself, as though this were a theme park ride. Catherine simply seemed to regard it as a routine part of spying; I actually saw her look at her watch on the way down.

Bizarrely, this wasn't the first time I had plummeted into a river with Erica and Alexander during a mission—and even if it hadn't been, we had covered plummeting in Self-Preservation 202, in a special seminar, so I knew how to brace for impact. So did my friends. As the Thames rushed up to meet me, I held my arms tightly to my sides and pointed my toes downward.

This allowed all of us to slice into the water rather than smacking into it; even water could be hard enough to break bones if you hit it wrong. The impact still hurt, though, like a punch to every single part of my body at once. The water was cold, too, and that packed its own punch. I shot down deep into the river. The water was too murky to even see my own hands, but I could hear the thunking noises of my fellow spies plunging in around me. I kicked back toward the surface, which turned out to be disturbingly far above me—I had sunk much farther than I'd realized—but I eventually broke through, gasping for breath.

To my immense relief, all six of my fellow spies emerged around me, coughing and spluttering and looking like drowned cats but otherwise all right.

Unfortunately, our ordeal wasn't over yet.

Our emergency drop had taken us away from Claire and the rest of the British spy school students, as well as the MI6 agents who had been running up the stairs, but of course they were all capable of running right back down again. There were also a few British agents who hadn't even bothered to run up the stairs in the first place, along with some of the guards for the bridge, clustered around the base of the tower on the north shore.

So we swam toward the south shore instead. My limbs were tense from the drop and the cold, and the Thames smelled like fish that had gone bad, but my adrenaline was pumping so hard, I barely noticed. We all swam like professional triathletes, making it to the pedestrian walkway on the south side of the river just as Claire, her classmates, and a dozen MI6 agents exited the southern tower and charged after us.

Fortunately, we were still a good distance away from them, and there were too many tourists around for them to take a shot at us. A large crowd had amassed on the walkway. Many of the tourists came to our aid, helping us from the water, mistakenly believing that we were fellow vacationers who had just had our visit to the Tower Bridge go horribly wrong. We were quickly wrapped in jackets and scarves by good Samaritans.

"Are you all right?" the woman who helped me out of the Thames asked, placing her husband's raincoat around my shoulders.

"I'm all right," I told her.

She didn't seem to believe me. "You just fell out of the bottom of the Tower Bridge and into the Thames!"

"I've had worse," I said, which sadly was the truth.

"This way!" Catherine ordered, and she bolted through the crowd.

The rest of us followed, slipping into the sea of people before MI6 could get to us. Our shoes squelched wetly as we fled, and we left trails of water behind us. If it hadn't been for the clothes we'd just been given (or possibly stolen) we might have frozen to death in the cool air. As it was, even with my newfound jacket, I was still chilled to the bone.

We raced away from the riverbank and into the city, passing London City Hall, a lopsided steel-and-glass structure that looked like a beehive in a tornado, and then through the large park beside it. Behind us we could hear the shouts of MI6 as they shoved through the crowd.

"Do you still have Joshua's flash drive?" Erica asked Catherine, concerned.

"It's safe and sound and wrapped in a watertight pouch with my phone," her mother reassured her.

Sirens echoed off the river. The London police had now joined MI6 in pursuit of us. Three patrol cars were speeding across the Tower Bridge, their bubble lights flashing. They paused just long enough by the southern tower for a few MI6 agents to jump in, then sped off after us again.

"We're not going to be able to outrun those," Alexander observed.

"Then let's take the bus." Erica pointed to a traditional red London double-decker that was pulling up to the curb ahead of us.

"A bus barely moves!" Mike protested. "The police will catch us in no time if we ride it."

"I didn't say let's *ride* it," Erica corrected him. "I said let's *take* it." She barreled through the crowd of riders getting off, climbed the steps, and announced to the driver, "Sorry. I need to commandeer this vehicle."

The driver laughed, amused. "I say, you Yanks are a cheeky lot. . . . Yoinks!" He yelped as Erica forcibly yanked him from his seat and deposited him on the curb.

By now the rest of us had piled onto the bus as well. Erica gave us a cursory glance to make sure we were all accounted for, then slammed her foot on the gas pedal.

The bus sped away from the curb with surprising speed

for something built like a cinder block, pitching half the passengers to the floor. The bus driver chased after us, yelling British words that I didn't recognize but which I assumed were curses.

My fellow spies all grabbed seats. Neither Catherine nor Alexander looked particularly concerned that their daughter was driving the bus instead of them. In fact, both looked relieved that they weren't doing it—the same look my parents got when I handled the TV remote instead of them. I was about to grab a seat myself when Erica said, "Ben, navigate for me. The streets in this town are crazy."

So I stayed beside the driver's seat. Erica grabbed a map from a pocket beside her and pulled into the right lane of traffic. Unfortunately, since the British drive on the left, we suddenly found ourselves facing a horde of oncoming cars.

"Erica," I said worriedly. "You're driving on the wrong side of the street!"

"I'm not driving on the wrong side," Erica argued, gunning the engine. "*They* are."

The cars ahead of us swerved out of the way, crashing into one another and plowing through the storefront windows of several shops that had, up until that point, been very quaint and picturesque.

Alexander sighed and turned to Catherine. "She obviously gets this from your side of the family," he said.

The police cars slewed onto the street behind us, but they had to slow to navigate the maze of wrecked cars Erica had left in our wake.

I unfolded the map. To my dismay, the street plan of London was incredibly confusing. Instead of being in a nice, neat grid, the roads went every which way imaginable. The map looked like someone had vomited up a plate of spaghetti.

"Which way do I turn up here?" Erica asked me.

I didn't want to admit I didn't have the slightest idea where we even were in the city. "Where do we want to go?" I asked.

"Anywhere that gets us away from *them*." Erica jabbed a thumb over her shoulder toward the police cars pursuing us.

The intersection was coming up quickly.

"Go left?" I said, with far less conviction than I'd intended.

Erica swerved left. The road turned out to be a one-way street, but thankfully, we were going the right direction. Unfortunately, the road had been built well before anyone had ever imagined there could possibly be a vehicle as large as a bus. It was old and cobblestoned and there were cars parked along both sides. There was barely enough room for the bus to squeeze through them. Erica did her best to thread the needle, but it was an impossible job, even for her. We clipped several cars, smashing off rearview mirrors, gouging deep gashes in the vehicles' paint, and sending up showers of sparks as metal ground against metal.

"Next time I ask you where to go," Erica said through gritted teeth, "try to remember I'm driving a bus, not a bicycle."

"So," Zoe said to Catherine, a few rows back. "Why do you think this Orion fellow won't decrypt that flash drive for us?"

Catherine arched an eyebrow at her. "You want to discuss this *now*?"

"Looks like Erica has things under control," Zoe said, then winced as the bus jumped a curb and flattened a bike rack. "More or less. We might as well deal with our other problems."

Catherine considered this a moment, then gave in. "Orion doesn't work cheap. He charges in the millions. And right now I'm guessing we've only got a few hundred quid on us. Plus, if Orion *did* do this for Joshua, he'll never *undo* it. That's not his way."

"Then let's not ask nicely," Erica said, blowing through a red light. "Let's make him do it. The security of the free world is at stake."

A street vendor wheeling a fruit cart across the road from us abandoned his wares and ran for his life. The cart exploded as the bus plowed into it, splattering the front windshield with smoothie.

"Which way now?" Erica asked me.

I had made no progress with the map at all. Not only were the streets impossible to figure out, but they seemed to change names every block. "Right?" I suggested.

Erica went that way, smashing through a sidewalk café that thankfully hadn't opened for dinner yet. The road we ended up on was much wider—but it turned out to be only for pedestrians. Everyone scattered, diving for cover in storefronts as we plowed through it all.

"I'm all for forcing Orion's hand," Catherine said. "But we can't make him do anything if we can't get to him. And we can't get to him."

"Why not?" Mike asked. "Don't you know where to find him?"

"Oh, I know exactly where to find him," Catherine said. "MI6 has used his services before. The problem is, his home is a fortress. We won't be able to get inside unless he wants us to, and unless we're paying, he won't want us to."

"Why's it so hard to get inside?" Alexander asked. "Are there guards?"

Catherine shook her head. "Orion doesn't use guards. Guards are human, and humans are fallible. He's designed his own security instead. Every door, window, and vent is protected by six separate systems, each with its own shifting eighteen-digit entry code. The only person smart enough to figure out how to get inside Orion's house is Orion himself."

The three police cars were managing to stay in pursuit of us despite the wreckage we were leaving behind. And another three dropped in behind them, joining the chase.

"Excuse me," an exceptionally polite bus rider seated behind Erica said, "but you seem to have passed my stop. And the next four stops after that. I don't suppose you could let me off at Waterloo Junction?"

"Sorry, old chum," Murray told him pleasantly. "This is an express bus now."

"Orion must leave his home on occasion," Zoe was saying to Catherine. "Can't we wait for him to do that and approach him then?"

"There are a few problems with that," Catherine said. "I suspect that Orion certainly leaves on occasion, but that happens rarely and he is extremely clandestine about it. MI6 has been watching his home for years and we have never seen him go in or out his own door. We suspect he has a secret entrance that we have never found the access point for. Furthermore, we don't know what he looks like."

"But you've worked with him," Alexander said.

"We've *used* him," Catherine corrected. "That doesn't mean we've ever seen him. Orion never presents himself to his visitors. He doesn't even let them into his home. All contact is conducted electronically. So there is no way to reach him if he doesn't want to be reached. And I can guarantee you he doesn't want us to reach him, especially with our current high profile."

We were coming to the end of the pedestrian promenade. "Which way?" Erica asked once more.

I had completely given up on the map. All I could do was guess a direction and pray it worked. "Left," I said.

Erica went that way.

I gulped in alarm. I couldn't possibly have guessed worse. Not only was this road so old and narrow that it looked like it had been laid by the Normans, but up ahead of us was a narrow arch where a train track crossed the road.

I made some estimates, did some quick calculations, and didn't like what I came up with.

The double-decker bus wasn't going to fit under the arch. Even if it had had only one level, the arch wouldn't have been wide enough to accommodate it.

The six police cars came around the corner behind us, boxing us in.

"Nice going, Ben," Murray said sarcastically, failing to hide his concern. "You led us right into a trap."

I couldn't even respond, because I knew Murray's words were true. I had failed miserably at my job.

Erica didn't chastise me, though. She didn't brake, either. Instead, she sped up.

"Erica," Murray said. "This bus won't fit through that."

"I don't have any intention of fitting this bus through it," Erica replied. "Crash positions, everyone!"

Everyone took cover, tucking into tight balls.

The bus sped into the arch . . . and jammed fast in the middle of it. There was a horrible rending noise, and the metal sparked as it scraped on the stone. We came to a dead stop, like a cork jammed into a bottle.

Erica calmly delivered a karate kick to the front windshield. As it was designed for emergency exits, the window popped out easily and smashed onto the cobblestones in front of us.

The six police cars screeched to a stop behind us. The bus was now blocking the way through the arch, wedged in so tightly, a mouse couldn't even get through.

Erica slipped out through the space where the windshield had just been and dropped to the street in front of the bus. "Escape route," she said proudly, then looked to me. "Very clever of you to realize that would work, Ben."

I smiled weakly, doing my best to make it look like this had all been my idea.

The rest of us filed out after Erica, ignoring the complaints of the bus riders. With the bus preventing the police and MI6 from coming after us, we hurried down the road half a block to the closest Tube station and descended into the subway.

"Does Orion have a dog?" Mike asked.

The question was so out of the blue, it caught Catherine—and all the rest of us—by surprise.

"A dog?" Alexander asked, confused.

"Yes," Mike answered. "It's a four-legged mammal. Comes in all shapes and sizes. Likes to lick its own private parts. Lots of people have them as pets. If Orion has one, then I know how to get into his house."

Zoe grinned at Mike, fluttering her eyelashes again, seriously impressed by his ability to come up with a plan yet again.

"As I recall, Orion has *three* dogs," Catherine said to Mike. "So what shall we do?"

VEHICLE ACQUISITION

Somewhere in the London Underground

March 31

1200 hours

There were more security cameras in London than in any other city in the world: hundreds of thousands, recording everything. I noticed dozens in the subway station alone as we hustled through it. "MI6 and the London Police are certainly scanning the feeds from every last one of them," Catherine warned us. "So we're going to have to move fast and stay out of sight."

Luckily, Catherine had a great deal of knowledge about how the cameras worked—which meant she also had some very good ideas on how to avoid them.

The first trick was to hop a train in the Underground, knowing full well that we'd be recorded getting on it—and then hop *off* before it got to the next station. I had my concerns about this when Catherine first suggested it, but it turned out to be easier than I'd expected. (Or at least it was easier than dropping out of the Tower Bridge and then racing a double-decker bus through the city; sometimes what you considered easy was all a matter of experience.)

We all positioned ourselves at the rear end of the subway car, where Catherine dismantled the alarm on the emergency exit. When the train slowed to a near crawl to make a tight turn, we popped the door open and leapt out into the tunnel.

It turned out there was a massive network of tunnels underneath the streets of London: not just subway tubes, but maintenance tunnels for the tubes, sewer lines, routes to access the power lines, gas mains, and a thousand other things that had been buried down there. There were so many passages that many appeared to have been forgotten. "People have been digging their way through here ever since the Romans," Catherine explained as she led us along. "There are some people who can get from one end of this city to the other without ever poking their heads aboveground."

Catherine was not one of those people. She didn't know much of the system at all, except a few choice routes under

MI6 headquarters, which we were quite a long way from. Still, there were no cameras down below, and we were able to work our way from one tunnel to another for quite a way until we ran out of options. We ended up in a shaft that simply led upward, so we climbed the metal rungs bolted into the ancient concrete along the sides and emerged through a manhole into a radically different part of London than we had first descended from.

This part was far less touristy. Instead, it seemed like the sort of place that tourists' guidebooks would specifically warn you to steer clear of, unless you wanted to spend the rest of your vacation in either a police station or a hospital. There were no brand-new shiny steel-and-glass buildings or exciting attractions. Instead, there were a staggering number of run-down pubs. Although all the pubs looked like the type of place you might be stabbed for merely asking directions, each had a bizarrely cheerful, somewhat cryptic name: the Knave's Head, the Tickled Chicken, the Elephant and the Plumber, the Moldy Cheese. Their entire economy appeared to be based on beer.

There weren't many security cameras, even though this was exactly the sort of place I would normally have been worried about security. Still, we stayed off the main roads and stuck to the smaller alleys, pulled our newfound coats and scarves up around our faces, and kept our heads pointed downward. While this helped keep our faces from being recorded by the few cameras, it also forced us to stay in dimly lit areas filled with shadowy people. I could feel almost everyone we passed glaring at us, as though they were angry at us for even crossing their paths.

All of us were uneasy, but Alexander was the most on edge by far. "We need to get out of here, and fast," he told Catherine as we passed down a murky alley. "All these men are itching for a fight, and since I'm the alpha male here, they're going to come for me first."

"The alpha male?" Catherine asked, amused.

"Yes. It won't look good for them to attack women or children. So they'll attack me."

"And me," Murray seconded nervously. "I'm definitely the beta male here."

Catherine seemed to be fighting the urge to laugh. "Don't worry, heroes. I'm working on some transport." She stopped suddenly behind a pub called the Pig and Knickers. The alley there smelled as though people vomited in it on a regular basis. Four large men were loitering behind it next to a large beer keg delivery truck. The men looked like they were the ones who did the vomiting on a regular basis. They reeked of beer, even at that early time of day, and glowered as we approached.

Despite the fact that the men were as welcoming as a

pack of rabid Dobermans, Catherine smiled at them cheerfully and said, "Hello, gentlemen. I don't suppose any of you know who owns this lorry? I'd like to rent it." (I presumed at the time—correctly—that "lorry" meant "truck" in Britain.)

The biggest of the men stepped forward. He was six and a half feet tall and built like a tree. "You got money for the lorry?" he asked, although his accent was so thick, it sounded more like "Oogatch unny cor de orry?"

"I do," Catherine said brightly. "Quite a lot, in fact."

Alexander's and Murray's eyes both went wide with fear. Mine probably did the same. Catherine's words were like waving raw meat in front of lions.

The other three thugs perked up in interest. They stepped forward, looming over Catherine. The big one smiled menacingly, revealing gums that were missing half their teeth. "How about this, then, pigeon? You all hand over your money." Once again it didn't really sound like that. It barely even sounded like he was speaking English at all.

"That is not what I suggested," Catherine said sternly. "I am warning you, many of my friends here are from overseas, and you are not making this city look good to them at all."

With surprising speed, the leader grabbed Catherine's arm and snapped a large, sharp knife from his belt, which he then pressed against her neck. "Your money," he repeated.

Mike suddenly burst into laughter.

The four thugs looked at him curiously.

"What's so funny?" the leader asked.

"You're mugging *her*?" Mike asked. "That is a very bad career move." He didn't seem the slightest bit nervous about how things were going. Instead, he was amused. He turned around and scanned the alley.

"What're you looking for?" the leader demanded. He seemed extremely upset that Mike wasn't properly worried.

"I'm looking for a good place to sit," Mike said. "So I can watch the show."

"What show?" the big man asked.

"This one," Catherine said, and then she attacked.

Until only a few months before, I had thought Erica Hale was the best fighter I had ever seen, but her mother was even more talented. The four thugs were crowded around her and she caught them completely by surprise. Within a second she had wrenched the leader's arm around, making him whimper in pain and drop his knife. Then she whipped him into his pals, knocking them all back into the brick wall. Before the men even had a chance to realize what was happening, Erica and Zoe had joined the fight as well.

It was like releasing three coyotes into a henhouse. The poor criminals never stood a chance.

Mike had spotted an old crate lying close by. He took a

seat on it to watch, just as he'd said he would, then motioned for me to join him. Aware that the three women had far better fighting skills than me and that if I tried to help I'd only get in the way, I sat down too. Murray quickly joined us, pulling up a crate of his own.

The battle didn't last long. The women were quick and talented, while the men were slow and dull. Every time one of the thugs tried to land a blow, they hit nothing but air, while the women made each punch and kick count.

Alexander looked uneasy about the whole thing, like he really ought to be helping out instead of letting the women do all the fighting. However, Alexander was even worse at fighting than I was. He tried to punch one of the thugs in the face but missed when Zoe decked the guy instead and ended up driving his fist right into a brick wall. Alexander staggered backward, howling in pain, tripped over yet another thug (whom Erica had just rendered unconscious), and tumbled into a pile of trash that had been set out for pickup.

It was over in less than a minute. The thugs, who had appeared so tough and menacing, were all sprawled on the cobblestones, either out cold or clutching wounded body parts and whimpering. The leader was curled in the fetal position, wide-eyed with fear and disbelief. He cringed as Catherine loomed over him.

"Now, then," Erica's mother said, "on behalf of all the

English, I believe you owe these people an apology for your behavior."

"I'm dreadfully sorry," the leader said meekly. "Please don't let the poor conduct of my friends and myself adversely affect your visit to this lovely country."

At least, that was probably the gist of what he was trying to say. I couldn't really understand him, given his strong accent and the fact that he'd now lost some more of his teeth and his nose was swollen like a candied apple.

"That's better," Catherine said. "Now, if you'd be so kind as to hand over the keys to this van, I'd appreciate it."

The thug pulled the keys from his pocket as quickly as he could, then passed out from either pain or fear.

Catherine picked them up off the ground, smiled proudly, and said, "Right. Let's get a move on."

9

SELF-DOUBT

The Cotswolds, England
March 31
1800 hours

"This can't be right," Zoe said, staring at Orion's home in astonishment. "We must have the wrong address."

"This is the right place," Catherine said, sounding slightly offended by the idea that she might have made a mistake. "I've been here once before."

"Only *one* person lives *here*?" Zoe asked. "This isn't a house. It's a palace."

She spoke the truth. The building we were staring at was even referred to as a palace on our map. Wickham Palace, to be specific. Back in London I had caught a brief glimpse of Buckingham Palace, where the royal family lived. This appeared to be bigger. In fact, it appeared to be larger than most shopping malls I had seen.

Wickham wasn't even the only palace in the area. We were in a part of the British countryside known as the Cotswolds, about two hours west of London—or five hours west if you got stuck in rush-hour traffic, as we had. According to my map, the Cotswolds were lousy with palaces. There was one every few miles, some of which, Catherine said, were even bigger than Wickham.

Wickham was big enough, though. The grounds were so large that we had to observe the place from a hillock a mile away, using binoculars and scopes. The palace was sprawling and ornate, built from beige stone, and was several football fields wide. It was designed symmetrically, with grand wings that extended out on both sides and a four-story building in the center. The front doors were flanked by columns the size of redwood trees. The roof was adorned with clocks, statues, and thirty-eight separate chimneys.

"How much money can you make in the illegal coding business?" Mike asked, amazed.

"A lot more than you can make in espionage, obviously," Alexander muttered. "I'm working for the good guys and I can barely afford to pay my electric bill."

"And yet you have five designer tuxedos," Catherine said.

"Those are a necessary expense!" Alexander protested. "A good spy has to infiltrate plenty of high-end social events. You don't expect me to go to a fancy cocktail party in jeans and a T-shirt, do you?"

"No," Catherine replied. "Although during my entire career I've almost never had to infiltrate a fancy cocktail party."

"We *met* at a fancy cocktail party!" Alexander exclaimed. "One that you had infiltrated to meet me in the first place. So that you could con me into giving up American secrets."

"Secrets that America should have been sharing with England in the first place," Catherine countered.

"Our entire relationship is built on a foundation of lies!" Alexander cried, so loud that a covey of quail spooked and took to the air.

"Guys, this is not the best time," Erica said, sounding embarrassed by her parents' behavior. "We're supposed to be doing surveillance here."

"You're right, darling," Catherine agreed, looking embarrassed herself. "What have you got?"

Erica returned her attention to Wickham Palace, staring through the collapsible scope she always carried in her utility belt. "Orion has a serious security system here. There are plenty of entry points to the palace itself: at least two hundred windows, by my count. But they all appear to be protected by laser grids, and I've counted five hundred and sixty security cameras so far. So we're not breaking in there."

"We won't have to," Mike said confidently. "He has dogs."

The dogs were out at that very moment. There were three of them, gorgeous golden retrievers that were gamboling about the grounds. They appeared to be of average size, but it was hard to tell. From our distance, they were so dwarfed by the giant lawns that they looked like fleas on a carpet.

The property around Wickham Palace was as staggering as the house itself. According to Catherine, it was larger than Central Park in New York City, more than fifteen square miles of rolling hills, woods, and lakes. Much of it had been professionally sculpted by landscape designers for maximum beauty. Waterfalls had been erected; creeks had been gouged; forests had been planted. Orion had installed ponds the way most people put in swimming pools.

Everything was extremely well tended and beautiful. The only thing that stuck out as odd was a large warehouse to the side of the palace. The walls were aluminum siding, and though it had been painted the same color as the palace to make it blend in with its surroundings, that didn't work so well. It still looked extremely out of place, like a mustache on a frog.

"What do you think is in there?" I wondered aloud.

Murray said, "With a guy this rich, it could be anything. Expensive cars. Wine. Art. I always figured, when I cashed in big, I'd get myself some elephants. But that was back when I thought SPYDER was actually going to pay me off rather than kill me."

"Elephants?" Zoe asked.

"Yeah," Murray said. "They're really big mammals. Have tusks and very strange noses. You can see them in zoos."

"I know what they are," Zoe said. "I'm just surprised that's what you were going to spend your money on. I figured you more for the type who'd get a yacht."

"Oh, I was planning on getting a couple of those, too," Murray said. "And my own spaceship."

Mike was contemplating the shed too. "If Orion had wine or art, you'd think he'd have plenty of room to store that inside. And it looks like there's already a garage for cars. So what's the point of a giant storage shed?"

I couldn't come up with an answer to that. And neither could anyone else. Besides, there were more pressing things to deal with. Like the wall.

A big, imposing wall surrounded the entire property, and it was dotted with yet more security cameras and crowded with electrical wire and lasers. "Anyone know how we're supposed to get over that?" I asked.

"Shouldn't be a problem," Erica said, her eye still to the

scope. "It's too big to fully secure. There must be twenty miles of it. Somewhere, there'll be a chink we can take advantage of."

I nodded miserably. Even that little bit of good news didn't make a dent in my mood, which was dismal and anxious.

I wasn't upset merely because enemy agents had tried to kill me that day. Or because I was wanted by the British authorities for the malicious destruction of antiquities. Or because I had just spent five hours crammed in the back of a stolen delivery van that reeked of stale beer. Or because the weather in the countryside was lousy; it was gray and grim and we were all getting rained on yet again. Or because I was still wearing the wrong clothes for England. On a normal day, any one of those would have been more than enough to upset me. But there was something else going on.

I felt like a failure.

By my accounting, I hadn't contributed very much to our mission at all. Mike and Zoe had figured out the font on the key, leading us to the British Museum. Catherine had been our leader, and she and Erica had got us out of trouble several times over. Even Murray had contributed: He'd inspired the whole mission with his knowledge of Joshua's key in the first place. Whereas I had done very little except take up space.

Yes, I had figured out the math to allow us to escape the gallery at the British Museum, but the plan itself had been Mike's.

Everyone had *expected* me to be the one to come up with a plan, but in the heat of the moment I had drawn a blank.

Similarly, when Erica had asked me to help her navigate through the streets of London, I had failed. I had sent her down one wrong road after another, and if it hadn't been for her quick thinking, I would have led us right into a dead end and gotten us all nabbed by MI6.

I was in the same category as Alexander Hale: deadweight. Neither of us was helping at all. But at least Alexander looked good while he was failing.

To make matters worse, it appeared that Zoe had also noticed Mike was better than me. The two of them had been clicking ever since the mission had begun. They had spent the entire van ride chattering about fonts and typefaces, happily bonding over things like how much they preferred Baskerville over Monaco. Zoe had barely even looked at me.

I morosely turned from Wickham Palace and scanned the surrounding countryside. It probably would have been beautiful on a sunny day, with gorgeous green hills and quaint towns and adorable flocks of sheep, but it was close to sunset, the sky was full of ominous clouds, and it was raining. So the countryside was dark and dingy, and all the sheep were damp.

A beat-up pizza delivery car approached the massive front gates of the palace. The driver pulled up to a speaker box mounted on a stone pillar. He was much too far away for us to hear his conversation, but he was obviously receiving instructions about how to get the pizza to the house. The gates didn't open for him. Instead, he had to get out in the rain and place the pizza box in a hatch built into the pillar. Then he simply closed the hatch and drove away.

"You think Orion even knows that pizza is there?" Murray asked. "Because I'm starving."

"The pizza isn't still in the pillar," Zoe told him. "That's certainly a pneumatic delivery system designed for fast food. That way strangers don't get access to the property."

"Any chance we could go get a pizza, then?" Murray asked. "As much fun as it is to stand here in the cold rain, staring at a rich guy's house, I'd rather be someplace warm and dry where there's hot food."

"Orion's definitely home if he's ordering pizza," Erica said, as though Murray hadn't even spoken. "And he must be by himself. Because that was only a single-serving pizza."

"You think he's really in that huge place all alone?" Zoe asked. "With no servants or anything?"

"My intel says Orion doesn't even have so much as a cleaning woman," Catherine said.

"Sounds awfully lonely," Zoe observed.

"Yeah, I feel terrible for the guy," Murray groused. "He's got more money than he knows what to do with, he owns a freaking palace, and he's dry and cozy. Unlike us. Honestly, exactly how much longer do we need to watch this place? It's not like we're going to suddenly spot a secret entrance. Can we please go and get some food?"

"I could go for a bite myself," Mike said. "Plus, my plan won't work until tomorrow morning anyhow."

In the distance the dogs ran up to one of the forty-eight doors of the house. It opened just enough to allow the dogs inside, then closed again, too quickly for us to get even a glimpse of Orion.

Erica collapsed her scope in a brusque way that indicated she had seen everything she needed to. "All right. We can go."

We all piled back into the beer delivery truck, which was parked on the side of a dirt road that was quickly degenerating into mud, then jounced along through the muck.

The towns in the Cotswolds seemed to have been christened by the same folks who had named all the pubs back in England. Every place sounded charming, but also a little bit quirky: Notgrove, Uckington, Oddington, Guilting Power, Bourton-on-the-Hill, Mourton-in-Marsh, Stow-on-the-Wold, and the unfortunately named Upper and Lower Slaughter. Catherine insisted both Slaughters were quite delightful, but I felt we should steer clear of them just to be safe.

So we went to Brockton-in-the-Mire instead (the Cotswoldians certainly liked their hyphens). Once again it probably would have been picturesque on a nice, sunny afternoon. But now, in the last light of day, it appeared dreary and decrepit. It was a small farming community perched on a low hill, and the newest building in the place appeared to be five hundred years old. The whole town was crumbling.

Like every other town in England, this one was centered around a pub. The pub was called the Whinging Sprat, and it had rooms for travelers as well. Given the foul weather and the fact that Brockton-in-the-Mire was probably not at the top of anyone's list of holiday destinations anyhow, the entire place was available, save for a traveling sheep-dip salesman.

The rooms were small and damp and the plumbing was prehistoric, so we didn't spend much time there. I took a quick shower—although the "quick" part wasn't really my choice. I had been in it for only two minutes before the hot water ran out. After being doused in what felt like water that had recently melted from a glacier, I quickly toweled off and dressed.

As I started down the old stairs to the pub for dinner, Erica emerged from her room.

"Oh," she said, like our emerging at the same time was a coincidence. However, I doubted that was the case. Erica left very little to chance, and the stairs were so creaky, she certainly would have heard me coming. Which meant she was only faking our coincidental meeting. "Hi."

She had cleaned herself up as well, washing her hair and scrubbing some blood from the thugs in London out of her clothes. As usual, she looked and smelled amazing. Normally, Erica saying "Hi" would have made me feel warm all over, but I was so glum, even that failed to lift my spirits.

"Hi," I replied, trying to sound upbeat and failing miserably.

Erica paused on the stairs. "What's going on with you?" she asked.

I stopped beside her. The stairs were narrow, so we were awfully close together. "Nothing," I said.

"Really?" she asked. "Because you kind of seem like you're depressed because you've contributed diddly-squat to this mission."

If I had felt like there was a cloud over my head before, I now felt as though that cloud had drenched me with rain. And possibly hit me with a lightning bolt as well. I thought about denying this but then realized it would be pointless. Erica would have seen right through it. "That's true."

"It also seems like you feel like a failure," Erica went on. "Especially given that Mike has succeeded when you haven't, and so Zoe is getting interested in him when she used to be interested in you."

"This talk really isn't helping improve my mood," I said. "I kind of liked it better when you didn't understand human emotions very well."

"I still don't understand them," Erica said matter-of-factly.

"There's no point to being depressed. It doesn't help anything."

"I know. But I can't help it. I've been useless. I couldn't figure a way out of the gallery at the museum. I haven't beaten anyone up. I couldn't even give you directions properly on the bus. I didn't lead you to the archway knowing you'd be able to jam the bus into it. That was a mistake."

"Oh. I know that."

I blinked at Erica, surprised. "You do? But afterward you said I was very clever to come up with that escape."

"Well, if I'd said, 'Way to bollix up the directions,' it would have made you look like a moron in front of everyone else."

I sagged against the wall. "I guess so."

I heard water churning through the pipes in the wall, followed by a startled yelp. "Oh dear Lord!" Alexander cried.

I figured he had just discovered there was no hot water. Given how clearly I could hear him, I realized the walls of the inn were extremely thin, which would make it very easy for someone else to overhear my conversation with Erica.

Erica seemed to realize the same thing. She crooked a finger and led me down the stairs.

Zoe, Mike, and Murray were already in the pub. True, its primary purpose was to serve beer, but England seemed to care far less about age restrictions than America did. Plus, it was the only place in town to get food. Murray had already tucked into a chicken pot pie; his face and the front of his shirt were covered in gravy and chicken bits.

Erica led me past the pub door before any of the others noticed us, and we headed out the back door into the rear yard. It was still pouring rain, but there was a small roof that protected a few square feet of patio, and the sound of the water on the roof was more than enough to drown out our conversation to anyone more than two feet away.

There were three sheep in the yard, grazing on a small patch of grass, lacking the sense to get out of the rain. They were so waterlogged, they looked like soggy cotton balls.

Erica said, "If you're upset about failing to contribute to the mission, then stop moping around and start contributing."

"Oh," I said. "I see what the problem is now. I've been trying *not* to contribute all this time. In fact, I've actively been trying to fail. But now I'll just try to do the opposite and everything will work out perfectly fine."

Erica gave me a hard look. "That was sarcasm, right?"

"Yes. If I could contribute, I would have done it already. I *have* been trying. That's the problem."

"Maybe. All I'm saying is, don't dwell on it. If you *think* you're a failure, you'll become a failure. You'll lose your confidence and then lose your edge. But if you want to contribute, then you need to buck up and get your head in the game. It's not enough for me to think you can help. *You* have to think you can help."

I turned from staring at the sodden sheep, surprised. "*You* think I can help?"

"Of course I do. You've helped on missions before. We never would have figured out what the bad guys were plotting before without you." Erica didn't say this in a particularly emotional way, like most people would have when trying to raise my spirits. Instead, she stated it as a simple fact, which might have meant more to me. It seemed that Erica wasn't saying she believed in me. She was saying that she didn't *need* to believe in me at all. And that did make me feel better, despite the rain and the musk of wet sheep.

"All right," I said. "I'll try."

Erica nodded appreciatively, then started to go inside. Then she stopped herself and looked back at me. "There's something I need to tell you. When you first came to the academy, I thought you were the worst spy-in-training I had ever met."

"Gee, thanks."

"The point is, I was wrong. Not only have you proven yourself, but you've also taught me something."

"Really?" I asked, unable to hide my surprise. "What?"

"That other people have value. When we first met, I thought I was better solo than with a team. I thought other people could only hinder me. But that's not true . . . with the right team. And we have the right team here now. If I thought anyone on this mission wasn't able to contribute, I wouldn't have allowed them to come along."

"Even your father?"

Erica considered that for a few moments before answering. "Yes. My father might be a fraud and a charlatan, but even he has talents."

"Like what?"

"I'm not sure yet. But my mother says he's not as bad as I think, so I trust her judgment. The man has survived as a spy for a long time. He can't be a total idiot."

This was the nicest thing I had ever heard Erica say about her father. And she had also admitted that I had taught her something. I wondered if Erica was finally feeling close enough around me to drop her guard—or if there was an ulterior motive to her behavior. I hoped it was the former, but my previous experience with Erica made me think it was the latter.

Her brief bit of emotional openness appeared to have made Erica uncomfortable. "I'm going back in," she said abruptly. "You should come get some food too. And some rest. We've got a big day tomorrow. We don't want to screw anything up."

With that she headed back into the pub, leaving me alone in the rain hoping I could live up to her expectations.

INFILTRATION

The Whinging Sprat

Brockton-in-the-Mire, the Cotswolds, England

April 1

0430 hours

One of the key indicators the Academy of Espio-nage used to determine who would be a decent field agent was to simply test our ability to wake up very early in the morning. As Sanchez's Maxim on Preparedness put it: "Everything important tends to happen at the least convenient time possible. Usually in the middle of the night."

We had determined at dinner that our mission needed to begin at 0500 hours on the dot, so I decided to set my alarm for 0430 to give myself time to get properly outfitted and prepared. Waking up at that time wasn't easy, especially given how exhausting the events of the previous few days had been, but I pried myself out of bed nonetheless. My fellow spies rose in different styles, generally in line with their talents. Mike and Zoe both shuffled into the lobby at 0445, drowsy but dressed (save for a few missed buttons), while Catherine and Erica were already there, wide-awake, on their second pot of tea, already having dressed, groomed, reviewed the mission, scrounged up a few scones for us, and done some calisthenics, even though both had spent a good portion of the previous night on a second scouting expedition to Wickham Palace. Meanwhile, Murray and Alexander each required additional goosing to get out of bed.

Erica deftly picked the locks on both their rooms so we could wake them.

Alexander had slept through the four separate alarms he had set for himself, swatting each one off in his sleep. (Somehow he'd even managed to toss the hotel's alarm clock in the toilet without waking up.) He was dreaming when we roused him, murmuring, "Don't worry, Princess Daphne. This isn't the first nuclear bomb I've defused." When we roused him, he snapped awake, startled and disoriented, and promptly fell out of bed, tangled in his sheets. But at least he got up.

Murray, on the other hand, did everything he could to stay in bed. He cocooned himself in his blankets, buried his head under his pillows, and groaned, "Can't you guys infiltrate this place without me? I'm only borderline competent anyhow. I'll probably screw everything up." Normally, that would have been a decent argument, but we knew we couldn't let Murray out of our sight. Rather than debate the point, Erica simply went to the bathroom, filled a cup with frigid water, and upended it over Murray's head.

Fifteen minutes later, we were all ready to go. Murray was still half asleep and grumpy, and so his clothes were all askew, like he had gotten dressed in the middle of a tornado. Alexander, however, was impeccably dressed in his bespoke suit, as usual.

We all piled into the van and clattered back through the countryside to Wickham Palace, where Catherine and Erica had found the best place to get over the wall. A centuries-old oak tree stood only a few yards from the property line, with enough low limbs that it wasn't too hard to climb. None of the branches extended over the wall, but one got close enough that we could rig a pendulum swing to it, using some heavy rope Erica had scrounged from a toolshed at the inn.

The ability to swing over the wall also corresponded well with our general spy-worthiness. Erica and Catherine both performed the feat with the deft grace of Cirque du Soleil cast members. (I almost felt as though I should applaud for them afterward.) Mike and Zoe handled it well, if a bit clumsily. I didn't embarrass myself, though I did slip on a wet patch of sod on the landing and tumbled to my knees. Murray missed landing on his feet entirely, belly flopping in the mud.

Alexander fell out of the oak tree. Twice. When he finally managed to grab the rope and swing over, he somehow got his ankle tangled in it and ended up oscillating helplessly while dangling upside down until Catherine—who seemed to have come prepared for this—threw a kitchen knife at the rope, severing it cleanly just below the branch when Alexander was on the proper side of the wall. Alexander came crashing down into a gorse bush and emerged spitting out leaves.

Thankfully, this didn't trigger any of the alarms, as it happened well above the wire and laser sensors atop the wall.

"You're *sure* he might come in handy?" Erica whispered to her mother.

"Everyone has their special talents, my dear," Catherine whispered back.

"It's been quite a long time since I used the old rope pendulum trick," Alexander told us, trying to save face, while extracting a gorse berry that had somehow gotten lodged in his right nostril. "The last few times I've scaled walls, we've used grappling hooks, so I guess I'm a bit rusty where ropes are concerned. Why, one time, I was using a grapple to break into the Taj Mahal in Cambodia. . . ."

"We need to be quiet, Dad," Erica admonished him, then quickly added, "And the Taj Mahal is in India."

"There's a secret one in Cambodia," Alexander said quickly, but then clammed up.

We set out across the grounds of Wickham Palace. Once we were past the wall, there didn't appear to be much security. The property was simply too big to wire it all up, and the wildlife would have been constantly tripping the alarms. There was a lot of wildlife at Wickham, much of which was also stirring at that early hour. Herds of deer grazed in fields. Waterfowl gabbled in the lakes. A badger lumbered across our path and scared the pants off Murray.

Besides that event, we made it across the property relatively quickly and quietly, arriving at the palace before the sun rose. The size of the building was even more startling up close. Although I had been able to tell it was four stories high while surveilling it, I now discovered each of those stories was much taller than I'd realized, twice the size of those in a normal house, and the fancy gables atop the roof added even more height.

We moved stealthily, sticking to the shadows, until we arrived at the door we had seen the dogs enter through the previous night. The door, like everything else about Wickham, was oversize, looking like it was meant for a giant. The wood at the base was marred with thousands of scratch marks and the jambs reeked of dog urine, indicating the dogs often came and went this way.

We all set ourselves down on the patio, our backs to the stone wall, and waited.

There is quite a lot of waiting in the spy business. That morning, it was damp and cold, but we all knew we had to bear it and sit still, without making a sound. (Most of us did this because we didn't want to mess up the mission. Murray did it because he knew Erica would punch his teeth out if he screwed anything up.)

The seconds crept by. We didn't really have to wait all that long, but it felt like hours.

After a while the sky brightened to the east. Shortly afterward, we heard the dogs barking. It wasn't the agitated barking of dogs who smelled intruders on the property. It was simply early-morning, I'm-up-and-I-want-to-go-outside-to-pee barking.

Because of the size of the house, it sounded like they were very far away, which was probably the truth. The barking went on for a few minutes and eventually began to come closer. As the dogs neared the door, I caught the faint sound of someone grumbling to them, sounding quite a bit like Murray had that morning. "Stupid dogs. Can't sleep in like intelligent beings. Nooo. You have to get up the moment the sun rises. Every stinking day."

This was the brilliance of Mike's plan. He had realized that Orion, in trying to protect himself by not having any staff, had created a major weakness in his own protection: He would have to do everything in his household by himself, and thus there would certainly be times when he let his guard down. "Anyone who has a dog has to let it out first thing in the morning," Mike had explained. "And very few people are totally alert first thing in the morning."

That certainly seemed to be the case with Orion. He didn't seem to have his guard up at all. Instead, he was going through the motions, as though this routine had played out every single day for years. He didn't sound angry at his dogs, so much as teasing them, but there was still a sense of the annoyance that came with having been woken up too early. We heard him trudge through the room closest to us, then a *thud* and a yelp as he groggily bashed into a piece of furniture.

We all took our positions outside the door.

On the other side, the dogs were still barking excitedly. If they had a sense that we were outside, I couldn't tell.

"Calm down," Orion said. "Give me a chance. I'm getting the door."

I heard some beeps from inside, the sounds of someone dismantling the alarm system, and then the door opened.

As the dogs rushed out, Erica and Catherine shoved their

way in. The dogs obviously weren't bred for security. Instead, they were your standard golden retrievers. Their reaction upon seeing strangers on the property was surprise, followed by excitement. Two of them mobbed me, having already forgotten about needing to go to the bathroom, wagging their tails so vigorously that their rear ends shimmied. The third ran to Mike.

Zoe grabbed one of the dogs lightly by the collar so it couldn't run off. Not that it had any intention of doing this. Instead, it turned its attention to her and licked her.

I reluctantly took out the dart gun Catherine had lent me and pressed it to the dog's head.

Mike did the same thing to the dog with him.

Through the open door, Orion was sleepily trying to make sense of what was going on.

He was much younger than I had expected, only a few years out of college, if that, and unlike the geeky, awkward computer nerds that tended to be depicted in movies, he was a handsome, athletic guy. He was still in his pajamas, with a robe slung over them. The only thing remotely geeky about him was his footwear: He was wearing Chewbacca bedroom slippers.

"Hey!" he said drowsily. "What's all this about . . . ?"

"We need you to decrypt something," Catherine told him. "Something we believe you encrypted in the first place.

And if you don't do it, my associates will be forced to put your dogs down."

Orion seemed to notice us for the first time. Suddenly, he was wide-awake. He had no idea that our guns didn't fire bullets—or that, even if they had, we would have only been bluffing. "Whoa!" he cried. "There's no need for that! I'll do whatever you need! Just let Porthos and Aramis go!"

I was surprised how quickly he had caved, although this had also been part of Mike's plan. "People will do anything to protect their dogs," he had said. "More than they'll do to protect themselves."

Still, I hesitated in stowing my gun, unsure whether he was bluffing or not.

"I mean it," he pleaded. "You're not asking me to do anything evil here, right? Like hack into NORAD and fire nuclear missiles or anything?"

"No," Catherine said.

"Then I don't have any problem with it. Don't hurt my dogs, okay?"

There was worry and concern in his eyes that I read as genuine. Catherine and Erica had the same reaction. They turned to Mike and me and nodded.

We let the dogs go. The one I'd been aiming at looked at me expectantly, as if hoping I was going to throw the gun so he could fetch it.

Erica held out Joshua's flash drive. "Recognize this?"

"Oh yeah!" Now that his dogs were no longer under threat, Orion didn't appear upset in the slightest that we had invaded his house. Instead, he seemed kind of happy, like he was excited to have guests. "I did that about ten months ago for Captain Hook!"

We all could figure out exactly who he meant by that—except Alexander, who reacted slowly. "Captain Hook?" he asked.

"Joshua," Zoe explained. "Ten months ago, he had a hook instead of that mechanical prosthetic. And without an eye or a leg, he looked kind of like a pirate."

"He did, didn't he?" Orion asked, with surprising friendliness for someone whose home had just been infiltrated. "I kept expecting him to say 'Arrrrrr, matey' or 'Yo-ho-ho and a bottle of rum.' Are you guys friends of his?"

"We work together, in a way," Erica said. "How long will it take to decrypt that?"

"Oh, not too long," Orion replied. "Do you folks want some breakfast while you wait? I've only got frozen waffles, but I've got a couple thousand of them, so there's plenty to go around."

"I could go for some waffles!" exclaimed Murray, who always thought with his stomach. He hurried into the house excitedly.

Erica caught him by the collar. "We're not here for breakfast. We're just here for the decryption."

"Oh," Orion and Murray said at once. Both sounded equally sad about it.

The dog at my side finally seemed to remember that he had to pee and ran off into the enormous yard, as did the other two dogs. So the rest of us filed into the house.

We found ourselves inside what was probably supposed to be a grand living room. The walls and ceiling were covered with intricate paintings of cherubs and mythological creatures surrounded by gilded frames. Ornate chandeliers dangled from the ceiling, bedecked with thousands of pieces of crystal. There was no furniture, not even a carpet, which made the unusually large room echoey and cavernous. At the far end, which seemed a good fifty yards away, there was a self-standing basketball hoop. A lot of the plaster on the walls down behind it was cracked, as though many of the cherubs had taken basketballs to the face.

"Yeah, sure, I can do this," Orion said. "We just need to go to my office." He started to leave the room, then paused, confused.

"What's wrong?" Mike asked.

"I'm just trying to remember where my office is," said Orion. "There's over two hundred and fifty rooms in this place. I get lost in here all the time."

"You do?" I asked before I could catch myself.

"Yeah. I'd always dreamed about having a palace like this, ever since I was a kid. But there are some serious problems with it. I mean, it's exhausting to live here. It's like half a mile from my bedroom down to the kitchen." He snapped, suddenly remembering where he needed to go, then reversed direction and led us out of the makeshift basketball court.

We followed him into another enormous room. The only furniture in this one was a large-screen TV and a few beanbag chairs.

Orion rambled on. I was definitely getting the sense that his self-imposed exile had made him lonely and desperate for company. "Also, I can't ever find anything. My car keys, my wallet, my phone. I think I bought a pool table last year, but I have no idea where it is. And another bummer: The palace is haunted."

"Haunted?" Alexander asked, so worried that he stumbled over his own feet.

"Yeah," Orion said. "The sixteenth Duke of Earlchester died here. Or maybe it was the sixteenth Earl of Dukechester. It was a couple hundred years ago. Supposedly, the guy was a big jerk. The peasants all rose up against him and burned him alive, and now his ghost roams the property, looking for a fire extinguisher or something like that. I haven't seen him, but some nights, when there's a full moon, you can hear him wailing. Sounds like a guy whose pants are on fire."

"You knew about this and you still bought the place?" Alexander asked, startled.

"No, I didn't know about the ghost. There's no law that you have to disclose a domain of the undead in this country. Apparently, you could buy a castle full of zombies and it'd be totally legal." Orion led us through another completely empty room. "Sorry about the decor. That's another problem with a place like this. It's impossible to furnish. Do you have any idea what two hundred and fifty sofa and chair sets costs? Half a million dollars. And that's at IKEA. So I opted out. Not that I'm doing a whole lot of entertaining anyhow."

"Still, you must have friends over sometimes," Zoe said, sounding truly concerned.

"Not really. It's not so easy being a secretive criminal genius. I mean, the pay is great, but it's hard to have a social life. After I decrypt this, do you guys want to hang out for a bit? I just got a new croquet set." Orion led us through another door, and we finally arrived at our destination.

This room was considerably smaller than the others and was the first one that looked like someone lived in it. The walls had no fancy paint or gilding, which led me to believe that the room had probably been a servant's quarters. Now they were plastered with posters and framed jerseys for the Manchester United soccer team, along with assorted other sports memorabilia. A large desk sat in the corner, topped by an enormous computer monitor and a dozen hard drives, attesting to a tremendous amount of computing power. The desk was a mess, covered with piles of papers and other random items, like several dirty plates of half-eaten waffles. A tower of empty pizza boxes teetered in the corner. Obviously, Orion's no-servants policy had left him without any housecleaning.

"I'm sorry," Catherine told Orion earnestly. "But we will have to leave very quickly. This is a precision operation. In and out."

"Oh," Orion said sadly, then looked Catherine over and smiled. "What are you doing after the operation's done? Want to meet for dinner sometime?"

Catherine took a step back, surprised yet flattered. "Orion! I'm old enough to be . . . well, not quite your mother. But a young aunt." She then took a good look at him. "Although, if I were your age, I would definitely say yes."

"Mother!" Erica gasped at the exact same time that Alexander gasped, "Catherine!"

"Face it," Catherine said. "He's handsome."

I wasn't sure if she really meant this or if she was merely saying it to make Orion feel good, but it certainly put him in a positive frame of mind. "All right," he said, jacking the flash drive into his computer. "Let's see what I did here. . . ."

"Careful!" Zoe warned. "You built a worm into that file!"

"Not a problem," Orion said confidently. "I build worms into everything. But my own system knows how to get around them."

His hard drives whirred into action, but they didn't get fried. A window popped open on his monitor, filled with gibberish. It wasn't merely letters and numbers, but all sorts of other random symbols and emojis.

Orion examined it thoughtfully. "Looks like I used a Snodgrass encryption system on this with a hexidecimal Watusi overgrid."

"Can you undo it?" I asked.

Orion snorted disdainfully, as though I'd asked him if he knew how to breathe. "Of course I can undo it. I did it in the first place." He turned to Catherine and grinned proudly. "No one does this as well as I do," he boasted.

"That's why we came to you," Catherine said flirtatiously. "You're certainly the best."

"I think I'm going to be sick," Erica muttered under her breath.

Orion's fingers flew across his keyboard, typing so quickly I could barely see them. The gibberish on the monitor began to change, though at first all it changed into was even more gibberish.

Mike noticed something lying on the desk haphazardly

atop a pile of papers and picked it up reverently. "This is a Honus Wagner baseball card!"

"Hey!" Orion exclaimed. "I've been looking for that!"

"This sold for more than two million dollars at auction a few weeks ago!" Mike said.

"Two and a half million," Orion said.

"And you just left it sitting around?" Zoe asked, stunned.

"I've been meaning to get it framed," Orion said sheepishly. "I told you it was hard to keep track of things here."

"Exactly how much money is there in illegal encrypting?" Mike asked earnestly.

"Oh, most of the work I do isn't illegal," Orion replied. "It's for corporations and banks. They're the ones with the serious cash. The contract for one Swiss bank alone nearly paid for this whole place."

Murray opened one of the pizza boxes and reacted with almost the same level of excitement that Mike had upon finding the Honus Wagner card. "You only ate one slice of this pizza! Can I have the rest?"

"Sure," Orion replied. "Though that might have been sitting around for a few days."

Murray shrugged. "Can't be worse than those scones we had for breakfast." He took a bite and groaned with ecstasy. "Oh, this is good. I haven't had pizza in more than a month."

Zoe leaned in to Erica and said, "Now *I'm* going to be sick."

Orion finished typing with a dramatic flourish. "Done! Here we go!"

The gibberish vanished and was suddenly replaced with good old, completely unencrypted English. There was a huge amount of information in the file. It scrolled rapidly across the monitor, filling up the entire screen.

"Pay close attention now," Catherine told us.

We all crowded behind Orion to see it.

The first block of text was a long list of names and dollar amounts, although they hadn't been spaced apart so they were difficult to read. I caught a glimpse of "Warren Reeves $250" before it scrolled off the screen, but I didn't recognize any of the other names.

"Can you pause the scrolling so we can read this?" Catherine asked.

"Sure thing." Orion tapped a button on his keyboard.

The information stopped scrolling. Instead of names, it was now showing lots of what looked like bank account information, but again, it was so run together that it was hard to make sense of.

Toward the bottom of the screen, I spotted a line that said "Mr. E +48.851764, +2.354130, UnicornsRule!!! Watch out for Operation Wipeout."

I knew the head of SPYDER was known only as "Mr. E," so I figured the numbers might be important. I focused on them and quickly tried to commit them to memory.

I had just done it when the computer monitor went black.

In the exact same instant, the hard drives shut down. And the lights in the room went off.

"What happened?" Alexander asked, startled.

"The power went out," Orion said, perplexed. "But that shouldn't have taken out the main computer. I have my own backup generators on the property so that I'm off the grid in case there's a blackout."

Erica and Catherine looked to each other, worried. "Someone's cut the power on the property!" Erica exclaimed.

At the exact same time, Catherine told us all, "We need to get out of here. Now."

None of us needed to be told twice. Even Orion. He might not have been a spy-in-training, but he was highly attuned to security issues. He snapped the flash drive out of the hard drive, leapt to his feet, and raced out of his office. "This way!" he announced.

We followed him into the hallway . . .

Where Joshua Hallal was waiting for us.

EVACUATION

Wickham Palace

Near Scumbly-on-the-Marsh

The Cotswolds, England

April 1

0700 hours

Joshua was coming down the hallway, flanked by a team of bad guys.

To his immediate left was Dane Brammage. Dane had been through quite a lot in the last few days, thanks to us: He had been thrown off a moving ATV, partially consumed by sharks, and nearly squashed by a collapsing waterslide. Plus, he had a nasty sunburn—although that wasn't really our fault; he hadn't used enough sunblock in Mexico. And yet he was still imposing. The man was built like a rhinoceros, a wall of muscle on legs. If anything, the red sheen to his skin made him look even more like a comic strip villain, possibly one from another planet.

To Joshua's right was Ashley Sparks. Somehow she had escaped police custody in Mexico as well. She was so different from Dane that aliens might have thought they were two entirely different species. She was only the size of one of Dane's legs, with her hair done up in a scrunchie and a combat outfit bedecked with sequins, but she still looked imposing herself. The submachine gun cradled in her arms probably had something to do with that.

Behind them were three other henchmen from Mexico, who had somehow escaped as well. Warren Reeves was almost invisible behind them—not because he was wearing some impressive camouflage, but because he was hiding behind them to keep out of danger.

And at the forefront was Joshua. His remaining human arm and leg were both in casts, so that he needed crutches, which mitigated his imposingness a bit. However, with his metal hand, his single eye full of anger, and the heavily armed bad guys around him, he was still awfully frightening.

We were unarmed, save for some dart guns—and we had only a few darts left for those. The only thing that really worked to our advantage was that Joshua and his team were at the far end of the hall. In most homes, this wouldn't have been a big deal, but in Wickham Palace, this meant they were still half a football field away from us.

For a brief moment we all gaped at one another, startled to see each other there.

"You!" Joshua screamed in rage, pointing a metal finger our way.

In theory he might have been pointing at all of us, but I had the distinct sense that all his rage was directed at *me*. I felt his lone eye boring into me hatefully, like I was somehow responsible for all the damage his body had suffered.

"Captain Hook!" Orion exclaimed, surprised to see him again.

Mike and I grabbed Orion and dragged him along with us. We all raced out of the hallway and into the next room as Joshua gave the order to his team. "Kill them!"

Bullets tore through the hallway we had just evacuated.

We were now back in the room with the TV and the beanbag chairs. We raced through it, unsure where we were going, except that we were going away from the bad guys.

"Hey!" Orion yelled angrily at Joshua's team. "No shooting in my house! Do you have any idea what it will cost to repaint this place?"

"There'll be no negotiating with him," Catherine said. "We need a way out of here. *All* of us."

"Right," Orion said. "Follow me. I have an idea." He started to go through one door, then paused, like he was trying to remember the right way through his house, changed his mind, and led us in the other direction.

"You *do* know where you're going, right?" Murray asked. Even though our lives were in danger, he was still carrying the box of cold, half-eaten pizza.

"I do now," Orion said. "I was a little confused back there for a moment. But I've got it figured out."

Mike and Zoe both gave me worried looks, concerned that our fate was in the hands of a guy who couldn't even remember how to get through his own house.

However, as we ran along, I realized that I might have the same problem if I lived at Wickham Palace. We passed through one giant unfurnished room after another, and while there were differences between them—one might have light green walls adorned with cherubs and woodland creatures while the next might have light yellow walls decorated with nymphs and pixies—it was hard to imagine that I could ever keep them apart. I found myself wondering what the original owners of the palace could have possibly been thinking. Exactly how many ballrooms and dining halls did one family need? How many people could they have possibly been entertaining—especially when you considered that the population of the countryside had been considerably smaller back then? Did they routinely invite entire villages to dinner?

The only advantage of the maze of rooms was that Orion had at least some idea how to get through it while Joshua and his team didn't. I could hear them racing through the palace somewhere behind us, but we had temporarily shaken them, so they weren't right on our tail.

"Split up!" Joshua ordered. "Find them and get that flash drive!"

"I'm on it!" Ashley's perky voice responded.

"How is she even here?" I asked Erica, struggling to keep up with her as we ran through the palace. "She's supposed to be in jail!"

"Joshua must have busted her out." Even though we were fleeing for our lives, Erica wasn't the slightest bit out of breath. She seemed as calm and relaxed as if she were merely out for a morning jog. "Or maybe he bribed the police to let her and the others go. But now at least we've learned something important."

"What?" I gasped.

"Isn't it obvious? They're not working with Jenny Lake. Otherwise, Jenny and her henchmen from the museum would be here too. And since Joshua has gone rogue from SPYDER, then Jenny must be working *for* SPYDER, trying to recover the stolen information before Joshua can—or with a rival evil organization that's trying to get that information to undermine SPYDER."

"And meanwhile, MI6 is after us too," Mike observed. "Is there anyone in this country who isn't trying to capture or kill us?"

"Possibly a few shepherds," Murray said. "Though I might be wrong about that." He was still clutching the pizza box in his arms and doing his best to eat a cold slice as we ran.

We finally entered a room that wasn't a ballroom or a dining hall. It was the grand entryway for the palace. Two massive doors led out to the main courtyard in the front. It was large enough to hold my entire house and was lined with enough marble to build a monument. Staircases that could each accommodate a herd of elephants swept along both sides of it, leading to a second floor that most likely had fifty bedrooms.

Alexander pulled up alongside Catherine as we passed through it, looking very peeved. He made sure Orion was out of earshot, then whispered angrily, "You were *flirting* with that hacker."

"You should talk," Catherine hissed back. "You flirt with anything that has a pulse. And you even did it back when we were married."

"That was always for business reasons," Alexander said, not quite believably. "A good spy has to manipulate people to his will. . . ."

"What do you think I was doing with Orion?" Catherine asked. "I needed him to decrypt that flash drive. It wouldn't have done a whit of good for me to reject him outright. You men always get so pouty when that happens."

We passed into yet another large room. This one had a pool table in it, still wrapped in its original protective packaging.

"My pool table!" Orion exclaimed. "I *knew* I'd bought one of those!"

There was an unusual sound behind us—although it was a sound I had become somewhat familiar with back in Mexico. Joshua's new mechanical hand had weaponry built into it, and I now recognized the sound of it preparing to fire. Which meant Joshua had found us.

I whirled toward the sound. The pool room connected to four other similarly enormous rooms in a row. Joshua and Dane were way down in the fourth, which was a good hundred yards away, but since the rooms were unfurnished, they had a straight shot at us. "Take cover!" I yelled. "Incoming!"

An explosive rocketed out of Joshua's metal palm and streaked through the palace toward us.

Most of us dove to the sides of the entrance to the room, placing walls between us and the artillery, then curled up in balls to protect ourselves.

Unlike us, however, Orion hadn't gone to class in taking

cover. He started to duck behind the pool table, unaware that it wouldn't provide much protection in a blast.

Mike was there for him, though. He threw himself into Orion, knocking him away from the table and behind the wall instead.

The flash drive tumbled from Orion's hand and clattered to the floor.

There was no time to grab it. Even Erica realized this, fighting her usual urge to be the hero in the name of self-preservation. We all tucked our heads down and wrapped our arms over them.

The explosive screamed into the room and blew the pool table to smithereens. I was showered with splinters of wood. The eight ball rocketed right over my head and embedded itself in the wall.

I raised my head. Felt from the pool table was drifting down like green snow.

The flash drive had been incinerated. All that remained was a smoking lump of plastic.

"My pool table!" Orion shrieked. "I never even got to use it!"

The chandelier in the room, weakened by the blast, dropped from the ceiling and shattered in the wreckage.

The fallen chandelier was the size of a minivan, big enough to give us some cover. We dashed into the next room before Joshua or Dane could fire again, though Erica stopped just long enough to snatch a pool ball and half a busted pool cue off the floor.

"We lost the flash drive!" Zoe exclaimed.

"And my pizza!" Murray wailed.

"Without that drive, we don't have anything on SPY-DER," Mike said despondently. "Our mission's a bust."

"Not necessarily," Catherine said, although it sounded like she was struggling not to despair herself. "We all saw a bit of data on the monitor. If everyone memorized some of it, perhaps we can reassemble some of the important information."

We passed into a kitchen. It appeared to be the second kitchen for the house—or maybe even the third or fourth—as it had apparently never been used. All the appliances were still shrink-wrapped and spotless. And yet, even for a backup kitchen, it was huge. Enough food for an army could have been prepared there.

"Whoa," Orion gasped. "I completely forgot about this."

"You forgot about an entire kitchen?" Murray asked, startled.

"No," Orion said. "I forgot about this entire wing of the house."

There was another ominous clicking behind us. Once again Joshua was at the far end of a line of rooms, preparing to launch an explosive our way.

While most of us immediately took cover, Mike turned to face Joshua and yelled, "Whoa! Time-out!"

"Time-out?" Joshua asked, surprised. "You can't call 'time-out' in the middle of a gunfight!"

"The flash drive you're after got destroyed," Mike explained. "It's useless. So there's no longer any point in killing us for it, is there?"

Dane turned to Joshua, confused, like he was trying to work out the logic of this. "He has a point."

Joshua simply raised his metal arm and fired at us. Maybe he thought Mike was bluffing. Or maybe he simply wanted to kill us because he was pure evil. Either way, the result was the same. The explosive rocketed through the house toward us.

"Uh-oh," Mike said, then dove behind the island in the center of the kitchen.

However, this time Erica was prepared. She hurled the pool ball she'd been carrying back toward the explosive. I was too busy cowering to see what happened, but it was obviously a direct hit. The explosive detonated a room away, instead of right where we were. The concussion of the blast caught Erica before she could dive to safety, tossing her across the kitchen. She slammed into the refrigerator and crumpled to the floor.

Flames licked through the doorway, setting the kitchen on fire.

I heard the distinct sound of yet another chandelier

crashing to earth in the room behind us and hoped that this one would also shield us from our enemies.

"Erica!" Catherine and Alexander cried at once. They raced toward their daughter.

"I'm all right!" Erica yelled, leaping to her feet as though she'd merely tripped over the curb. "Let's move!"

So we ran again.

"Oh man," Orion said sadly, observing the flaming wreckage of his kitchen. "I really hope I have insurance for this." Then he led the way onward through the palace.

Erica paused by the kitchen door while her parents ran ahead. "Ben," she said quietly as I neared her.

I stopped, warily glancing back toward Joshua. Thankfully, the ruined chandelier was sitting between us and him a room away. "What?"

Erica slipped her hand into mine. "I need you to lead the way for me. I was sort of blinded by that blast."

"Sort of?" I asked.

"Shhh!" she hissed. "Don't freak my parents out. I'm sure it's only temporary."

I ran after the others, clutching Erica's hand as tightly as I could. She dropped in beside me. With me guiding her, she moved just as quickly as before.

The others had got a little ahead of us, but we quickly made up the ground.

Beyond the kitchen, the rooms got significantly smaller. We had reached what would have been the quarters for the enormous staff that previous owners had required. There was no longer any attention to decor. Apparently, the help wasn't entitled to luxuries like gaily painted walls or large living spaces. We found ourselves moving through narrow hallways, flanked by drab rooms that reminded me of our dorms back at school, only these appeared to have working heat and didn't smell like the communal toilets had backed up again.

The cramped architecture now worked to our advantage. No hallway ran straight for more than a few yards, preventing Joshua from taking another long-distance shot at us.

Still, it felt as though we had covered a half mile inside the house. I was getting a major cramp in my side, but I worked through it.

"Now, then," Catherine went on. "Let's discuss what we saw on that flash drive. I noticed a long list of names."

"That's what I saw too!" Zoe agreed. "With dates and dollar amounts beside them."

Mike said, "It looked like a list of spies they've paid off to be double agents. The cash values were probably the amounts SPYDER gave them, and the dates were when they were bought."

"That's what I figured as well," Catherine agreed. "Did anyone memorize any names?"

"Warren was on that list," I said, struggling to catch my breath as we ran. "They only paid him two hundred and fifty dollars."

"That's it?" Zoe asked, stunned. "He turned to the dark side for less than the price of a video game system?"

"Warren was never the sharpest tool in the shed," Erica said. "But I'd guess his anger about you was his primary reason for joining SPYDER. He probably would have done it for free, so the money was a bonus."

She was giving no sign that she'd been blinded. If it were me, I would have been freaking out, but she was acting perfectly normally. Or at least, as perfectly normally as someone could act while being chased through a palace by a bionic ex-boyfriend who had turned evil and was now trying to kill her.

"Any other names?" Catherine asked. "Ones we didn't know were evil already?"

"Harlan Kelly," Erica reported. "And Lydia Greenwald-Smith."

"Our professors?" Zoe exclaimed. "I *loved* Dr. Greenwald-Smith's class."

"Not me," Mike said. "I suspected she was evil. She gave me a D on my counterespionage exam last week."

The rooms were growing even smaller and more cramped the farther we got from the grand entry foyer, as though we were now where the lowest-ranked servants would be. I figured we had to be running out of house.

Catherine looked to Alexander. "How about you? Did you notice any names?"

"Er . . . no," Alexander said weakly.

"Not a single one?" Catherine sounded extremely disappointed.

"I was distracted," Alexander replied, then thought to add, "by something very important to the mission."

"What?" Catherine challenged.

"A . . . uh . . . well . . . ," Alexander stammered. "I sensed the enemy was coming."

"Then why didn't you give us a heads-up so that we'd have more time to save our lives?" Catherine demanded.

"Oh, all right, it wasn't the enemy," Alexander admitted. "It was a duck."

Catherine lost her temper. "We've been risking our lives to get this information, and at the only moment we got to see it, you were distracted by a *duck*?"

"In my defense, it was an emerald-crested Welsh Harlequin," Alexander said. "They're very rare."

"I put my neck out to bring you on this mission!" Catherine exclaimed. Despite all the adventures we'd had, this was the first time I had ever heard her lose her cool. "I knew it was risky, but I figured you couldn't be totally useless! And yet you haven't done us one whit of good the entire time.

I *told* everyone to pay attention to the screen when that information came up! That shouldn't have been too difficult! Look forward, read some words, try to remember a few of them. And you couldn't even manage that! Because some jade-faced waterfowl wandered across your path!"

"It was an emerald-crested Welsh Harlequin . . . ," Alexander corrected.

"I don't care if it was a pink elephant wearing a baboon for a hat!" Catherine exploded. "All I needed you to do was focus for five seconds, and you couldn't even do that!"

I grimaced, feeling terrible for Alexander—but also feeling miserable about my own lack of contributions again. Yes, I had noticed Warren's name on the list of double agents, but that wasn't exactly news. I had also noticed Mr. E's listing with a few numbers next to his name, but I had no idea what they meant, or if they were even remotely important. Which meant that my own contributions to the mission were barely better than Alexander's.

Everyone's general sense of fear and exhaustion was now mixed with a bit of awkwardness as well; it was uncomfortable to listen to Erica's parents bicker. And that started to segue into panic as we all noticed the rear of the palace coming up ahead. At the end of the hall, there was a door with a window, and out the window, there was nothing but acres of open lawn.

"Speaking of ducks," Mike said, "we're about to become sitting ones."

"Maybe not," Orion said, without as much confidence as I would have hoped. He made a sudden turn to the left, shoving through a door that didn't look like any of the others in the hallway.

Instead of leading into a servant's room, this one led into a small antechamber, which led to a set of doors that appeared to have been put in the exterior wall relatively recently. Orion pushed through those . . .

And we found ourselves inside the large warehouse structure I had noticed while casing the property before. Once inside, I discovered it was much larger than I had thought. Wickham Palace was so large that the warehouse had looked smaller next to it. But in reality it was the size of an aircraft hangar.

Because it *was* an aircraft hangar.

The floor was a vast expanse of concrete. The ceiling was retractable. And right in the middle of the hangar sat a military helicopter.

It was one of the most beautiful things I had ever seen.

Not because it was literally beautiful. It was actually quite homely, squat and blocky and painted a bilious green. But it would allow us to escape, assuming we could get it going before Joshua and his team arrived.

"What is it?" Erica whispered to me, blinking blindly into the hangar.

"A helicopter," I whispered back.

Erica heaved a sigh of relief, then handed me the busted shaft of pool cue she'd been carrying. "Barricade the doors."

"Right." I quickly jammed the cue through the handles, then threw the dead bolt too.

"That's a Russian Yukutsk 260!" Catherine exclaimed excitedly. "Orion! What on earth are you doing with it?"

"I'm twenty-six and I have more money than I know what to do with," Orion explained. "I also own a private submarine, a minor league baseball team, and forty percent of Madagascar." He yanked on a chain by the door. It set a series of cogs in motion, which started the ceiling retracting.

Something slammed into the opposite side of the door, followed by the distinct sound of Warren Reeves yelping in pain. The doors, with the dead bolt and the pool cue jammed through the handles, held fast.

"Joshua!" Ashley shouted from the other side. "Come this way! I think they're through here!"

Catherine threw open the doors of the helicopter, her anger at Alexander totally forgotten. Inside, the craft wasn't cushy—it had been built for military transport—but there was plenty of room for all of us on jump seats lining the walls. "It's gorgeous, Orion! How long have you been flying?"

"Um . . . ," Orion said. "I was kind of hoping one of *you* knew how to fly it."

Catherine spun around, her mood instantly shifting once again. "You have a helicopter you don't know how to fly?"

"I've been meaning to take lessons," Orion said. "But I kind of got distracted."

Erica looked to Catherine as I helped her into the helicopter. Or, still being temporarily blinded, she looked in the general direction she thought her mother was, which wasn't quite accurate. She directed her attention to an empty jump seat. "You don't know how to fly this, Mom?"

"No!" Catherine was too distraught to notice Erica's lack of sight. "A British helicopter, I can fly. But Russian ones are completely different. Can *you* fly one?"

"How would *I* know how to fly a helicopter?" Erica asked. "I'm only a teenager!"

"I thought Cyrus might have taught you! You know how to drive a double-decker bus and—" Catherine was cut off by a loud whirr as the helicopter rotors suddenly started spinning.

To our surprise, Alexander Hale was sitting in the pilot's seat—and for once he appeared to know what he was doing. His hands moved rapidly across the control panels, flipping on switches. Monitors sprang to life on the dashboard. Alexander snapped a headset over his ears to cut out the sound. "Everyone, buckle up right away," he said, sounding like the confident charlatan he'd been when I had first met him. "We're going to have to take off very fast."

Everyone scrambled for the jump seats, except Catherine, who slid into the copilot's seat, and Erica, who stayed rooted fast to her spot behind the cockpit, resisting my attempts to drag her away. "*You* know how to fly this?" she asked, stunned.

"Of course I do," Alexander said. "I've told you that."

"You've told me lots of things," Erica said. "Like how you prevented the French from invading Turkey and how you thwarted an evil plot to turn all the gold in the world into soup. I figured this was a lie like all the rest."

"It wasn't." Alexander flipped a few last switches. "I learned while on a covert operation in Siberia—but it was quite some time ago and I'm probably a bit rusty, so please go strap in right now, young lady. That's an order."

"You heard your father," Catherine said. "Do it."

Erica stared in surprise at her parents—or at least at the point where she thought her parents were—but then allowed me to lead her to the body of the helicopter.

Catherine was looking at Alexander with newfound respect. Though maybe it was old respect that she had just rediscovered. I could imagine her looking at him that way when they were much younger and had just met and she hadn't realized what a sham Alexander was.

Everyone else was strapped into their seats. Orion didn't

seem quite as bummed about leaving his palace to a horde of criminals as one might have expected. Instead, he was brimming with excitement, thrilled to have an adventure—and to finally get to use his helicopter—after a long period of loneliness.

Erica and I strapped in as well.

Across the hangar, the doors to the palace smashed off their hinges as Dane Brammage bulldozed through them.

Ashley, Warren, and Joshua raced through the gap behind him. Joshua aimed his bionic hand at the helicopter.

Alexander yanked back on the stick just as Joshua fired. The helicopter shot upward. The explosive raced beneath us and blew out the opposite wall of the hangar.

The other thugs poured into the hangar as well. Together with Dane, they opened fire on us, but we were already rising through the retracted roof. The bullets rattled off the armored hull of the helicopter but didn't punch through.

Alexander took us straight up as fast as he could before steadying the helicopter out of range of the bullets. For a moment we hovered above the property, high enough to see the grounds laid out like toys beneath us, and then we raced off across the countryside.

A sense of relief fell over everyone, though it was slightly tempered by the feeling that we had failed in our mission to recover the information on the flash drive.

Beneath us, the Cotswolds were a carpet of green fields

and forests, speckled with the white puffs of a staggering number of sheep.

"Where are we heading now?" Alexander asked.

Everyone looked to one another blankly, unsure what the answer to that question was.

Except me.

I had a sudden, wonderful surge of insight into what I had seen on Orion's computer, followed by the even more wonderful feeling that I had just become useful to the mission as well.

"Paris," I said.

INVASION

10,000 feet above the Cotswolds

April 1

1000 hours

"There were three things written next to Mr. E's name," I explained. "+48.851764, +2.354130, and Unicorns-Rule!!! The first two are extremely specific points of latitude and longitude."

"What's the third?" Mike asked.

"I don't have the slightest idea," I admitted. "To be honest, it threw me off for a bit, because I was figuring all three items were a set. But they're not. The first two are a location. The plus signs indicate north and east, while minus signs would have meant south and west."

"Makes sense," Erica said excitedly. "What would the single most important piece of information be about Mr. E? What secret would SPYDER desperately want to protect more than any other?"

"Where to find him," Zoe said.

"Exactly," Erica agreed.

"I can't say where the exact spot is that those coordinates pinpoint," I went on. "But I know forty-eight latitude north and two longitude east is Paris."

"You know the latitude and longitude of every city?" Zoe asked, surprised.

"Not every one," I said.

"Almost every one," Mike put in. "He memorized them all when we were in elementary school. One of his crazy math things he came up with. Watch this. Ben, what's Sydney, Australia?"

"Thirty-three degrees south, one hundred fifty degrees west," I said before I could stop myself.

"See?" Mike asked. "And he thinks liking fonts is dorky." He was teasing as he spoke, though, indicating he was proud of me.

"And you're sure you memorized those coordinates perfectly?" Orion asked.

"Ben never forgets a number," Erica told him, then looked at me. "Cairo, Egypt."

"Thirty north. Thirty-one east," I said.

"Sounds like we're going to Paris," Alexander said. He tapped the coordinates onto a touch-screen monitor, got directions, then veered that way.

"How far away is it?" Mike asked.

Alexander consulted one of the screens in the cockpit. "About two hundred and thirty miles. We ought to be there in around two hours."

"Hold on," Zoe said. "Are we really sure going after the head of SPYDER is the best thing to do right now?"

"Absolutely," Catherine answered.

"Really?" Zoe pressed. "Because it's going to be awfully dangerous. We saw a few names of corrupt teachers at spy school. Why don't we just start with reporting them to the CIA?"

"To *whom* at the CIA?" Catherine asked in return. "That list was much longer than the few names we saw. There were dozens of corrupt agents on it, if not hundreds. For all we know, one of them might be the very agent in charge of rooting out corruption. Or perhaps the head of the CIA himself. All we have learned so far is that we can't trust anyone in the CIA—and quite likely any other spy agency as well—except those of us in this helicopter. Now that Joshua's flash drive has been destroyed, the only way to retrieve the list of double agents and root out this corruption once and for all is to get it from SPYDER. And the only lead to SPYDER we have is those coordinates. Therefore, I see no other options for us except infiltrating Mr. E's compound."

"Oh," Zoe said. "I see." She sank a bit in her seat, looking as nervous as I felt.

"Maybe it won't be that dangerous," Mike said. "Maybe Mr. E will be so confident that he can't be found that he won't have that much security."

Catherine said, "While that would be a nice surprise, I think it's best if we keep our guard up and assume this won't be a walk in the park. So far, SPYDER has never done what we've expected."

"I'm just saying it's possible," Mike said, settling back into his seat.

I turned my attention to Erica. She was sitting next to me, her eyes closed, looking amazingly serene for someone who had just nearly died several times over and had been temporarily blinded in the process.

"How are your eyes?" I whispered to her.

"Not great," she admitted. "But they're improving slightly. I'm starting to pick up some light in my peripheral vision. If I rest them for the flight, they ought to be fine. Thanks for helping me through that, by the way."

"You're welcome."

"And that was nice work, picking up on those coordinates," she said softly. "See? You're not totally useless."

I wasn't sure, but I thought I saw the slightest flicker of a smile play across Erica's lips, as though this last comment had been more of a tease than a flat statement. Which made me smile back. "Thanks."

"You ought to get some rest too. We're going to need to hit the ground running in Paris."

"Right," I agreed, and noticed that I was nodding off even as I said it. Although it was still morning, it had been a crazy day. The adrenaline that had been surging through me had now drained, leaving me feeling exhausted, and the rumbling of the helicopter was having a strangely soothing effect on me, lulling me to sleep. In their seats on the opposite side of the chopper, Mike and Zoe appeared to be nodding off as well, though Zoe managed one brief, surprisingly angry stare at me before conking out.

The next thing I knew, it was ninety minutes later.

"Rise and shine," Catherine said pleasantly, gently shaking me awake. She sounded so calm and peaceful that for a moment I felt as though I were back home, being roused by my mother late on a Sunday morning. It was upsetting to realize that I was in a helicopter, infiltrating French airspace on my way to a dangerous confrontation with the head of an evil enemy organization—although things got even more upsetting two seconds later, when Catherine handed me a parachute and said, "Put this on."

"We're parachuting into Paris?" I asked, stunned.

"Well, we can't possibly land there," Catherine said matter-of-factly. "We're all fugitives from justice, and we're not entering the country through legal channels. The moment we set down, the French police would be all over us. Plus, there's a severe lack of decent heliports in the city."

"No one said anything about parachuting," I said.

"I said we would have to hit the ground running in Paris," Erica told me. She was already wide-awake and calmly strapping on her parachute, with the facility most girls her age would put on a pair of shoes. "What part of that didn't you understand?"

"All of it, apparently," I replied. "I thought you meant we'd need to move fast. Not actually hit the ground. I've never parachuted before!"

"You haven't?" Catherine asked, amazed, as though I had said I had never had a glass of water. "But you're already into your second year. . . ."

"MI6 students take parachuting early in their second year," Erica explained. "Spy school students don't get Rudimentary Airdrops until our third year." She returned her attention to me. "It's not that hard. All you're really doing is falling. Gravity handles most of that for you."

"I still have to jump out of the helicopter!" I reminded her. "That's terrifying!"

"So is being shot at," Erica said. "But you've done that plenty."

"Not because I wanted to," I pointed out. "In fact, I would be perfectly happy to never get shot at again. Or to never jump out of a helicopter, for that matter. Why didn't anyone tell me about this part earlier?"

"Because we were hoping to avoid this reaction you're having for as long as possible," Erica replied.

"Sorry, Benjamin," Catherine said. "It's the only way. Thankfully, Orion had this helicopter nicely stocked with parachute gear for everyone."

"It all came as a package," Orion said, by way of explanation. "I also got two years of free maintenance!" He was still wearing his robe, pajamas, and slippers, looking very out of place in the helicopter. He was not putting on a parachute, as his service was done.

"When we jump out, what happens to Alexander?" I asked.

"He'll be staying with the helicopter," Catherine said. "There's no other way. He'll have to fly off and leave us to our own devices." There was a hint of sadness to her voice, as though she had been enjoying having her husband along and didn't want him to go.

There didn't seem to be anything else for me to do except suit up. I reluctantly got to my feet and let Catherine help me into my jumpsuit. I did my best to act calm, cool, and collected in front of her, but my heart was racing and my stomach was threatening to get rid of that morning's scone via the way it had come in.

On the other side of the helicopter, Mike looked much calmer than me. In fact, he seemed downright excited about the upcoming jump.

Zoe didn't look so good. She was a shade of nauseous green I feared I might be as well.

Murray was also suited up, but he was seated in a yoga pose on the floor, doing his best to relax. The Murray I knew hadn't seemed much like the yoga type, but I figured maybe he'd picked it up during his month of incarceration at spy school.

Once Catherine had me dressed, she informed me, "You'll be doing a tandem jump with Erica to guarantee you pinpoint your landing. I'll leave you two to work out the details."

A tandem jump would involve Erica and me being strapped into the same parachute, most likely with my back to her chest, so she could be in control. I was torn about this. On the one hand, I was relieved, as I trusted Erica far more to work the chute and guide us to the proper landing spot than I trusted myself. On the other hand, if I panicked on the way down and started crying in fear, Erica would be strapped to me for the whole show.

"This is really quite easy," Erica assured me. "There's nothing to worry about."

"I suppose not," I said quietly. "I guess you've got your eyesight back."

"Oh, not at all," Erica replied. "I can barely see my hand in front of my face."

I gaped at her, startled she could be so calm under the circumstances. "You're still blind?"

"*Mostly* blind," she corrected. "My sight is starting to clear up slowly."

"But you put your parachute on without any trouble."

"Yes. Because I've practiced doing it blindfolded."

"Why?!"

"In case a situation like this ever came up. You have to be prepared for any eventuality in this business, Ben. I can also scale a brick wall while blinded, fight two enemy agents at once, or put on a scuba tank while surrounded by sharks."

"You practiced with sharks?"

"Don't be ridiculous. It's almost impossible to get your hands on live sharks. So I had to use grouper. Anyhow, since my sight's wonky, I'll need your help targeting our landing spot."

"And where is that?"

"The roof of the Musée d'Orsay."

"Right," I said with resignation. The Musée d'Orsay was

yet another museum that I had always wanted to visit, the finest repository of Impressionist art in the world. Of course, I had always imagined that I would be entering it through the front door and possibly even paying admission, rather than parachuting onto the roof, but this was the way my life seemed to be working out. I could only hope that we didn't end up destroying any priceless Monets.

"Which way is my mother?" Erica asked me. "I need to discuss some tactics with her."

"Fifteen steps to your left," I said.

"Thanks." Erica headed across the helicopter without giving away that she couldn't see.

I noticed Zoe was still looking as nervous as I felt, so I headed over to talk to her. "How are you feeling about this?" I asked.

Zoe glared at me angrily. "Oh. *Now* you want to know how I'm feeling?"

I took a step back, caught off guard. "What's that supposed to mean?"

"You didn't seem to care much about my feelings when you and Erica decided to hold hands back in the palace."

"You saw that?" I asked, surprised. Which, in retrospect, was probably the exact wrong response.

"Of course I saw it! You two were running along, right in the open, like it was a date."

A date where her ex-boyfriend was trying to kill us, I thought, though this time I had the presence of mind not to say that out loud. Instead, I said, "It wasn't what you thought it was. . . ."

"You held hands with *me* back in Mexico," Zoe reminded me. "Was that not what I thought it was either?"

"Um," I said, unsure how to answer that, in part because *I* wasn't even sure what to make of the fact that Zoe and I had held hands. We had never done it in any remotely romantic situation. Instead, we had always found ourselves holding hands when we were in danger. I was never even quite sure how it had happened.

"You can't just hold hands with me and then go off and hold hands with her and expect me to be okay with that," Zoe said.

"Hey!" I snapped back. "I'm not the one flirting with Mike every chance I get!"

At the time, I actually knew that was the wrong thing to say. But I couldn't help myself. My own jealousy just spilled out before I could stop myself.

Thankfully, the rotors of the helicopter were so loud, no one else overheard us—as far as I knew. But they could all see Zoe's reaction. She stood up and glared bullets at me. "How dare you?" she demanded. "I'm not flirting with him! I'm just being friends! And you don't have any right to be jealous. I told you I couldn't wait around for you forever to make a decision about us. But given the hand-holding, it's pretty clear you've picked Erica." Then she stormed away. She couldn't storm very far inside the helicopter—only a few steps—but it got the point across.

Mike came up alongside me. "Was that about you holding hands with Erica?"

I turned to him. "You saw that too?"

"No. But Zoe told me. She was awfully upset about it."

"It's not what she thinks . . . ," I began, although this time I didn't get far in my explanation, because Catherine announced, "Five minutes to drop zone! Let's get prepared!"

This news set my stomach roiling again. I glanced out the window and saw the city of Paris coming up quickly ahead of us.

"This probably isn't the best time," Mike told me, "but you need to make things right." Then he headed over to Zoe, who was his tandem jump buddy.

Catherine took her place beside Murray. She didn't look pleased about being teamed up with him, but then, if he tried anything crazy, she was probably best equipped to handle him.

A phone started ringing.

Whoever had their ringer on had it set to the highest level, so the phone rang out loud and clear and echoed inside the helicopter, even with the noise from the rotors. We all looked at one another, wondering whose phone it could be, until we pinpointed the noise and settled on Alexander.

He sheepishly fished the phone from his pocket and answered. "Alexander Hale speaking." He then listened a moment and, somewhat confused, looked to me. "Benjamin, it's for you."

Everyone now looked at me curiously, wondering who could possibly have been calling me there. I could only shrug in response. I went to Alexander's side, figuring that whoever had gone through that much trouble to reach me must have had a good reason.

"Hello?" I asked.

"Ben! It's Jawa!"

"Jawa?" I repeated, shocked. Jawaharlal O'Shea was one of my good friends back at spy school, an excellent student and future spy. Even so, there was no way he should have had Alexander Hale's phone number. "How did you . . . ?"

"I hacked the call logs off your phone a couple of weeks ago. Nothing personal. It was for class. Alexander had called you before and forgotten to block his caller ID. I've been trying to call you, but your phone seems to be turned off."

"It is," I lied, because I couldn't admit it had been destroyed on a top secret mission, seeing as that was what "top secret" meant.

"Three minutes to drop zone," Catherine announced.

We were now dropping lower over Paris. I could make out many of the famous landmarks: the iron spike of the Eiffel Tower, the blocky arch of the Arc de Triomphe, the sprawling mass of the Louvre. The Seine River curled through it all, with the Île de la Cité and Notre Dame sitting in the center.

Jawa asked, "Where are you, Ben?"

"I'm spending spring break at school, working on a project." That was the official story I was supposed to give to everyone.

"Then why are you wanted for breaking into the British Museum?"

"Ah," I said. "That's a case of mistaken identity."

"And Erica, Mike, Zoe, Alexander, and Murray Hill all happen to be wanted for the same thing?"

"Er . . . It's a very complicated case of mistaken identity."

"You're on a mission, aren't you?"

"No."

"I knew it! You *are* on a mission!"

"I just said I wasn't!"

"Because you're not allowed to say that you are. Which means you're on a mission!"

"It could also mean that I'm not. . . ."

I heard the sound of the phone being grabbed from Jawa, followed by the voice of Chip Schacter, another friend from school. Chip wasn't quite as bright as some of the other spies, but he was still loyal and true. "Ripley! You guys all went on a mission without us? You suck!"

"I'm not on a mission, Chip!"

"Liar. Would you be cool if I went on a mission without you?"

"Yes," I said, thinking that I would have been very happy at that moment if Chip and Jawa were the ones about to jump out of a helicopter rather than me.

"Well, if I *was* on a mission, and you asked me if I was on it, I'd at least tell you the truth."

"No, you wouldn't. You'd be under orders not to."

"One minute to drop zone," Catherine said.

Alexander slowed the helicopter. The city of Paris now radiated out around all sides of us.

It was still disturbingly far *below* us though, given that we were about to leap out of a helicopter.

Erica suddenly snatched the phone from me and spoke into it. "Chip, this is Erica. Ben has to go. We have a very important study session right now. But I have a favor to ask first. . . ."

That last part surprised me. Erica wasn't the type to ask anyone for favors.

I didn't get to hear what it was, though, because Catherine threw the side door to the helicopter open.

The craft now filled with the whirr of its own rotors.

Wind howled through the chopper, chilling us and making Orion's bathrobe flap behind him like a cape.

Murray presented himself at Catherine's side. He didn't say anything cocky or ask if she had any snacks on her. He seemed resigned to his fate.

Catherine quickly buckled her harness to his, so she was strapped to his back.

Mike followed her lead and did the same thing to Zoe.

Erica handed the phone back to Alexander and said, "Thanks, Daddy. See you soon."

As far as I knew, that was the first time she had ever called him "Daddy." Or "Dad." Or anything that would have acknowledged he was her father.

Then she clipped her harness onto mine.

Catherine and Murray leapt out of the helicopter.

Then Mike and Zoe went.

One second they were all there, and the next they had dropped out of sight.

Erica and I shuffled to the open door.

I made the terrible mistake of looking down. Directly below us, my friends were plummeting toward Paris at sickening speed.

"Ready?" Erica asked.

"Not really," I said.

"Too bad," Erica said, and then yanked me out of the helicopter.

BLENDING IN

High above the Musée d'Orsay
Paris, France
April 1
1230 hours

Parachuting out of a helicopter turned out to not be nearly as bad as I had expected.

Then again, I had been expecting it to be horrible, so my expectations were quite low.

The first few seconds *were* pretty bad. Watching the ground rush upward to meet you is simply not my idea of a good time. But then Erica yanked the cord on our chute and suddenly, instead of plummeting to our doom, we were gently drifting downward toward Paris.

It was far nicer than suddenly dropping through the glass floor of the Tower Bridge and plummeting into the Thames had been.

And it was even nicer than parasailing with Erica back in Mexico, because while that had been part of a plan to infiltrate a stronghold full of enemy agents, our target this time was one of the finest art museums in the world.

All in all, I had been through a lot worse lately. Even though Erica was semi-blinded, I still trusted her to land us properly, so I wasn't too concerned about that. The view of the city was quite lovely as well. My only real concern was that lots of people could see us coming down, as it was very hard to camouflage ourselves against a blue sky in the middle of the day—and quite a few of those people who could see us were police. It's illegal to parachute into the middle of most major cities, and Paris was no exception. As we got closer to the ground, I noticed many patrolmen watching us intently. As they determined we were heading for the museum, they began heading there too. In droves.

The museum was a large target. It had once been a train station, so the roof was wide and flat, and since the building was right on the edge of the Seine, it was easy to keep track of. That didn't mean I could have directed myself there alone, but Erica had little trouble getting us to it—although I did have to give her some guidance, given that her eyesight still wasn't fully recovered. We stuck the landing right in the dead center of the roof.

The others were already down. Catherine had parked herself and Murray perfectly, and even though Mike had never parachuted before, his innate athletic ability had served him well. He and Zoe hadn't executed a flawless landing, but they had made it to the proper building and had not injured themselves.

The roof of the museum was seven stories up, high above much of the surrounding city, affording us a gorgeous view of Paris. It was a beautiful spring day. The temperature was perfect and the rooftop was warm after baking in the sun. It would have been a lovely place to sit if we hadn't just flagrantly broken the law and attracted the attention of every policeman in Paris.

Sirens wailed in the streets below. Dozens of squad cars were racing toward the museum. The cops probably didn't know we were the same fugitives wanted for the attack on the British Museum yet—but parachuting onto a national landmark was already enough of a crime for them to be coming en masse.

"We need to move fast," Catherine said.

We quickly unhooked ourselves from one another and shed our jumpsuits. Erica tightly knotted the silk from two parachutes together, then wrapped the harness from one around a safety railing and tossed the rest over the northern edge of the roof.

Shortly beyond the rail, the roof curved gracefully downward. "Follow me," Erica ordered, then hopped over the rail and used the parachutes as a rope to rappel down over the curve.

The rest of us obediently fell into line even before she was off the end of the parachutes, with Catherine bringing up the rear. There was a time when rappelling off a roof might have seemed scary to me, but I had done things like this in school several times by now, and as far as frightening activities were concerned, it paled in comparison to everything else we had done that day.

I stepped aside to allow Zoe the chance to go ahead of me, thinking she might at least appreciate my chivalry. She responded with a hard glare that indicated she was still angry at me, then got on the chute and disappeared over the edge of the roof.

I went next. Beyond the curve, the roof grew much steeper, but we weren't heading all the way down to the street. Instead, there was only a ten-foot drop to a long, broad terrace on the sixth floor that served as outdoor dining for a museum café. Since it was a nice day and lunchtime, the terrace was crowded with tourists, most of whom were surprised to see us rappelling down from above.

Erica set the tone for how to handle this; she acted like

our unorthodox arrival was no big deal at all. She didn't even so much as say "*Bonjour*" to anyone. This was a perfect example of Bernetti's Third Principle of Going Unobserved: If you pretend like your behavior is perfectly normal, most people will assume it's perfectly normal, even if it's not. The tourists watched us as we descended one after the other, but they didn't make a fuss or alert security. If anything, some seemed jealous that we were doing this. I observed a few Americans desperately searching their guidebooks for roof-top tours of the museum.

We might have made it out without any trouble at all if Murray, the fifth one down, hadn't lost his grip on the parachute and fallen onto one of the lunch tables, landing squarely in the middle of the charcuterie plate and catapulting several bowls of French onion soup into the laps of unsuspecting diners. Now tourists leapt to their feet, yelping in surprise and causing a commotion. One unfortunate elderly woman had gotten the worst of it: She was coated in bits of meat, and the cheese cap from her soup was now perched atop her head like a beret. Murray didn't help matters much when he plucked a gob of goose liver pâté off her shoulder and asked, "Are you going to eat this, or can I have it?"

Catherine rappelled down into the midst of the chaos, ordered, "After me, children," and quickly led the way off the terrace and into the museum. We crossed through the café, hooked a left into the Impressionist galleries, and promptly slowed our pace.

My instincts had been to run like crazy for the exit, but I instantly grasped why Catherine's plan was better: We were not the only group of students in the museum. In fact, the galleries were mobbed with school groups, and there were dozens of small clusters of kids our age being herded about by adult chaperones like Catherine. We blended right in.

This was one of several times when being kids had worked to our advantage. Chances were that when the police arrived, looking for whoever had illegally parachuted onto the building, they would assume the perpetrators were all adults. And while the tourists on the terrace knew we were kids, it would be a while until the police got all the way up there and questioned them. In the meantime, if we didn't draw attention to ourselves, we might have been able to walk right out the exit.

Sadly, that didn't mean we had time to see the museum. Even though we were acting like kids on a school tour, we still had to move quickly—like kids on a school tour who had just discovered that their bus was about to leave without them. Once again, we had to rush right past numerous incredible works of art that I was dying to see: Monets, Renoirs, van Goghs, and Cézannes. I barely had a glimpse of them through the crowds as Catherine hustled us past.

The galleries were so tightly packed with tourists, it was

like being in a subway train at rush hour. And since the tourists were all focused more on the art than on everyone else, they kept wandering into our path. It was difficult to wind our way through them all, especially for Erica, who still hadn't completely regained her sight. After colliding with someone for the third time, she slipped her hand into mine once more, indicating that I needed to lead the way for her.

Zoe noticed this and promptly misinterpreted the reason for it yet again. I couldn't really explain why it was happening at the moment, though, and I couldn't release Erica's hand. Zoe gave me an icy stare, then made a show of taking Mike's hand as they wove through a display of sculptures by Edgar Degas. Mike seemed surprised by this, but he didn't let go, either.

The Impressionist galleries were only a tiny part of the Musée d'Orsay. They ended at a wide metal balcony that gave us a great view of the main portion of the museum: a cavernous space, several stories high.

We could see all the way across it to the main entrance at the far end. Several policemen were clustered on a much lower balcony there. Some were scanning the main portion of the museum as well, while others were poring over museum maps, trying to figure out how to get to the roof. None of the police seemed to take any notice of us, most likely dismissing us as yet another school group, dozens of which were swarming around them.

We descended a large metal staircase and then crossed the main floor toward the exit.

The police now began to fan out into the museum. Several came our way, but as they approached, Catherine launched herself into a school chaperone act, speaking to us in perfect French. (I could tell because I spoke French myself; it was one of the few talents I had acquired before spy school.) "Move along, children! If we don't meet the rest of our class at the entrance soon, we'll miss lunch!"

Even though I knew Catherine was a secret agent, she still looked far more like a member of the PTA. The police bought her act, hurrying past us without a second glance.

We finally arrived at the entry hall. It was filled with tourists, but most were still streaming in, rather than heading out, so we finally had enough space around us that Catherine felt comfortable enough to talk without being overheard. "Those coordinates Benjamin found for us are on the Île Saint-Louis. It's only a brisk walk along the Seine from here. We can be there . . ."

She was interrupted by a sudden, startled shout from behind us. I fought the urge to turn around and give us away, as did Catherine and Erica—but Mike, Zoe, and Murray all gave in to it. In the reflection of the glass doors ahead, I saw a French policewoman staring after us suspiciously. When the others turned toward her, her eyes widened in surprise, and she promptly glanced at her phone, as if comparing us to an image there. "That's them!" she shouted, but in French.

I had no idea how she had noticed us. But we weren't going to stick around to find out.

Catherine bolted for the doors, and the rest of us followed her lead. We raced out into the plaza in front of the museum, which was jammed with tourists. Long lines of them snaked up to the ticket booths, while others clustered around mimes, musicians, and caricaturists. We used the crowd as cover, slipping through it as fast as we could. Behind us, the police burst from the museum and scanned the plaza for us.

There was a subway entrance at the corner ahead, a stairway descending into the ground. More tourists were surging up to the surface from it.

Murray suddenly broke away from us. "I'll distract them!" he cried. "Get to the subway!" And with that, he dashed in the other direction.

His actions caught all of us by surprise. Perhaps, if Erica's sight hadn't been compromised, she wouldn't have let him get the jump on her, but now he had several steps' head start on us. I glanced after Murray, unsure what to do, as did everyone else. I had a hard time believing he could possibly be doing anything so chivalrous—and yet he was definitely trying to attract the attention of the police. If he had really wanted to escape free and clear, he could have skulked off quietly, but he was making quite a scene, bumping into as many tourists as possible. He also shoved over a mime who was performing for a small crowd, though he might have done this only because he hated mimes. The police quickly spotted him and homed in on him. Now if we went after him, we would certainly end up captured.

So Catherine led us in the other direction. While the police were watching Murray, we raced toward the subway. Just as we reached the stairs, I heard a policeman shout, "Over there! The children! At the Metro!"

Murray had bought us some time, but not quite enough to fully escape. We had perhaps a thirty-second head start.

Unfortunately, that wasn't quite enough time to buy subway tickets. There was a line for the machines, and even though I could read French, the instructions were long and complicated enough that I feared it would take me several minutes to sort them out. The turnstiles had gates, so we couldn't jump them, and there were Metro police patrolling them anyhow.

However, there was a door halfway down the stairs marked DEPARTMENT OF SANITATION. NO ADMITTANCE. (In French.) The door was old, with an outdated lock that any decent thief could have picked in thirty seconds.

Erica picked it in fifteen. Even with her eyes in bad shape.

We slipped through the door and found ourselves in a

wide, dark tunnel with a narrow concrete walkway running along a deep trench. It was too dim to see what was in the trench, but I could certainly smell it. Running parallel to the subway line, which shuttled millions of human beings from place to place, there was a sewer line, which shuttled what came *out* of millions of human beings from place to place. The odor assaulted us so hard, it was like being punched in the face.

The concrete walkway ran only a few feet before coming to a large iron grating that blocked the entire tunnel. There was a gate in the grating, but it had a lock on it that looked far more time-consuming to pick than the one on the door we had come through. We were trapped.

Erica locked the door behind us. Through it, I could hear the police approaching.

The lock on the door probably wasn't going to stall the police much longer than it had stalled us.

Catherine turned to us and spoke in the same tone my mother did when she had to inform me that my goldfish had died. "I'm afraid there's only one way out of this."

Sadly, I knew exactly what she meant.

NAVIGATION

The sewer

Directly underneath Rue de Lille

Paris, France

April 1

1300 hours

I had often dreamed of going to Paris. I had already done plenty of research for that day. There were hundreds of places I wanted to visit.

The sewers were not one of them.

I had imagined that my first hours in Paris would be delightful: visiting museums, strolling through the parks, taking in the sights. Instead, within half an hour of arriving there, I had been thrown out of a helicopter against my will, chased by the police—and then fully submerged in human waste.

My first visit to Paris wasn't a dream. It was a nightmare.

Mike had been the most resistant to getting in the sewer. While the rest of us had dutifully held our noses and prepared to dive in, he had held firm on the concrete walkway. "No," he said. "No, no, no, no, no. I'm not going in there."

"I'm afraid you are," Catherine had told him, and then shoved him in.

I leapt in right afterward. I had assumed it was going to be the most disgusting thing I had ever experienced in my life—and it turned out to be far worse than I had imagined.

Judging from the gagging and retching sounds my friends were making around me, they weren't enjoying it any more than me.

A second later, the door we had come through rattled. I heard a policeman on the other side say, "Maybe they came through here!"

"It's locked," said a second.

"They might have locked it behind them," the first replied. "We should check."

The door rattled again, harder this time.

"Stand aside," said the second policeman. Then the door flew open as he drove his foot into it.

I took a deep breath and sank into the sewage. Through

the murk, I could hear the police react with disgust as they were hit by the smell. I listened to them as they swept the trench with their flashlights. They spent only a few seconds doing it, but in my position, a few seconds was an eternity. It was the worst thing I had ever experienced—and I'd had people try to kill me on a regular basis.

Finally, the first policeman said, "No sign of them."

"Must have gone into the subway, then," the second said.

Even with my ears clogged with human waste, I could tell the police didn't want to spend any more time down there than they had to.

Then I heard them leave, shutting the door behind them.

I burst out of the sewage, gasping for air—and then found that my mouth was filled with toxic sewage fumes, which made me want to vomit. Mike and Zoe emerged beside me, having almost the exact same experience.

Erica and Catherine were much calmer as they emerged, though neither of them looked happy.

We all scrambled out of the trench as quickly as we could, not that our situation was improved much by standing on the concrete ledge, still covered head to toe with effluent.

"This is not what I signed up for when I agreed to be a spy," Mike grumbled. "Spies are supposed to go to swanky parties and visit fabulous places and have car chases and cool stuff like that. No one said anything about being covered up to my head in poop!"

"Sometimes we all have to make sacrifices for the greater good," Catherine said.

"James Bond never had to hide in a sewer!" Mike exclaimed.

"James Bond isn't real," Erica informed him. Instead of heading out the door, she took her penlight from her utility belt and shone it around the concrete ledge.

"You know who should have been down in here with us?" Zoe asked. "Murray. That weasel chose the perfect moment to sacrifice himself—if he was even really sacrificing himself at all."

"It certainly *looked* like he was sacrificing himself," Catherine said. "Those were real police up there, and he wasn't going to get away from them."

"Murray isn't the sacrificing sort of person," Zoe said. "He's the 'What's in it for me?' sort of person. I've seen him shove a nun out of the way to get to a doughnut."

"People can change," Catherine suggested.

"*I'd* like to change," Mike said. "I'd like to change into clothes that aren't saturated in human waste. And then I'd like to spend the rest of the day in the shower, scrubbing myself clean."

"What are you looking for?" I asked Erica.

"There must be a hose around here somewhere," Erica replied. "The concrete walkway's clean. Or it was until we showed up. The sewer people must have some way to rinse it off. . . . Ah! There it is!"

Sure enough, there was a thick red hose wrapped around a spigot off in a dark recess of the wall. The hose was grimy and caked with muck, but it was still one of the most beautiful things I had ever seen in my life.

We quickly turned on the spigot and hosed ourselves off. It was a far cry from a warm shower, but it was still wonderful to get clean. We passed the hose back and forth quickly, washing the gunk off our bodies, flushing the filth from our hair, and rinsing our clothes out while we were still wearing them. After a few minutes, we were sopping wet, bedraggled, and chilled, but that was still a big step up compared to how we had been feeling shortly before.

"We still don't smell great," I observed.

"We're in France," Mike said. "No one even uses deodorant here. We'll fit right in."

Catherine wandered over to the iron grating that blocked the rest of the sewer and peered down the tunnel through it. "This looks like it runs right along the Seine," she observed. "That's the exact direction we want to go."

"Oh no," Mike groaned. "You're not suggesting we stay down here?"

"We've already been submerged in that filth," Catherine replied. "This couldn't possibly get worse than *that*. Besides, the police are probably still combing the area for us up above. This will keep us out of sight almost the entire way to where Mr. E is holed up."

"Yes," Mike said. "But this is a *sewer*. It smells like the inside of ten million people's bowels. I'm willing to take my chances on the surface."

"I'm sorry, Michael, but this is the prudent choice." Catherine checked her utility belt, then looked to Erica. "Do you have any small explosives, darling? I think I used the last of mine last week."

Erica checked a pocket on her own belt. "Nitroglycerine or C-4?"

"Oh, a spot of nitro ought to do the trick just fine. C-4 is a tad too loud. Don't want to alert the police. Then we'd be in a pickle."

"Sure thing." Erica and Catherine appeared to have already fully recovered from the morning's adventures, chatting about explosives the way most families might talk about doing the dishes. They had weathered everything far better than I had, looking relaxed and bizarrely stylish. Like they had merely been caught in a light spring rain, rather than plunged into a trench full of human waste and then doused with cold water.

Erica cautiously placed a dollop of nitroglycerine in the lock on the iron grating, then ignited the fuse and ran back to the rest of us. We all curled into protective balls, just in case something went wrong.

Nothing did, though. The charge worked exactly as it was supposed to. There was a hiss from the fuse, followed by a slight pop, and when we looked back at the gate, it was hanging open and tendrils of smoke were curling up from the lock.

"Very good," Catherine said brightly. "Let's move on, children."

She led the way through the grating and along the sewer.

The tunnel remained wide and high enough for us to walk without stooping, and except for the contents of the trench, it was surprisingly clean. If we hadn't been walking along a river of human excrement, it would have almost been pleasant.

The tunnel curved slightly as we walked, following the bend of the river. We could hear cars rumbling along the road above us and subway trains hurtling past on the other side of the wall. Every so often, a few weak shafts of light would spear down into the darkness, indicating a manhole cover above. At each of these, metal rungs would be bolted into the concrete wall, leading up to the surface.

Erica's vision seemed to have fully returned to her—or perhaps, in the dark tunnel, she realized that she could see just as well as me and no longer needed my help to guide her.

She stayed close behind Catherine, who was leading the way, while Mike, Zoe, and I followed in single file.

Operation Screaming Vengeance was now down to only five members. We had lost Cyrus before we even got started. Alexander had flown away in the helicopter. Murray was off with the French police—or maybe he'd pulled a fast one on us. Either way, he was gone.

As we worked our way through the sewers, our team seemed awfully small to me. Yes, I trusted and believed in every member of it, but the idea that only the five of us were going up against the top rung of SPYDER still filled me with dread. Especially when I considered that Joshua Hallal, the police forces of two major cities, and possibly even a third team of bad guys, led by Jenny Lake, were after us.

Rather than obsess about all that, though, I turned my attention to the one thing I *could* handle at the moment.

Zoe was bringing up the rear of our team as we headed through the sewer. I fell back and joined her. "I need to explain why I was holding Erica's hand," I said quietly, hoping we were far enough away that the others wouldn't hear.

Zoe gave me yet another glare in the dim light. "I know exactly why you were doing it. Because you two like each other and you always have."

"Erica couldn't see anything," I said. "She was temporarily blinded by that blast at Orion's house. The one in the kitchen."

"Yeah, right."

"I'm telling the truth. Think about it. I wasn't holding her hand before that, right?"

There was a long silence. When Zoe spoke again, there was no longer an edge to her voice. "No."

"She needed my help after that. She couldn't see anything."

"Then why didn't she say anything to us?"

"Because she's Erica. She didn't want everyone to freak out when there was already so much going on. So she only told me."

"And not her parents?"

"Her parents probably would have freaked out the worst. No matter how competent Catherine is, Erica's still her daughter."

There was another silence. Then Zoe said, "Ben, I'm sorry. I didn't realize. . . ."

"It's all right," I said. "I understand why you got upset."

"Back in Mexico, when you were trying to explain how relationships mess everything up in this business . . . This is the sort of thing you were talking about, right?"

"I guess so."

Another silence followed. But instead of saying anything at the end of this one, Zoe slipped her hand into mine.

I laced my fingers through hers and held tight.

We continued on like that through the darkness. I wasn't

sure if we were holding hands because we were friends, or if we were doing it because we wanted it to be something more. But for the time being, it made me feel better.

That lasted until we came upon the cavern filled with human skulls.

We were alerted to its presence by Mike completely flipping out. He was a little bit ahead of us and a little bit behind Catherine and Erica, and he suddenly shrieked at the top of his lungs. "There are dead people in here!" he howled.

Zoe and I let go of each other's hands and raced up to where he was. A tunnel branched off of ours there, but it was much older, rougher, and narrower. It looked like it had been hacked through the rock with pickaxes centuries before, and then at some point, whoever had put the sewer line through had run across it. The old tunnel had been gated off, but the chain that held the gate shut had been clipped open by someone with bolt cutters.

That all might have been eerie enough, but to top it off, the walls of the tunnel were lined with human skulls. Hundreds of them. Like they were some horrible form of wallpaper.

"Oh, that's just one of the catacombs," Catherine said pleasantly. "Paris is filled with them. There are thousands, really."

"There are thousands of tunnels lined with the skulls of dead people?" Mike asked, horrified. "And everyone in Paris is totally fine with that?"

"I'm not sure everyone knows about them," Catherine said. "The tunnels weren't originally dug out as catacombs. They were quarries for all the rock that the city is built from. But then the city grew out over the quarries. And at some point, some religious sects decided it'd be nice to inter their dead down here."

"And they did it by stacking their skulls up along the walls?" Mike asked. "How mentally disturbed were these people?"

"Someone's gone through here," Zoe observed, pointing to the severed chain.

"There are a lot of people who like to explore these catacombs," Catherine explained. "It's illegal, but still quite popular. I understand that there are even a few communities living down here."

"Living down *here*?" Mike repeated. "With hundreds of skulls lining the walls and the stench of sewage everywhere? Man, there are some really deranged people out there."

"At least they're not trying to make money off of human misery," Catherine said. "Unlike SPYDER. Speaking of which . . ." She paused and checked her phone. "According to my GPS, the location of those coordinates is directly above us."

"You mean . . . ," Zoe began.

"That's right," Catherine said. "We're on the doorstep of Mr. E."

ANALYSIS

The sewer

Directly underneath Quai de Montebello

Paris, France

April 1

1430 hours

A new feeling crept over me, replacing the sense of the willies the skulls had given me. I now felt excitement at the prospect of being so close to the leader of SPYDER. The rest of the CIA had barely been able to confirm that Mr. E even existed until I had come along (except for the agents who'd been corrupted by him, of course), and now we were right outside his house.

My excitement was tempered with a great deal of fear as

well. Mr. E ran one of the most evil organizations on earth, so chances were good that we were in for some trouble.

There was a manhole directly above me, fifteen feet over my head, with a ladder of iron rungs leading up to it. A few feeble beams of light filtered down through the holes in the cover, though they blinked out every few seconds as a car drove over us.

"Let's see what security Mr. E has." Erica withdrew yet another device from her utility belt: a very small camera with a long, thin cable attached. She handed the end with the plug to her mother, then scampered up the ladder of iron rungs with the other end. When she reached the top, she fed the camera through one of the holes in the manhole cover.

Catherine jacked the cable into her phone. The image from the camera came up on the screen. It was of quite high quality, allowing us a good look of the buildings above, although it was a very low worm's-eye view. Mike, Zoe, and I huddled around Catherine to look at it.

The first thing Erica did was turn the camera in a full circle, giving us a 360-degree sweep of what was above. The road was directly along the edge of the right bank of the Seine, but since the banks were built so high, street level was a good three stories above the river.

Directly to the north of us, a large pedestrian bridge—the Pont au Double—extended over the Seine to the grand plaza in front of Notre Dame. Once again, I was close to a tourist attraction I had always dreamed of visiting, and yet I was stuck in a sewer, viewing it through a camera.

Even seen this way, the famous church was beautiful, its graceful stone spires, buttresses, and gargoyles gleaming in the sun. Hundreds of tourists were teeming around it, taking group shots and selfies with their phones in the plaza, streaming across the Pont au Double, and crowded all along the bank of the Seine.

The raised riverbank had a wide pedestrian walkway that was lined with booths selling everything from fruits and vegetables to paintings of street scenes to secondhand books. On the opposite side of the road was a small park (though we couldn't see much of it given our low angle).

Finally, on the corner across the street from the park was the building in question, the home of Mr. E and thus the power center of SPYDER.

Frankly, it didn't look like much.

It appeared to be a decent enough building, and it certainly had an incredible view of Notre Dame, but I had expected something more. I had thought that the head of SPYDER might live in some place large and lavish, like Orion's palace. Or perhaps a heavily armed fortress. Or maybe a remote chalet at the top of a mountain in the Alps. This building was simply, almost disturbingly . . . normal.

Which, I suddenly realized, was exactly what I should have been expecting all along. SPYDER was never ostentatious. The organization always hid in plain sight, whether it was building its own gated community in the suburbs of New Jersey or renting a suite in the middle of a Mexican vacation resort. So it made sense that Mr. E would, at least on the surface, live someplace as normal-looking as possible.

The building was six stories tall, although the first story was a restaurant. This being Paris, I would have expected a nice little bistro where everyone was eating brie and baguettes and sipping coffee at outdoor tables. Instead, it was a Burger King.

Above the restaurant, there was nothing particularly intriguing about the building at all. It looked like a million other buildings in Paris: It was made of dull beige stone, the windows had wrought-iron railings, and the balconies were so small and narrow that there was barely room for a person to stand on them. The front door was wedged between the Burger King and a Starbucks.

"Are we sure this is the right place?" Zoe asked.

"Definitely," Catherine answered. "I've counted at least seven men guarding it so far."

"Really?" Mike asked.

Catherine said, "There are two sitting outside the Burger King, three in the park, and two on the bank of the river, one of whom is pretending to be a used book dealer and one of whom is posing as a grocer. They look relatively normal, of course, but they're all packing heat. I recognize two of them from the British Museum."

"So . . . Those guys *were* working for SPYDER then," Zoe surmised.

"I suppose so," Catherine said. "And that's just the ones I've detected in a cursory sweep. I'm sure there must be at least a dozen others."

"That'd make sixteen people!" Mike exclaimed.

"Nineteen," I corrected. "At least."

"Nineteen," Mike agreed. "Sorry. Math's not my best subject. Point is, that's an awful lot of bad guys protecting one building. How are we supposed to get past them all?"

"Especially when the building probably has a dozen separate security systems?" Zoe added. "We'll never get in off the street."

"Then let's not go in off the street," I said, suddenly struck by an idea.

The others looked to me, intrigued.

"What are you thinking?" Catherine asked.

I said, "When we came across SPYDER's old headquarters in New Jersey, it looked completely normal, but there was a whole lot hidden beneath the surface. I'm guessing that's the case with this place too. There's no way Mr. E is living in a completely normal building. SPYDER must have altered that place somehow. At the very least, there's bound to be a secret entrance, so Mr. E can sneak in—or sneak out if he thinks there's trouble. And where's the best place to put a secret entrance?"

Everyone realized what I was talking about at once. "Underground," they all said.

"Right," I agreed. "If Paris really does have this whole maze of sewers and catacombs and other tunnels down here, then that'd be the perfect way for Mr. E—or any other members of SPYDER—to get around unnoticed."

"And it'd be a good way to move all sorts of illegal goods as well," Erica added. She yanked the camera back through the manhole and then climbed down the ladder of rungs. "Although it doesn't look like there's an access from the sewer."

"No," Catherine said thoughtfully. "It'd be too hard to build that without someone from the sanitation department noticing. And that doesn't seem like SPYDER's style, either. I doubt Mr. E likes the idea of coming and going through a tunnel filled with sewage."

"The catacomb!" Zoe exclaimed. "That goes right along the basement of the building."

"Buildings in Paris don't have basements," Catherine said, but then caught herself and added, "but perhaps this one does."

We all returned to the catacomb. The tunnel seemed even creepier than before, knowing it might provide access to Mr. E's home somehow, but we headed into it anyway.

The only light we had was from Erica's and Catherine's penlights, which wasn't much. It turned out, the walls weren't only lined with skulls, but with a whole assortment of human bones, which were stacked up like firewood. And occasionally, a rat would scuttle past our feet. Heading through a narrow, dark, rat-infested tunnel lined with human bones was so unnerving, it actually made me nostalgic for our trip through the sewer.

About twenty feet along, we came to a fork in the tunnel where some ancient, depraved interior decorator had arranged the bones into a pattern, with the skulls making a series of concentric circles, like a target. Erica paused there, scrutinizing the wall on the opposite side of the tunnel, right where the basement of Mr. E's house would have been. This side had no decorative patterns, only a random assortment of skulls.

"What's wrong?" Zoe asked.

"These skulls are newer than the ones on the other side," Erica observed.

"How can you tell?" Mike asked, then said quickly, "Come to think of it, don't tell me. I really don't want to know the answer to that."

"Really?" Erica asked. "Because the forensics are quite fascinating. . . ."

"I agree with Mike," Zoe said. "I'm perfectly happy not knowing."

Erica sighed with disappointment. "Fine. The point is, these skulls have been put here relatively recently. I'd say they're only a few years old." She grabbed one by the eye sockets and gave it a good, hard yank. It stayed right where it was.

"It's bolted to the wall, too," Erica said. "I'll bet the ones on the other side of the tunnel aren't. Ben, check and see."

"No thanks," I said. I really didn't want to stick my fingers into the cranial cavity of one of my great-great-great-great-great-great-ancestors.

"Ben," Erica said firmly.

"Okay. I'll check." I reluctantly stuck my fingers into a random skull and tugged on it.

It was mortared to the wall, but the mortar was hundreds of years old and crumbled. The skulls popped free relatively easily, revealing the stone behind it. I quickly replaced the skull and wiped my hand on my shirt. "This is *sooo* not how I wanted to spend my first day in Paris."

"You should consider yourself lucky," Catherine told me. "My first day in Paris, I was undercover with a group of neo-Nazis who didn't believe in bathing. That was no picnic."

"The way this day's going, we'll probably run into them by dinnertime," Mike muttered under his breath.

Catherine aimed her penlight between the newer skulls and examined the wall behind them. "That looks like concrete to me. Must be the wall of Mr. E's basement." She turned to Erica. "Now might be a nice time to use that C-4 explosive of yours."

"All right," Erica said.

"Wait!" I exclaimed. "You're going to blow through that wall?"

"I'd ring the doorbell, but it doesn't look like there's one down here," Erica said.

"I thought the whole idea was to sneak in," I said. "If you blow the wall, won't that alert everyone?"

"The idea is to get in, period," Catherine informed me. "Maybe this will trigger the alarms. Maybe it won't. But it will at least get us inside. If we move fast, we might be able to get a jump on Mr. E before his security team can react."

"Might?" Zoe repeated, concerned.

"We'll have to figure this out as we go," Catherine said. "I know that's worrisome, but I don't think we have the time to wait around for another option to present itself. With all the various factions of rogues and scoundrels on the hunt for us, as well as the police, we're on borrowed time as it is." She stepped aside and looked to Erica again. "Darling, do the honors."

Erica removed a wad of C-4 from a small bulletproof case she kept in her utility belt. She broke it into four chunks, jammed each one into the skulls, and then jabbed wires into them. "Get back," she ordered us.

We all hurried back toward the sewer. Erica followed us, playing out more wire, until we were a safe distance away. Then she connected the wires to a small detonator. "Here goes nothing," she said, and pressed the plunger.

The explosion wasn't as loud as I had expected, but it was big enough to jolt the earth around us. The skulls in the tunnel rattled, and tiny flakes of stone rained down on us from the ceiling. A large cloud of dust, debris, and human bone fragments billowed through the tunnel in the distance.

No alarms went off, though.

We pulled our shirts up over our faces so we wouldn't breathe in any dust—or human bone fragments—and hurried back through the cloud. It was dissipating as we got to the place where the explosives had gone off.

The skulls had all blown away, revealing a relatively new concrete wall behind it. That wall now had a hole in it big enough for us to climb through.

So we climbed through it.

Catherine went first, and when no one jumped out from the shadows and clubbed her unconscious, Erica followed. The rest of us filed through after her.

For once, luck briefly seemed to be on our side.

We didn't find ourselves surrounded by enemy agents lying in wait for us with all sorts of deadly weapons pointed our way. Instead, we were in a storage room in Mr. E's basement. It was a rather normal storage room, with concrete walls and fluorescent lights and lots of shelves. It was filled with items that had been smuggled into the country, but in this case, most of it wasn't illegal contraband; it was American junk food that the French didn't approve of. There were plastic bins filled with Hostess Ding Dongs, nacho-flavored Doritos, peanut butter, Pop-Tarts, and Hershey bars.

"From the looks of this, Mr. E is American," Catherine observed quietly.

"Or he knows Murray is coming to visit," I said.

There were many household items in the storage room, like cleaning supplies and toilet paper—and, because it was SPYDER's storage room, there were also weapons. One wall held an array of guns, crossbows, grenades, explosives, and a flamethrower.

"Who on earth needs a flamethrower?" Zoe asked. "I mean, I know SPYDER is evil and all, but honestly, when does that come in handy around the house?"

"You'd be surprised," Erica said, taking a bit of C-4 to refill her utility belt. "We're just lucky all this wasn't on the wall we blew open, or this entire place would have come down on top of us."

Catherine selected two handguns and some ammunition for herself. "We'd best take advantage of this and arm ourselves, children," she said, then looked to me. "Including you, Benjamin."

"I'm not so good with weapons," I reminded her. "I got an N on my last exam in firearms."

"An N?" Catherine asked, surprised. "Is that supposed to be five times worse than an F?"

"Kind of. I think Professor Crichton made it up just for me. He said the N stands for 'Never ever let this person use a gun.'"

"Perhaps only a grenade or two, then," Catherine suggested.

I gingerly picked up a grenade while everyone else grabbed weapons. I didn't like being responsible for something potentially deadly at all, but I reluctantly crammed it into my pocket. We were in the lion's den now, and Catherine was right; I ought to be prepared.

I also took some Ding Dongs, because we had missed lunch.

Once armed, we passed out of the storage room. Catherine and Erica led the way, their newly pilfered weapons at the ready.

We emerged into a basement that was a little more like what I had expected from SPYDER. It looked like a relatively normal basement, only with some evil touches. There was a foosball table and a dartboard, but there were also a rocket-propelled grenade launcher and some metallic cases of the sort that stolen nuclear weapons were stored in. The whole place was austere concrete and appeared to have been built within the last five years.

The dartboard had my photo on it. Three darts were plugged directly into my face.

I groaned upon seeing this.

"You shouldn't be upset," Mike told me. "You should be flattered! You're the number one enemy of the most evil organization in the world!"

"That's not really making me feel better," I said.

Also, I noticed that Erica looked the tiniest bit jealous that *her* photo wasn't on the dartboard.

A stairwell led up to the rest of the house, while a door with multiple security systems led into the catacombs.

"That's probably camouflaged with skulls on the outside too," Erica said. "Luckily for us, SPYDER didn't realize anyone might breach any place down here besides their own door." She nodded toward an elaborate security system mounted over the door. "That looks like it drops poison gas on whoever enters uninvited."

I breathed a sigh of relief. It appeared that, in this case, SPYDER might have been too clever for their own good. They had disguised their secret door so well that we hadn't noticed it and had thus come in through the storage room wall instead.

At the top of the stairwell, we heard a door creak open and then footsteps coming down.

They weren't the heavy, plodding footsteps of one of SPYDER's usual thugs. Instead, the footsteps were light and soft, as though the person making them didn't weigh much. We heard a woman speaking in French, though so softly, I couldn't make out the words.

Catherine signaled for all of us to hide. She and Erica flattened themselves up against the walls on opposite sides of the stairwell, weapons at the ready, while Mike, Zoe, and I ducked behind the foosball table.

A maid came tottering down the stairs. She appeared to be in her sixties, with glasses perched on her nose and her gray hair drawn back in a bun. She wore a traditional maid's black uniform, complete with a little headband and sensible shoes, and she was cradling a cat in her arms. It was a skittish orange tabby, and she was speaking to it in a slightly dotty fashion. "I know, Gaspard. I heard something down here too," she said in French. "I hope the rats haven't gotten into the Pop-Tarts again."

As she reached the bottom of the stairs, Catherine and Erica stepped out on both sides of her, aiming their guns.

The maid was so startled, she dropped the cat, which yowled when it hit the floor and scampered back up the stairs. *"Zut alors!"* the maid exclaimed, which was French for something much more offensive in English, and then fearfully raised her hands over her head.

"I'm terribly sorry to frighten you like this," Catherine said in French. "Or your cat, for that matter. We mean you no harm. Do you speak English?"

The maid nodded her head.

Catherine switched to her native tongue. "Very good, then. Is Mr. E here?"

The maid nodded again.

"Could you please take us to him?" Catherine asked.

The maid nodded a third time, then obediently turned and headed back up the stairs.

"Is anyone else in the house?" Erica asked.

"N-n-no," the maid stammered.

"No guards?" I asked.

"They all are being outside," the maid said in broken English. She seemed so terrified, I was worried she might wet herself.

We followed her upstairs to the first floor of the house, which wasn't what I had expected at all.

It turned out SPYDER didn't own only one house. They owned the entire block. They had bought every building, torn down the walls between them, and combined them all into a single massive home. Although the front door looked nondescript from the outside, it opened into an opulent living room that was completely hidden from the rest of Paris. It was thirty yards wide and two stories tall and opened onto a central atrium that had a lovely garden. The room was all white marble, and the windows onto the atrium were enormous, so light spilled in, illuminating everything brightly. And as for the art . . .

I suddenly realized that I had no longer missed out on visiting the great museums of Europe—because this single room possibly had as much great art as all the rest of them. There were paintings by Monet and Picasso and van Gogh. Sculptures by Rodin and Bernini. Exquisite vases from China and Japan. And a painting that looked disturbingly like Leonardo da Vinci's *Mona Lisa*, even though the *Mona Lisa* was supposed to be in the Louvre.

My fellow spies seemed shocked by it all as well. Catherine gaped at the *Mona Lisa*. "Is that the . . . ?" she began.

She didn't get to finish her question, though, because the maid suddenly whirled on her with startling speed. Her tottering walk and meek persona had all been an act. In an instant, she snapped the gun from Catherine's hand and spun it around so that it was now pressed against Catherine's head.

"Lower your weapons!" the maid yelled, in a voice that was far deeper and more ominous than the pretend one she had used before. "Or I'll blow her head off!"

It didn't sound like she was bluffing. Erica and Zoe, who now had their own guns aimed at the maid, did exactly as she'd ordered.

Four thugs raced into the room. Three were big and muscular, while the fourth was significantly smaller, but still quite menacing: Jenny Lake. They all aimed weapons at us.

The maid had obviously lied to us about no one else being in the house.

Catherine looked extremely disappointed in herself for underestimating the maid, but she remained surprisingly calm, given that there was now a gun pressed against her head. "There's no need for violence," she said. "You may have turned the tables on us, but the end result here will be the same. It'd be best if you brought us to see Mr. E."

"Catherine," I said. I had to struggle to keep from freaking out. Not only because we now were on the wrong end of a lot of weapons in the middle of our enemy's headquarters—although that should have been terrifying enough. I was worried because I had recognized the maid's real voice. I had heard it once before, late at night while on a mission at SPYDER's previous headquarters in New Jersey.

"What?" Catherine asked me.

"This woman doesn't have to take us to see Mr. E," I said. "She *is* Mr. E."

CONFRONTATION

Secret lair of Mr. E
Paris, France
April 1
1500 hours

A proud grin spread across the face of the woman
we had all assumed was merely a maid. "That's right, Benjamin," she said. "Though, sadly for you, this is one twist you
didn't figure out ahead of time."

I was already kicking myself for that. Looking back, it
seemed there were clues I should have caught. The "maid"
had claimed no one else was in the house, but unlike Orion's
palace, which had been dingy and dusty due to the lack of
help, this place was spotlessly clean. The floor was perfectly

polished, the windows onto the garden were immaculate, and the garden was meticulously cared for. All of that should have indicated the need for a team of servants and gardeners, at least some of whom would have been on duty in the middle of the day.

Or maybe it should have occurred to me that, with an organization as crafty as SPYDER, the fact that they called their leader "Mr. E" was an obvious misdirection. And yet the name had worked its way into my mind so that I had idiotically only been looking for a man.

Of course, everyone else on my team had been similarly caught off guard. Even now Mike and Zoe were gaping at Mr. E in surprise, while Erica and Catherine appeared extremely disappointed in themselves for not catching on sooner. And yet the attention of Mr. E remained firmly fixed on me.

"After all the trouble you've caused me, I was expecting more from you," she said tauntingly. "I'll admit, that little trick of yours, coming through the storeroom wall downstairs instead of the doorway, was decent, but now I'm wondering if you just got lucky. Given the look on your face when I caught Catherine here by surprise, it never even occurred to you for a moment that I might have been the leader of SPYDER, did it?"

Lying to someone who had multiple guns trained on me

always seemed like a bad idea. So I admitted the truth. "No."

Mr. E's glee at my predicament quickly turned to anger. "Just like everyone else at the CIA," she said with a sneer. "Incapable of thinking that a woman might be the slightest bit competent."

A different thug came up behind each one of us and frisked us for the weapons we had just stolen from the store-room. Jenny Lake handled Zoe. I got a guy who seemed to be only halfway up the evolutionary tree between gorillas and humans. He was big and smelly and extremely rough with his frisking.

Mr. E turned her attention to Catherine. "You don't even know who I am, do you?"

"I'm afraid not," Catherine replied.

"It figures," Mr. E spat. "I started in the CIA the same week as your moronic husband. Needless to say, I was a better agent than he was. Although that lamp over there would be a better agent than Alexander. And yet that charlatan rose in the ranks, getting all the plum assignments, while I got assigned to a desk in Wichita. I was talented. I was intelligent. And yet I was constantly overlooked and ignored."

"And that's why you turned evil?" Mike asked.

"It's not like I was rewarded for being good!" Mr. E said angrily. "I was working my butt off and no one even seemed to care! So I figured, maybe I'd get a little more respect if I was bad. Plus, it turns out the pay is much better." Mr. E cracked a smile again at the thought of this, then calmed herself. "Sorry for the digression. I just get so worked up whenever I think about the sexism inherent in the espionage game." She returned her attention to me. "So, appease my curiosity, Benjamin. How *did* you finally figure out it was me?"

"Well, Mr. E . . . ," I said, then paused. "Is there another name I can call you besides 'Mr. E' given that you're, well . . . not a mister?"

"No," Mr. E said.

"Really?" Mike asked. "I mean, if you're really upset about sexism in the evil workplace, it seems that not using the feminine form of address is playing right into their hands. Don't you want it known that a woman is running the most powerful, corrupt, and evil organization in the world?"

Mr. E considered that for a moment. "That's a good point. Call me Ms. E." She shifted her attention back to me. "You were going to say how you figured out who I was. . . ."

"I overheard you one night," I said. "At Hidden Forest."

Understanding flashed in Ms. E's eyes. "The night I was outside with Joshua! So you *were* creeping around out there after all."

"That's right," I said. "Although your voice sounded a lot deeper then."

"I use a voice modulator whenever I'm in the field," Ms. E explained. "Just in case some little twerp who can't be trusted is eavesdropping."

"Ah," I said.

"Also, I rarely ever appear in public, and when I do, I dress inconspicuously and make sure to travel with my guards. People always assume one of them is the important one and that I'm only a lowly secretary. Sexism at work once again. You wouldn't believe the places I've infiltrated by merely looking like the assistant to someone else."

The thugs finished frisking us. The one behind Erica had amassed a pile of weapons. He also snapped off her utility belt and took that as well.

The thug behind me relieved me of the grenade I had taken.

"So," Zoe said to Jenny Lake, "I guess you were working for SPYDER all along."

"Of course I was," Jenny said sharply. "Duh. Who else would I have been working for?"

"A rival organization that wanted the information to bring SPYDER down," Zoe replied, just as sharply. "So this isn't exactly a 'duh' situation. Even Murray wasn't sure who you might be working for."

"Murray Hill is a jerk," Jenny said. Then she added, "Does he talk about me much?"

"Not at all," Zoe replied, taking pleasure in saying it.

Jenny looked hurt. "Not at *all*?"

"Never," Zoe said happily.

"Not even—" Jenny began.

"Oh, for Pete's sake!" Ms. E snapped. Although, being evil, she used a different word than 'Pete's.' "Get ahold of yourself, Jennifer! Do you realize how difficult it is to be menacing when you're mooning over your boyfriend like a sap?"

"He's not my boyfriend," Jenny said quickly. "And *I* broke up with *him*."

"Just can it!" Ms. E ordered.

Meanwhile, my mind was racing, trying to figure out how we were going to get out of this alive. We had lost our weapons and the element of surprise. No one from the CIA or MI6 had any idea where we were—and there was a decent chance those agencies thought we were the enemy anyhow. However, instead of coming up with a solution to the problem, I found myself wondering why we were even still alive in the first place.

"I can see that you're wondering why you are even still alive right now," Ms. E said.

I reacted to this, surprised, then tried to act like I hadn't been surprised at all, which probably gave away that I had been surprised in the first place. "Well . . . yes," I said.

Ms. E gave me a crocodile smile. "That's a legitimate question, given how much trouble you have caused me. Sadly, as much as I would like to kill you right at this very moment, I still need to question all of you. You have all had access to information that traitor Joshua stole from me—and I need to know what it was."

I relaxed a bit upon hearing that, though not much. It had bought us a very small respite from imminent death. Our best chance was to draw out the release of what we knew, stalling for time until we could figure out a way to get the jump on Ms. E and her henchmen.

"I suppose you're now thinking that this gives you the opportunity to stall for time until you can figure out a way to get the jump on me and my henchmen," Ms. E said.

I reacted with surprise again, disturbed—and slightly impressed—by her ability to read my mind.

"I have something prepared to prevent you from doing that." Ms. E picked a remote control up from the coffee table and pressed a button.

A projection screen began to lower from the ceiling in front of the *Mona Lisa*.

"Sorry," Mike said. "I know this probably isn't an appropriate time, but I have to ask. . . ." He pointed at the painting before it was covered up. "Is that the *real Mona Lisa*?"

"It is," Ms. E replied proudly. "Originally, I thought I

could get by letting it stay in the Louvre. The whole reason I chose to live in Paris in the first place was because of the amazing museums and galleries here. I do adore art. But the painting was too hard to see at the Louvre. There were always these enormous crowds of annoying tourists gathered around it, taking photos of it with their stupid cell phones, gabbing like they were at a baseball game instead of standing before one of the greatest works of art of all time. So I liberated it from there and replaced it with a copy. Those fools at the Louvre haven't even noticed the difference. Or maybe they have and don't want the public to know. The end result is the same."

The screen clicked into place, obscuring the painting. Ms. E clicked another button. A projection system lowered from the ceiling and began broadcasting video.

The video appeared to be a live feed from a small camera, focused on a small suburban house. The house was two stories and slightly run-down, with an aging car parked in the cracked driveway and a front yard that was a good week past mowing. Overall, it was a rather ordinary house on an ordinary street, the kind of place most people wouldn't have looked twice at or thought was remotely special at all.

But it was special to me.

It was my parents' house.

FEAR

Secret lair of Ms. E
Paris, France
April 1
1530 hours

Up until that moment, I had thought I knew what fear was.

After all, I had certainly had plenty of occasions to fear for my life. I had nearly been blown up, nuked, buried under an avalanche, and eaten by crocodiles. I had faced the wrong end of a gun so many times, I had lost count.

But now it wasn't *my* life I was worried about. It was the lives of my parents. Because of me, they were in serious danger.

I looked back at Ms. E, who was actually laughing at my distress. It was a truly evil laugh; she thought my anguish was hilarious. "It *never* occurred to you that we knew where your family lived?" she asked. "You really thought you could cause us all of this trouble and we wouldn't ever retaliate?"

"Your problem is with me," I said. "Not my parents."

"Maybe you should have considered that before you kept thwarting my plans!" Ms. E roared, losing her cool. "Do you have any idea how much time and energy it takes to engineer the destruction of Antarctica? Do you have any idea how much money you have cost me? Do you know what you have done to my reputation? I used to be respected in the evil community! Now I'm a laughingstock who can't defeat a thirteen-year-old boy!"

"It wasn't personal," I pointed out. "You *were* trying to destroy a large part of the earth. . . ."

"Well, it's personal now!" Ms. E strode toward me, the soles of her sensible shoes squeaking ominously on the highly polished floor. "As I'm sure you realized, the men I have stationed outside your house aren't just aiming a camera at it. They have guns, too. And the moment I give them the signal, they will break in and take care of your mommy and daddy." She picked a small microphone up from the coffee table and spoke into it. "Blue Morpho Team, this is Monarch. Do you copy?"

The camera swung from my house to the face of one of the thugs keeping an eye on it. He was a big guy, dressed as a suburban dad to blend in in the neighborhood, though the menace in his eyes was anything but neighborly. "Roger, Monarch. Blue Morpho is in position and ready to proceed at your command." The camera then swung back toward the house.

"Monarch?" Zoe asked. "Blue Morpho? You're using types of butterflies as code names."

"So I like butterflies," Ms. E snapped. "That doesn't make me any less powerful." She turned on the rest of us. "If you don't want me to let those men loose on Ben's parents, then I want the information you've learned right now—and no tricks! Got it?"

I looked to my friends. The official protocol for a mission was that sometimes sacrifices had to be made. Including the parents of other people on the mission. The goal was to bring SPYDER down no matter what, and we couldn't let hostages get in the way.

But my friends all looked worried for my parents. Even Erica, who had always preached the gospel of not letting relationships interfere with our spying, seemed unsure about what to do. Maybe it was because her own mother was in the room, or maybe it was because she cared about me and thus my parents as well, even though she had never met them.

Whatever the case, the revelation that they were in trouble seemed to have shaken her.

"All right!" Mike exclaimed. "We'll tell you what we saw!"

In the heat of the moment, I had forgotten that Mike might have cared about my parents almost as much as I did. He had spent hundreds of hours at my house over the years, having dinners with us, playing games, watching movies. Once, Mike had even told me that he liked my parents more than his own.

Ms. E looked to him expectantly. "Spit it out."

"Sure thing, Ms. E," Mike began. "For starters, obviously, we got the coordinates for this place. Although that was really all Joshua had on you. Just latitude and longitude. Not any other details, like the *Mona Lisa* or the Burger King or the fact that there was a secret entrance inside a seriously creepy tunnel filled with rats and the skulls of ancient dead people. . . ."

"You're stalling for time," Ms. E said.

Mike feigned confusion at this, even though stalling was exactly what he'd been doing. "Don't you want as detailed a report as possible?"

"Listen up, smart aleck," Ms. E said menacingly. "I suspect you noticed that some of the skulls down there along my basement wall weren't ancient. They're relatively new. Would you like to know where they came from?"

Mike gulped. "Not really."

"Some of them were enemies of mine," Ms. E said, sounding very pleased with herself. "But others were people who were simply unfortunate enough to work for me. The architect who designed this place, for example. And all the people who helped remodel it. And the people who delivered the art. I mean, I couldn't just let them live with the information about what was here, could I? Sooner or later, one of them would blab about it to the wrong person, and the next thing you know, Interpol's knocking on my door."

"So you killed them all?" Zoe asked, aghast.

"I did," Ms. E said. "And for the record, I *liked* my architect. She was extremely talented. So at least I made her death very sudden and painless. She never saw it coming. If you all keep stalling me, though, I won't show you the same respect."

I suspected this was a lie. I was quite sure Ms. E planned to make our deaths as drawn out and painful as possible. And I was also sure, given her rage at me, that she wasn't about to let my parents go, either. But I had no idea how to protect them when they were thousands of miles away from me—let alone how to save myself and my friends.

Luckily, I was with Erica Hale, who excelled at saving people. She locked eyes with me and mouthed, *Stall her*. Or possibly *taller*. Or maybe even *stalwart*. Lipreading isn't that easy. *Stall her* made the most sense, though. It gave me hope that Erica was working on a plan to save my family, or maybe even had one already.

Of course, Ms. E had just threatened to use my skull as part of a subterranean decorating motif if she realized I was stalling . . . but I had to do *something* to save my parents. And there was one thing I could think of that might distract Ms. E for a little while. "There was an awful lot about Operation Wipeout on the flash drive."

Ms. E looked at me in the same surprised-but-trying-to-hide-one's-surprise way I had looked at her before. "Joshua knew about that?"

"He knew plenty." I was pleased Ms. E had bought my ruse—but also worried. I knew nothing about Operation Wipeout except the name, which I had seen for a split second on Joshua's flash drive. Now I had to hide that fact for as long as I could.

"Like what?" Ms. E asked.

"To begin with, there were lots of schematics," I said, forcing myself to talk as slowly as I could. "Not official blueprints or anything. Instead, they were hand drawn. Probably Joshua's. It looked like he might have copied them from the actual plans."

"What did the drawings show?" Ms. E was watching me closely now, her back to Erica. Erica still couldn't attack, given that there was a heavily armed thug right behind her, but she did nod to me encouragingly, recognizing that my stall tactics were working.

"To be honest, I didn't have the time to get a really close look at them," I went on. "There were dozens of them, and there was a tremendous amount of intricate detail. Joshua must have spent hours copying them all down. He had really taken his time."

Erica made a very slight signal, twirling her index finger in a circle, the international sign to me to keep going. She stole a glance at the video screen while she did it.

I glanced that way too, but the scene hadn't changed. It was still just my house, shown from the vantage point of some very dangerous men.

"Nothing's happening at your house," Ms. E told me. "*Yet*. Please continue."

"Right. Sorry. I'm just getting a little nervous, knowing you're plotting to kill the two most important people in the world to me." I took a deep breath and continued. "Anyhow, while I didn't fully grasp what Operation Wipeout was, it was pretty obvious that Joshua knows. He also had some notes about who to deliver it to at the CIA."

"Yes," Catherine agreed, coming to my aid. "Kind of a death-drop scenario."

"Death-drop?" Ms. E asked. Despite her tough exterior, it seemed that she was growing slightly worried.

"Yes," Catherine said. "It's a bit of espionage parlance that must have come up after you left for the dark side. What happens is, Joshua prepares these documents he's gathered and, in addition to placing them on that flash drive, he sets them up in a death-drop e-mail. Only, he doesn't send the e-mail. Instead, if he doesn't enter a password every day, the e-mail *will* be sent to the CIA. That provides insurance against you killing him. If you bump him off, he can't enter the password, and the e-mail goes out with all your plans to the CIA."

"Who at the CIA?" Ms. E demanded.

"I don't know," Catherine replied. "Though I must assume that it's someone you haven't bought off yet. After all, Joshua has the entire list of those moles as well, with every dime you've paid them. I suspect that list would be in the death-drop e-mail as well. Thus, if you take him out, your entire empire comes crashing to the ground. Not that there's much left of it anyhow."

"What do you mean?" Ms. E asked.

"Well, SPYDER has taken quite a lot of hits lately, thanks to this crew of young agents," Catherine replied. "You're really on the ropes financially now, aren't you? In fact, I'd be surprised if you weren't very deep in debt, given the debacle of your last operation."

Anger flashed in Ms. E's eyes. She wheeled on Catherine.

"Yes, SPYDER has suffered some setbacks, thanks to this gang of twerps—especially that one." She jabbed a painted fingernail at me while still keeping her eyes locked on Catherine's. "But I assure you that SPYDER is as strong as it ever was and that it will be even stronger as soon as I am rid of all you pesky rapscallions once and for all!"

Behind Ms. E, on the video screen, there was a groan of pain and the view of my house suddenly tilted sideways, as though whoever had been holding the camera had taken a heavy blow.

Ms. E spun around to see what was going on.

Her thugs, who had already been somewhat distracted by Ms. E's theatrics, now spun that way as well, dropping their guard even more.

Which allowed Erica and Catherine—both of whom didn't seem surprised by the sudden turn of events at my house at all—to launch themselves at their respective thugs, unleashing a devastating series of martial arts moves.

Zoe and Mike responded quickly, wheeling on their thugs as well.

As for me, however . . .

I did exactly the same thing. Except I went straight for Ms. E.

I might not have been the best fighter in my class by a long shot but I *had* learned a few things over the past year.

Plus, my parents being threatened had really pissed me off. And I wasn't about to let Ms. E give the order to kill them if I could help it.

While my friends were clobbering their various opponents, with punches and kicks—and in Mike's case, a very old, very expensive Chinese vase, which he had smashed over his thug's head—I ducked away from the gorilla behind me and charged at Ms. E. My thug came after me, but he was big and slow, and before he got two steps, Erica sent her own thug crashing into him, bowling both off their feet.

Meanwhile, I lowered my shoulder and bulldozed Ms. E. She slammed into a large Rodin sculpture so hard that her head bonged off of it. Her gun flew from her hand and skittered across the polished marble floor.

Unfortunately, Ms. E was tougher than most older women. (Not that I had ever fought an old woman before.) She spun on me, her eyes full of fury, and socked me in the jaw so hard, I saw stars.

I dropped like a bag of cement, crashing to the floor.

Ms. E laughed and came toward me, ready to kick me while I was down.

Which was just what I was waiting for.

Professor Simon, my self-preservation instructor, had devised a new move for me based on the idea that I couldn't fight well, so we ought to play to my strengths. It was called the Wounded Duck. Basically, when someone hit me hard—which Professor Simon was 100 percent sure would happen to me in any fight—then I was to drop, act dazed, and wait for them to come in for the kill. At which point I was to suddenly spin around, catch them by surprise, and sweep their legs out from under them. Or, if that didn't work, I could always bite them on the ankle.

The leg sweep *did* work, though. I probably couldn't have upended one of the muscle-bound thugs that my friends were fighting, but I could trip a relatively small woman.

Ms. E squawked in surprise and crashed to the floor beside me.

I'm not very proud of what I did next.

My parents had always told me that I should treat older women with kindness and respect—though I suppose they had never suspected that I would ever be confronting an evil woman in charge of a criminal organization who had killers poised outside our house. Therefore, I might not have treated Ms. E with kindness or respect, and I might have possibly punched her in the face a few times.

Not that she treated me with much kindness or respect either. Fistfights in real life are rarely as cool as the ones you see in the movies. Instead, there's a lot of writhing around on the floor, trying to get in a good shot at the other person and usually failing. At one point, Ms. E locked both of her pantyhosed legs around my head for a brief moment — which was an experience I would prefer to never think of again—but I then drove my knee into some part of her that made her yelp in pain, and I wriggled away.

I'm not sure if I would have eventually won the fight or not, because Erica and Catherine came to my rescue, Erica prying me off Ms. E while Catherine painfully wrenched the woman's arms behind her back and dragged her away.

I had missed what was going on elsewhere in the room while having my own battle, but we appeared to have won handily. Three of the thugs lay sprawled on the floor, out cold. Jenny Lake was fleeing for her life from Zoe, disappearing down the stairwell that led to the catacombs. Zoe was about to go after her, but Catherine caught her arm and said, "Let her go. We have bigger fish to fry."

Zoe didn't argue, but she didn't look happy about it either.

My friends didn't look nearly as bad as the thugs did. Sure, they weren't completely unharmed—they all had bruises and scratches, and everyone's hair was pretty badly mussed—but unlike the thugs, they were upright and conscious.

Meanwhile, the thugs outside my parents' house seemed to have suffered the same fate. The camera was now lying on the ground, showing a sideways view of my neighbor's pansies. Someone then picked it up and looked directly into the lens.

Jawa O'Shea. Chip Schacter stood behind him, looking into the camera as well.

Both of them were also slightly mussed and bloody, but in otherwise high spirits.

"Hi there," Jawa said. "I'm not sure who I'm talking to at SPYDER, but I wanted you to know that your thugs here have failed to complete their mission."

"Because we kicked their butts!" Chip crowed.

Zoe quietly grabbed the microphone Ms. E had used to speak to the thugs earlier. "Jawa! Chip! This is Zoe! Nice work, guys!"

Chip frowned, confused. "Zoe? You're working for SPY-DER?"

"No, you nimrod!" she snapped. "We've successfully infiltrated their headquarters! We kicked all their butts too!"

"Oh!" Chip grinned broadly. "Way to go, guys!"

I looked to Erica, who was strapping her utility belt back on again. "You told them to check on my parents?"

Erica shrugged. "I thought there was a distinct possibility SPYDER might play dirty once they knew you were on their trail. Like you always tell me, friends are assets, not inconveniences."

Mike grabbed the microphone from Zoe and said, "Hey, guys, it's Mike! While you're in the neighborhood, could you swing by my house and check on my family?"

"Done and done," Jawa reported. "No thugs around your place. Either SPYDER doesn't have all the info on you—or they really just had it in for Ben."

"Oh," Mike said. "Well, in that case, can I ask something else? When you get back to campus, I might have forgotten to feed my goldfish before I left. Can you make sure he's still alive?"

There was some movement behind Jawa.

Before I could even ask him to move the camera, Zoe saw what I had and said, "Hey, can you guys show Ben the view across the street?"

"Sure thing." Jawa shifted the camera.

My parents were leaving the house for work. Neither of them had any idea what danger they had just been in. They were simply going about their lives like it was a completely normal day.

"Don't worry," Chip whispered. "We hid the unconscious guys in your neighbor's hedge. Your folks won't suspect a thing."

They didn't seem to. They just climbed into the car and drove off together.

Still, I cherished every single second I saw of it.

"I hate them!" Ms. E screamed, then shifted her attention to me. "I hate them because they gave birth to you! And I hate you more than I hate anything! One of these days, Ben Ripley, I will destroy you and everything you hold dear!"

"Enough with the histrionics," Catherine told her. "I

want access to your computer now, or I'll rip off both your arms and beat you senseless with them."

"Bite me," Ms. E said.

Catherine wrenched her arms harder. A *lot* harder.

Ms. E screamed in pain. Her tough attitude immediately vanished and was replaced by a much meeker, more frightened one. "All right. I'll show you. You don't have to hurt me."

"Not so tough when you're not aiming a gun at people, are you?" Catherine asked.

Ms. E obediently started across the room. As we passed some of the shattered Chinese vases, Catherine sighed heavily. "Those weren't Ming dynasty by any chance, were they?"

"Yes," Ms. E said, sounding far more upset about the pottery than she had about my parents. "They were worth hundreds of thousands of dollars apiece."

"Gosh," Mike said. "I'd feel bad about that if, you know, your men hadn't been trying to kill me when I bashed those vases on their heads."

Catherine said, "Michael, will you be a dear and truss all these thugs so when they wake up, they won't be able to harm us again?"

"Sure thing!" Mike told her.

Catherine pulled some zip ties from her utility belt and threw them to Mike, who set about binding the thugs' hands and feet with them.

Ms. E led us out of the living room and into a stairwell. It wasn't as grand as the sweeping staircase at Orion's house, but it was still rather nice. Most of an entire brownstone had been gutted to provide the space for it. It spiraled upward in a graceful oval for five stories.

Erica caught us as we started up the stairs, having gathered the weapons the thugs had taken from her. "You forgot your grenade," she said, handing the explosive I'd stolen back to me.

"Thanks," I said, though I didn't really mean it. I had left the grenade behind on purpose. It seemed likely that there might be more trouble ahead for us, but even so, I hadn't enjoyed the feeling of carrying explosives so close to my private parts. Rather than explain this to Erica, though, I dutifully put the grenade back in my pocket.

We reached the second floor and entered a tidy, well-kept study with gorgeous views of Notre Dame and the Seine. The walls were lined with bookshelves, a half-knitted scarf lay across the arm of a plush armchair, and framed family photos were nicely arrayed on a burnished oak desk. It looked far more like the sort of room where a grandparent might write letters to their grandkids than where an evil person might plot chaos and mayhem.

A computer sat on the desk. It wasn't anything fancy. It was even a few years out of date. The screen saver showed the standard photos that came loaded on every computer. Some lavender Post-it notes were stuck to the screen, reminders of things Ms. E had to take care of: "Send card for Tina's birthday," "Order bullets," "Find Ben Ripley & kill him."

Ms. E started for the desk, but Catherine held her tight. "No," Catherine said. "I don't trust you. Erica, handle the computer, please."

"Sure thing, Mom." Erica quickly checked the desk and chair for booby traps, then sat down and woke the computer.

The first thing that appeared was a log-in screen asking for a password.

Erica looked to Ms. E expectantly.

"That's not going to be so simple," Ms. E said. "That's encrypted with a rotating sixty-four-digit code that changes every five minutes for maximum security. The only way past it is for me to press my thumb to the fingerprint scanner you see there, but that has been designed to assess my stress levels and heart rate. If it senses that I'm attempting to access it under duress, as I am now, the entire system will lock down for twenty-four hours. . . ."

"Try UnicornsRule!!!" I said, recalling it from my brief look at Orion's computer. "The U and the R are both capitalized, and there are three exclamation points."

Ms. E glared at me hatefully, in a way that indicated I was right.

Erica entered the code. It worked. We immediately had access to all of Ms. E's files.

"I assumed you were bluffing," I explained to Ms. E. "Erica once told me that the weakest point of any security system is the human element. I figured, even the head of SPYDER probably wanted a password she could remember and would never bother to change it."

Zoe gave Ms. E a disdainful look. "UnicornsRule? Really? How old are you? Seven?"

Now that Erica had access to the computer, her fingers raced across the keyboard, bringing up one file after another. "Let's see what we have here. Looks like that list of double agents. I'll bet that'll make for some interesting reading. Oh, and here's a list of all the leaders of SPYDER, along with their home addresses. I'll definitely want a copy of that." She took a flash drive, jammed it into the port, and started dragging files onto it.

I glanced at Ms. E, expecting that she would be glowering with rage. Instead, she seemed bizarrely happy. Jubilant even. It looked like she was doing everything she could to keep from bursting into laughter.

And if Ms. E, the head of SPYDER was happy, that could only mean one thing:

Something very bad was about to happen.

FAIL-SAFE

Secret lair of Ms. E
Paris, France
April 1
1600 hours

"What's so funny?" I asked Ms. E.

"The great Ben Ripley doesn't seem to know everything after all," she replied.

"He knows enough," Zoe said. "That information's going to put you and everyone else in SPYDER in jail for the rest of your lives."

"I don't think so," Ms. E said cheerfully. "You were bluffing about Operation Wipeout, weren't you? You morons didn't know a single thing about it. You started it the moment you downloaded those files."

A wave of nausea swept over me. I *did* know one thing about Operation Wipeout: On Orion's computer, there had been a warning, right after the code word to access Ms. E's computer. "Watch out for Operation Wipeout."

At that moment, a box opened on the computer screen. SECURITY BREACHED. OPERATION WIPEOUT INITIATED. A timer began to count backward from fifteen minutes.

Erica immediately started typing, trying to stop it, but had no immediate success.

"What is Operation Wipeout?" Catherine demanded.

"Like I'd tell you . . . ," Ms. E said, but then yelped in pain as Catherine twisted her arm again. "Okay! Fine! I'll tell you! It's not like you can do anything to stop it anyhow. It's a fail-safe I put in place in case anything like this ever happened. Once that timer is done, a massive electromagnetic pulse will be triggered, big enough to take out every major city in Europe, as well as those on the Eastern Seaboard of the United States."

My nausea got much worse. We had discussed electromagnetic pulses—or EMPs—in class as one of the biggest threats to national security. EMPs were short but incredibly disruptive bursts of energy. A large one could wipe out all electronics in a city, leading to instant chaos: Cellular networks, streetlights, and air traffic control systems would fail.

"Why?" I asked. "You're already captured. What's the point of this? Just to be a huge jerk one last time?"

"No," Zoe said, grasping Ms. E's plan. "Being a huge jerk is just a side benefit to her. A big enough EMP will take out the computer networks in all those cities. Law enforcement. Banking. The stock market. Everything. All that information is going to be wiped out. We'll lose all our evidence."

"But you'll lose all your money, too," I said to Ms. E. "Everything you have in the banks."

"Who says my money is in banks?" Ms. E asked gleefully. "People *rob* banks. I have millions in cash, gold, and jewels stored in a very safe place. Once the banks crash, the world's economy will be in shambles—and all the records of SPYDER's debt will be wiped out. I'll be able to buy anything I want. Including my freedom."

The timer was now down to just over thirteen minutes. Erica hadn't been able to stop it.

She yanked the flash drive from the computer and wheeled on Ms. E. "Where's the generator?" she yelled.

"Too far away for you to reach it in time," Ms. E replied. And then she actually giggled.

Catherine wrenched her arm behind her again.

"Ouch!" Ms. E yelled. "All right! It's at the top of the Eiffel Tower!"

Understanding came to all of us at once.

"The biggest antenna in all of France," I said. "Right. Where is it exactly?"

"To be honest, I have no idea," Ms. E said. "I'm not the one who installed it there. And in the name of security, the man who *did* install it provided another one of those skulls down in the catacombs. So I'm afraid there's no way to stop it."

"We still have to try," Erica said, more to us than to Ms. E.

Catherine looked to us in response. Her standard unruffled persona was gone. There was panic in her eyes. "It's impossible. The tower's all the way across town. You couldn't drive there in thirteen minutes in traffic, let alone climb to the top, locate the EMP, and defuse it."

"Who says we have to drive?" Erica asked. "Where's Dad?"

"Oh," Catherine said. And the panic in her eyes faded a tiny bit. She shoved Ms. E over to Erica, then snapped out her phone and called Alexander while Erica took over keeping Ms. E's arms wrenched behind her back.

The phone rang. And rang. And rang again.

Mike bounded into the room, blissfully unaware that

anything had gone horribly wrong in the five minutes since he'd last seen us. "I got those bad guys tied up nice and tight," he announced. "They won't be going anywhere for a . . ." His mood immediately sank as he read the tension in the room. "Oh no. What's happened now?"

Zoe said, "SPYDER has an EMP atop the Eiffel Tower set to wipe out civilization as we know it."

"Oh come on!" Mike shouted at Ms. E. "What is wrong with you? You can't go five minutes without doing something horribly evil?"

Alexander finally picked up on the tenth ring. He must have still been in the helicopter, because he was shouting loud enough for me to hear him across the room. "Catherine!" he said. "Sorry. I was on the other line with my mother. . . ."

"That's all right," Catherine said. "Listen—"

"And you know how she can natter on and on and on sometimes," Alexander continued.

"Yes, I'm well aware that runs in your family. . . ."

"I was trying to get her off, but she always has to say one last thing. . . ."

"Alexander!" Catherine shouted. "Shut up and listen! We have a crisis!"

"Oh. What is it?"

"Are you close by with that helicopter?"

"Yes! I'm parked on the helipad atop a hospital. . . ."

"I need you right now. On the rooftop at the location we pinpointed for SPYDER's hideout."

"On my way. What's the crisis?"

"Just get here!" Catherine exclaimed. She hung up, then tossed the phone to Zoe. "You know computers. Stay here and see if you can stop the EMP from this end."

Erica shoved Ms. E into Mike's hands. "And you see if you can get her to cough up anything helpful. Feel free to punch her teeth out if you have to."

"I think they're already false," Mike said.

Catherine, Erica, and I raced out of the room.

"You'll never make it!" Ms. E taunted, then burst into laughter again.

We ignored her and hustled up the circular stairwell. Even though it was only five flights up, I was beginning to feel the effects of our long day. My muscles were tired and achy after all the fighting and running, and the Ding Dongs I'd eaten had barely made a dent in my hunger. I was running low on energy.

At the top of the stairs, we found a grand bedroom with balconies on both sides. One set faced Notre Dame, while the other looked out onto the interior atrium. Catherine threw open the French doors on the atrium side, then scrambled up a drainpipe to the roof, as nimbly as a squirrel.

Erica followed her with just as much skill and speed.

I wasn't nearly as graceful, but with their help, I was able to clamber up onto the gravel rooftop.

Although we hadn't set a timer to match the one on Ms. E's computer, I had a good enough sense of time to know exactly how long we had to stop the EMP.

Nine minutes and forty-five seconds.

It was surprisingly quiet up on the roof, five stories above the traffic and the crowds. Below us, throngs of people swarmed the cafés, the walkways along the banks of the Seine, and the plaza in front of Notre Dame. They all were going about their normal lives, completely unaware that the electricity and the cellular networks and almost everything else they took for granted in their daily lives were about to disappear.

There are not many tall buildings in Paris. Most were shorter than the one we stood on, so I could easily see the Eiffel Tower sticking out over the other rooftops like a toothpick in a sandwich. By my reckoning, it was about three miles away. It looked completely innocent, and yet . . .

"Let me guess," I said to Catherine and Erica. "The Tower wasn't built as a tourist attraction. Some kind of French spy agency built it for security reasons, just like every other monument on earth."

"Yes," Catherine said. "Although Gustave Eiffel was quite

open about the tower being used as an enormous antenna. The fact that it was used to transmit classified information was never much of a secret."

Because of the quiet, we could hear the helicopter coming from far away. It raced along the river, then swooped over the riverbank and set down gracefully on the roof. Orion, still in his bathrobe, slid the door open. We clambered into the chopper, shielding our eyes against the dust and gravel the rotors kicked up. Alexander lifted off before we even had the door shut again.

"Hey, guys!" Alexander said cheerfully.

"Get us to the top of the Eiffel Tower!" Catherine ordered. "Now!"

We raced across the rooftops, quickly narrowing the distance to the landmark.

"And I'll need your phone," Catherine said to Alexander. "So I can stay in touch with the others."

Alexander reluctantly handed his phone to her. "I've almost used all my minutes," he warned. "And they charge an arm and a leg if you go over. So try not to use it unless there's an emergency."

"Like the possible destruction of the world's electrical, communications, and banking systems?" Catherine asked sarcastically. "Perhaps something like that will come up."

Erica grabbed a parachute off the wall and unfurled it inside the chopper.

"We're not jumping again?" I asked fearfully.

"No time for that," she replied. "We'll have to climb down. And we'll need to do it quickly."

She nodded out the window. Before, when we had approached the city, Alexander had kept the helicopter high enough not to draw attention until after we had jumped out of it. Now he had caught the attention of the police. It was probably against the law to be buzzing the rooftops like we were, as two police helicopters were homing in on us.

I helped Erica straighten out the chute so we could use it as a rope.

Orion was staring at us in a way that people generally stared at car wreck victims. Part horror and part shock that we were still alive. "What happened to you guys?"

It occurred to me that we had been through quite a lot in the brief period of time since we'd last seen him, during which I hadn't looked in a mirror. Now I didn't want to. I felt my face and realized that I had a large welt above one eye and a swollen lip.

"Long story," I said. "How are you at hacking into computers?"

"I'm far better at coding," Orion said. "But I'm not bad. Why?"

"Zoe is trying to get into SPYDER's computer to stop the EMP from detonating. Maybe you could talk her through it?"

"Good idea," Catherine told me, then turned to Orion. "Do you have a phone on you?"

"Of course." Orion fished his phone out of his pocket and handed it to Catherine, who entered the number for her own phone.

"How much time do we have?" Orion asked.

Catherine and Erica looked to me expectantly.

"Six minutes and fifteen seconds," I said.

"Oh jeez, there's no way," Orion said.

"You just said you weren't bad at hacking!" I exclaimed.

"I didn't say I was the god of hacking either, did I?" Orion asked. "And even the god of hacking probably couldn't pull that off. He'd need at least fifteen minutes."

"But in the movies hackers are always getting into enemy computers within seconds," I pointed out.

"Yeah, well, they also have talking animals and time travel in movies, don't they?" Orion asked. "Same level of reality."

"Still," Catherine urged. "Give it a try."

"We're here," Erica said.

We had already reached the Eiffel Tower—which was good from a trying-to-save-the-world perspective and bad from a now-it-was-time-to-do-something-exceptionally-dangerous-yet-again perspective.

Alexander brought us in right over the top of it—almost.

He couldn't hover directly above it, as he had to avoid the main antenna.

Erica threw the door open again. Wind tore through the helicopter.

Although I had probably seen thousands of photos of the Eiffel Tower, I had never realized how large the portion at the very top was. It was significantly larger than the top of the Washington Monument or the Statue of Liberty, practically the size of a small house, suspended high in the air over the city.

There were five stories at the top of the tower, two for tourists and three above that were devoted to various antennas and transmitters. The upper three stories were really a large metal dome bedecked with an exterior framework of metal struts, upon which all sorts of electronic equipment was mounted. At the very top of all that, the main antenna jabbed into the sky, as thick and as tall as a redwood tree.

"How are we supposed to find the EMP in all that?" I yelled over the wind.

"It'll have to be awfully big if SPYDER can take out the East Coast of the United States with it!" Erica had already knotted the top of the parachute to the seats inside the chopper. Now she threw the rope end out the door. "Let's go!"

With that, she belayed herself out of the helicopter. She didn't even pause for a moment to think about what she was doing. She did it as calmly as most people would hop out of a car.

I cautiously approached the door. Jumping out of the helicopter with a parachute on had been nerve-racking enough. Lowering myself down a rope hand over hand a thousand feet above the ground looked to be a million times worse.

And yet there wasn't any time to dwell on it. The police helicopters were closing in, and the fate of the free world hung in the balance.

So I gritted my teeth, grabbed on to the rope, stepped out onto the runner of the helicopter, and hoped I wouldn't die.

VERTIGO

Above the Eiffel Tower
Paris, France
April 1
1610 hours

It had been just over four months since I had last dangled from a helicopter.

Turns out it's not the sort of thing you get used to the more you do it.

Dangling from a helicopter sucks on about a hundred levels. It was terrifying and cold and the rope was whipping around in the wind from the rotors, but even though I wanted to simply cling on for dear life, I had to force myself to keep letting go with one hand and then the other as I lowered myself.

The descent wasn't really that long. Alexander was skilled enough to keep the helicopter about twenty feet above the roof of the Eiffel Tower. Due to my innate sense of time, I knew it took only thirty seconds to get down.

It felt like five years, though. Five long, cold, terrifying years.

Eventually, I felt the blessed sensation of something solid under my feet. It was a tiny metal platform without a safety rail over a thousand feet in the air, but still, it was better than where I had just been. I grabbed a random piece of transmission equipment and hugged it tightly before letting go of the parachute.

Catherine slid down two seconds later and alighted next to me with the casual grace of someone who hadn't done anything more life-threatening than coming down a playground slide. "Let's go, Benjamin," she ordered. "No time to lose."

Catherine waved good-bye to Alexander, who promptly banked away, so we were no longer being thrummed by the rotors.

One of the French police helicopters went after him in pursuit. The other bore in on us. It hovered in the air so that the pilot and the police inside could give us nasty looks. One spoke to us over a loudspeaker.

"You are breaking the law," she said in French. "Please remain where you are. The authorities are coming to arrest you."

That was certainly a concern, but I had other, more pressing things to deal with.

I turned my attention to the array of electronic equipment around me. There was a startling assortment of things I didn't know anything about. There were metal boxes with antennas and blinking red lights; big, round, humming things; weird lumpy objects that looked vaguely like robot porcupines, bristling with metal prongs; and all sorts of other technical thingamabobs and doohickeys.

And if all that wasn't enough to deal with, the tower was moving. The wind at high altitude was considerably stronger than it was at ground level, even on a bright spring day, strong enough to make the tower wobble. It was very subtle, so subtle that maybe the tourists below us didn't notice it, but up on the roof, with no railing, I was *very* aware of every tiny shift of the tower. It felt like I was at sea, which combined with my already anxious state to make me feel like I was going to throw up.

So I sat down. I sat and took deep breaths and focused.

"What are you doing?" Catherine yelled at me. She was anxious too, and her usual calm state had given way to near panic once more. "We need to find that EMP generator immediately! This is no time for tantric meditation!"

"I'm not meditating," I told her. "I'm *thinking*."

Catherine started to say something else, but Erica held up a hand, signaling her to be quiet. "Don't bother him, Mom. This is what Ben is best at."

I didn't quite have Erica's confidence in myself, but I also knew that scrambling around the top of the tower hunting for something I had no idea how to recognize wasn't going to do us any good. The far better use of my time—what little there was left—would be to take what I knew of SPYDER and try to imagine where they would have hidden the EMP generator.

Unfortunately, I had only two minutes and thirty seconds left to figure it out.

I found myself thinking about Murray Hill.

Murray was the quintessential SPYDER operative. Not in the way he dressed or behaved, but in the way that he *thought*. Murray never took any risk he didn't have to. He avoided putting his life on the line at all costs.

Being up on top of the Eiffel Tower where I was now, at the mercy of the wind and the elements and gravity, wasn't safe. It was also off-limits to the general public, which meant visiting it would draw the attention of the police—just as our arrival had done. Therefore, coming up there to bolt an EMP generator to the tower didn't sound like something anyone at SPYDER would do.

"I don't think it's up here on top," I said.

"It has to be up high, though," Catherine argued. "So that it can broadcast farther."

"Then it must be on one of the tourist levels," Erica concluded, scrambling down a ladder off the platform.

Catherine and I followed her.

The ladder led us down the exterior of the three-story dome at the top of the tower, until we reached a large opening that allowed us inside the dome itself. The interior of the dome was also filled with electronic equipment, as well as the motors and giant spools of cable that lifted the elevators, but it still seemed too difficult to access and exposed for SPYDER's tastes.

There was a trapdoor in the metal floor of the dome, leading to the lower levels. Erica twisted the handle and popped it open.

"Stop!" the policewoman in the helicopter shouted at us. "You were told to stay where you were! Do not violate the perimeter of the tower!"

We ignored her. We had plenty to worry about besides the police.

A metal staircase spiraled down into a small maintenance room. It was unheated and cold, but being out of the wind made me feel a thousand times better. The room was cramped and windowless. Another, larger spiral staircase led downward, to an exit, while a door to the side had writing on it in French. I could read it, though: EIFFEL APARTMENT. AUTHORIZED PERSONNEL ONLY.

I had learned somewhere along the line that Gustave Eiffel had kept a small apartment at the top of the tower for entertaining guests, and it was now a museum. The door to it had a simple key-based lock. Easy enough to pick for someone who knew what they were doing—like a member of SPYDER.

"Let's check this out," I said.

Even though Erica could have picked the lock in only a few seconds, that was still a few seconds we didn't have. Instead, she lashed out with a karate kick. The dead bolt tore from the jamb and the door flew open, revealing Eiffel's apartment.

It felt as though we had just gone through a hole in space and time.

The apartment was like a tiny piece of Victorian France that had been transplanted into the sky. It was designed to look like it had when Eiffel had used it in the late 1800s, with dowdy wallpaper and carpeting, antique wood furniture, an original phonograph, and light fixtures with Edison bulbs. Three mannequins were there in period dress: Eiffel himself sat at a table with Thomas Edison, while Eiffel's daughter hovered in the background, relegated to the corner.

Around the room there were windows that looked out onto the exterior tourist deck. Lots of tourists were now pressed against the windows, gaping at us in surprise, rather than at the view.

Behind all of them, I caught a glimpse of Alexander zooming around Paris, trying to ditch the police helicopter that was chasing him.

We had ninety seconds left to save the world.

The apartment seemed more like SPYDER's kind of place. It was more easily accessible than the roof of the tower, and it was cozy. Yes, it was visible to the public, but SPYDER had a penchant for hiding things in plain sight.

"How big is this thing we're looking for?" I asked.

Erica said, "If it's big enough to take out the East Coast of the USA, it'll have to be at least a hundred pounds. Probably more."

"About the size of an average human," Catherine said.

The moment the words were out of her mouth, we all had the same idea at once.

We looked more closely at the mannequins.

Despite being on display for tourists, the room hadn't been cleaned too recently. There was a thin film of dust on everything, including Thomas Edison and Claire Eiffel. Edison even had a strand of spiderweb running from one of his eyebrows to the table.

But Gustave Eiffel wasn't as dusty. And now that I looked at him, he seemed considerably newer than the others, his plastic skin shinier and his suit less worn.

Erica punched him in the face.

His head flew off—eliciting gasps from the tourists outside—and caromed off the wall.

We peered through the hole in his neck where his head had just been.

His body was filled with high-tech electronics.

We had found the EMP generator.

But we still had to stop it from going off. And now there were only fifty seconds left.

"Is there a plug for it?" Catherine asked.

"No," Erica replied. "Looks like it has its own power source."

"Is there a switch?" I asked.

"Like an on/off switch?" Erica asked. "I doubt it." She started to unbutton Eiffel's vest to get at the electronics.

This produced more gasps from the tourists. Not only had she beheaded the designer of the tower; now she was undressing him.

My mind was whirling. I had no idea how to shut off an EMP generator, and even if I did, it seemed like it would take a while to do that properly and possibly even involve a lot of tools that we didn't have.

But then it occurred to me that we didn't really have to shut it off. We just had to stop it from working.

We had to break it.

And I had a pretty good idea how to do that.

Unfortunately, I needed to be outside to put my plan into action. There was no door out onto the viewing platform, and even if there had been, the platform was surrounded by a metal cage to prevent people from falling off it. Which meant we had to go back the way we had come.

"Help me get Eiffel upstairs!" I exclaimed.

Erica didn't question me. It was possible that in that moment she understood exactly what I intended to do—but it was also possible that she was simply trusting me.

I grabbed the headless body of Gustav Eiffel under the arms while she grabbed the legs and we raced out the door, accidentally knocking over the phonograph on the way.

Then we ran up the staircase. Dragging a body up a spiral staircase isn't easy. The EMP generator was heavier than a hundred pounds, and the mannequin it was encased in was bulky and unwieldy, but we were cruising on adrenaline now.

We had nineteen seconds left.

We emerged through the trapdoor into the base of the dome and dragged Eiffel to the closest railing.

"Throw him over!" I ordered.

So Erica and I did. We tossed Eiffel as hard as we could over the railing.

It was only after we heard the tourists shriek on the level below us that I realized anyone who hadn't seen us steal the body might have thought it was a real one. So there were definitely some poor tourists who thought they had just seen someone fall off the tower. Someone without a head, no less. Which was probably a good way to ruin a family vacation.

I didn't have time to think about that, though. I leaned over the railing, forgetting all about being scared of the height, desperate to see if my plan worked. And hoping (a little belatedly, I admit) that Eiffel's body didn't land on any unsuspecting tourists.

Throughout my life, whenever I had broken something by accident, gravity had usually been involved. I had accidentally dropped glasses and plates, knocked things off shelves, and crashed model airplanes into the ground, and I figured there was no better way to break an expensive piece of equipment like an EMP generator than the sudden deceleration that came after dropping from a very high place.

And in Paris, there was no place higher than where I stood right then.

The route to the ground from the top of the tower wasn't exactly a straight shot, though. The tower curved away slowly beneath us, and there were two wider tourist levels before the ground.

I hoped that would be far enough.

Eiffel's body smacked off the metal girders of the tower and spun as it fell, like a man tumbling down an incredibly steep hill. The moments of friction slowed it slightly, but it still gained speed, the same way a real body would have. Those bounces off the tower, combined with the wind, pushed Eiffel away enough that he almost cleared the lower tourist level—although not quite.

Instead, the body slammed into the railing, traumatizing a whole new group of tourists, then flipped over and dropped another 200 feet, until it smashed into the ground and burst apart.

The timer in my mind had three seconds left.

I stared out at the city and waited.

The seconds ticked down to zero.

Nothing happened.

Or rather, technically, everything *kept* happening.

The traffic lights and neon signs far below us continued shining. The helicopter with the angry police hovering near us didn't drop out of the sky. The tourists who hadn't been traumatized by the sight of a falling person continued taking selfies and uploading them through a cellular network that still appeared to exist.

Catherine emerged through the trapdoor behind us, holding Alexander's phone triumphantly. "It's still working!" she exclaimed. "You did it!"

Before I even knew what was happening, she and Erica and I were all hugging one another, thrilled we had succeeded.

And then, as my adrenaline drained and the strength went out of me, I sank to the iron grating and sat, exhausted, looking out at Paris.

Erica and Catherine sat next to me. They didn't look nearly as exhausted as I felt, but it still seemed that everything that day had taken a lot out of them.

Catherine called her own phone from Alexander's and turned on the speaker.

Zoe answered excitedly. "Alexander?"

"It's Catherine," Catherine said. "Along with Erica and Ben. I believe we've destroyed the EMP generator. How do things look on your end?"

"Fantastic!" Zoe exclaimed. "The countdown ended at three seconds and said that Operation Wipeout had failed, and now we have access to all Ms. E's files again. Nice work, guys!"

Behind her, I could hear Ms. E's distinct voice shouting very angry things at us.

"Ms. E says hi," Zoe reported. "She's not happy. I think

we have more than enough evidence here to put her and everyone else at SPYDER away for a long time."

Erica, Catherine, and I all were overcome with relief—which lasted an entire half second.

"There's just one problem," Mike said, joining the call. "Remember all those dangerous people who were gathered outside Ms. E's house when we showed up? Well, they all took off the moment you flew away in the helicopter."

"Did you see where they were heading?" I asked nervously.

Mike said, "Unfortunately, I think they're all headed toward *you*."

SELF-PRESERVATION

The Eiffel Tower
Paris, France
April 1
1625 hours

"Think they're coming to kill us?" I asked.

"It's a definite possibility," Erica said.

"Why?" I cried, exasperated. "We've already defeated their evil plans. There's no point in killing us now. That's just bad sportsmanship."

Catherine said, "They might not realize their plans have been thwarted yet. Besides, it was never going to be easy getting off this tower. The French police are still after us. I'm sure they're on their way up here to arrest us by now."

"Yes, but I figured you could just call MI6 and have them explain everything to the French police," I said. "They're all on the same side, right?"

"As far as I know, MI6 still considers us criminals," Catherine explained. "Now, I'm sure we could sort everything out eventually, but I'd prefer not to let them capture us in the meantime. If they do, we'll be sitting ducks for SPYDER."

"We just saved Western civilization!" I exclaimed. "How can people still think we're the bad guys?"

"That's just the way things go sometimes," Erica told me. "Point is, we need to get off this tower, fast. The police *and* the bad guys all know we're here, and right now where we're sitting is a literal dead end." She got back to her feet and headed for the trapdoor.

I got to my feet as well, although I was so worn out, even that was exhausting.

Catherine cupped a hand under my arm to help me. "I know this is disheartening, but rest assured, we'll do our best to persevere."

"Do our best?" I repeated. "Don't you mean, we *will* persevere?"

"Right," Catherine said, though I knew she was trying to cover her mistake. "That's correct. We will persevere."

I took a deep breath, trying to steady my nerves, and wondered how we were going to get out of this.

I started for the spiral staircase to head down it again, but Erica caught my arm. "Not that way. We can't ride down the elevator. The police will be expecting that."

"You're not planning to rappel down the tower?" I asked, worried.

"No. We don't have any rope." Erica steered me to another trapdoor, this one set between the huge spools of cable that controlled the two elevators. "But we *do* have this."

There was a small window in the trapdoor, allowing me to see below us. We were standing directly over the elevator shaft.

Unlike most elevator shafts in buildings, this one wasn't a closed tube. The elevator simply rose up on a track that was open to the elements, but the basic idea was the same: Should the trapdoor give way, we'd have a nice long way to fall to our deaths.

The elevator was on its way up, rising toward us quickly, while the one in the neighboring shaft was on its way down. Both spools of cable were turning, one winding while the other unwound.

I understood what Erica intended for us to do. We weren't going to ride down *in* the elevator. We were going to ride down *on* the elevator.

I wasn't thrilled about that, but given everything else I had done that day, this practically seemed cautious.

Catherine and I stepped back from the trapdoor while

Erica popped it open. Cold air gusted up from the shaft and whipped around us.

The elevator slowed as it neared the top of the tower, then came to a gentle stop a few feet beneath us. We all carefully lowered ourselves onto the roof, taking care to not make any noise so we didn't alert the people inside the car.

As it was, the elevator roof wasn't thick and had vents in it, so we could hear the people inside as they were exiting. They were police. I could tell, because they shouted, "Police! Step aside!" to the crowds as they rushed out of the elevator. Then we heard them racing off, asking anyone if they had seen the terrorists who had landed on top of the tower.

I presumed that meant us.

Erica shut the trapdoor above our heads and jammed a hairpin in the lock.

A few police officers stayed behind to inform the tourists that no one was allowed to board the elevator down until the perpetrators were found.

Then they sent the elevator down so no one could escape, unaware that we were sitting on top of it.

We flattened ourselves onto the roof and held on tight as we suddenly dropped away from the top of the tower. The ride down was windy and cold but only slightly terrifying— and the closer we got to the ground, the better I felt.

Unfortunately, I discovered that our elevator wasn't heading all the way to the ground. We were going only about halfway, to the second tourist level, which was still a good four hundred feet above the earth. In a sense the tower was two different structures: The lower half was the legs, which splayed out at angles to the ground, while the upper half was a vertical shaft. The lower half had two tourist platforms, one at the top and one in the middle between the legs, forming a capital *A*, while the shaft sat atop it. Our elevator was descending the shaft, but to get all the way down, we still needed to travel down the legs. To do this, there were either specially designed elevators that worked on a slant, or staircases.

I peered over the edge of the elevator, assessing the layout of the second tourist level below us. We were heading down to a loading station. There was an extremely long line of people waiting outside it, all of whom appeared very annoyed that the police had commandeered the elevators. A few police were stationed on the second level, probably to keep an eye out for us, but they had their hands full dealing with angry tourists. As we neared the loading station, I could hear tourists berating the police in a dozen different languages.

No one had noticed us atop the elevator—yet. No one had been expecting anyone to ride down on the roof of it.

However, a new squad of police was waiting to board the elevator, meaning that if we didn't disembark, we would soon be on our way up to the top of the tower again.

Luckily, the roof of the elevator was flush with the roof of the loading station. The moment our elevator stopped, we crawled onto the station roof. From there, iron struts slanted gently down to the viewing platform. It wouldn't have been hard to run down them—but we couldn't do that right away, as the struts sloped past the glass elevators and we didn't want the police to see us. So we waited for the elevators to start upward again.

The moment they rose past us, the police spotted us atop the loading station and promptly went nuts. It took them a few moments to hit the emergency stop, pausing the elevator fifty feet above us, but they couldn't simply put it in reverse to come back after us. Meanwhile, the few police down on the platform who weren't dealing with angry tourists now thought something was wrong with the elevators and ran to the doors of the loading station.

Catherine, Erica, and I took advantage of the distraction to scurry down the iron struts and blend into the crowd. Once again, our ages worked to our advantage—as did Catherine's motherly appearance. We didn't look like spies or terrorists so much as a family on vacation—albeit a very disheveled one. We casually slipped through the hordes of tourists while, in the elevators above us, the police could only bang on the glass and shout mutely in frustration.

The staircase in the southeastern leg of the tower was closest to us. This one switchbacked down through the iron struts around the canted shaft of the lower elevator. A lot of disgruntled tourists were streaming down it, upset that the elevators to the top of the shaft weren't working and thus looking to visit somewhere else. We fell in with them and swiftly made our way down to the first tourist level.

For a moment I allowed myself to believe that we were going to escape without any trouble.

At which point everything went wrong.

I didn't *say* that I thought we were going to escape out loud, as this was a direct violation of Twomey's Rule of Premature Gloating. Even the most logical spies at the CIA were superstitious about this, afraid that the tiniest bit of gloating could jinx a perfectly good escape. But I still *thought* it, which was apparently bad enough.

Erica came to a stop so suddenly on the staircase that I ran right into her.

"What's wrong?" I asked.

"SPYDER's here." Erica pointed to the base of the leg far below us. Jenny Lake and a group of thugs I recognized from the British Museum were racing toward the stairwell.

So we abandoned that staircase and cut across the first

level, hoping to find a stairwell that didn't have people who wanted to kill us coming up it.

Given how many tourists were at the tower, the first level was surprisingly unpopulated. Although we were still twenty stories above the ground, the views were significantly better from the higher levels, so that's where the crowds gravitated. Plus, this level was quite large, so the few tourists who *were* there were spread out. Most were congregated at the railings on the exterior, or gathered in the gift shops and cafés, so that the wide expanse in the center was strangely free of tourists.

The middle of the level was an enormous void, an eighty-five-foot square of emptiness, surrounded by glass walkways. Just like the floor of the Tower Bridge, these allowed you to see the ground far below you. Apparently, glass floors had become mandatory for all extremely tall European tourist attractions.

We were halfway along one of the walkways when we got ambushed.

"Stop right there!" someone shouted.

The blood in my veins immediately ran cold. I knew the voice all too well.

Joshua Hallal.

COMBAT

Level one
The Eiffel Tower
Paris, France
April 1
1640 hours

Joshua was with Dane Brammage and Ashley Sparks, which led me to believe that Warren Reeves was around too, but I simply hadn't seen him yet. They had all been hidden behind some racks of cheap souvenirs outside one of the gift shops. Although they were wearing T-shirts, shorts, and baseball caps to blend in with the tourists, they still were an odd trio. Joshua had his metal limbs. Ashley hadn't been able to resist the most sparkly T-shirt she could find. And even the largest T-shirt still didn't fit Dane well; it was stretched so tightly over his muscles that it was coming apart at the seams. I was surprised that neither Erica nor Catherine had noticed them before they'd surprised us—and was annoyed that I hadn't either—but then, we were all tired and worn out and there had been quite a lot of other enemies for us to focus on.

Joshua had his arm extended, palm out, aimed directly at us, ready to fire an explosive charge. Erica and Catherine immediately reached for their weapons, but . . .

"Don't touch those!" a reedy voice said from right behind my ear. Warren Reeves. He was wearing an outfit that was the exact same color as the metal girders of the Eiffel Tower, and he'd painted his face to match, allowing him to blend in seamlessly. We hadn't even noticed him until that point, when he suddenly materialized behind me and placed a gun to the back of my head. "Get your hands in the air or I'll blow Ben's head off!"

Erica and Catherine complied, raising their hands.

I raised mine too, just to be on the safe side.

"Very good." Keeping his arm aimed at us, Joshua sauntered toward us from the gift shop. "Now, please remove all your weapons. Try anything funny, and you'll regret it."

Dane and Ashley followed Joshua. Both of them had guns in their hands, though they kept them close to their sides, so as to not draw attention.

Erica and Catherine started removing the weapons they had taken from Ms. E and setting them on the ground at our feet.

Through the glass floor, I could see the SPYDER agents heading up the stairs toward our level. They all looked to be in good shape, so I figured it wouldn't take them more than a few minutes to reach our level.

Which would be bad, assuming we lived through the next few minutes anyhow.

"You're making a mistake," I told Joshua and the others as they approached us. "SPYDER's people are on their way up here right now. They know you betrayed them. They'll be just as happy to kill you as they are to kill us."

"Oh, I don't think so," Joshua said. "In fact, I think they'll be quite happy to see me once they realize I've captured you. I know you've taken down Ms. E. I know you've got access to enough information to destroy SPYDER for good. But that's going to leave a power vacuum. Those idiots down there aren't leaders. They're followers. And they need someone with good, strong, evil ideas to follow. Like me. Once I show them I've captured the very jerks who brought SPYDER down, they'll be lining up to work for me. There really aren't many job opportunities out there for evil henchmen. It's a limited market."

Erica looked to Dane and Ashley. "You do realize, when

he's talking about idiots who aren't leaders, he means you guys too, right? Are you going to just take that?"

"You're the idiots," Ashley sneered. "In fact, you're midiots. Morons plus idiots."

Dane didn't say anything. He seemed a little confused by the entire conversation.

The SPYDER thugs were several stories up and coming fast.

Catherine and Erica had amassed a sizable pile of weapons at our feet.

"You're never going to get away with this," Catherine said. "This tower is crawling with police, and Interpol is surely on its way. You think you can negotiate a power play right here? You should run before you get caught."

"I'm not worried about the French police," Joshua said. "Or Interpol. There are always people who can be bought. You three moralistic fools are the exception, rather than the rule. And when people can't be bought, they have to die."

I said, "Actually, when you put it that way, I'd be happy to be paid off."

Joshua frowned at me. "You've had your chance to switch to our side. More than once. But instead of taking it, you had to be a Goody Two-shoes and thwart our plans."

"Well, maybe you weren't offering me that good a deal," I said. "I'm willing to discuss terms if you'd like."

"Can it," Joshua warned. "I'm through negotiating with

you. In fact, empty your pockets. Just to make sure you don't have any weapons either."

Up until that point I had forgotten all about the hand grenade I was carrying. I removed it from my pocket. "Sorry."

"Put it with everything else," Joshua said. "And then slide it all over to me."

I set the grenade down with all the other weapons and ammunition, then shoved it toward Joshua. It glided easily across the smooth glass floor, sliding the five yards over to our enemies, although a few stray bullets rolled off in random directions.

"Very good," Joshua said, and then went on to add something else. I wasn't really paying attention to it, however.

Instead, I was counting to ten, which was the amount of time you have to seek safety when you've pulled the pin out of a grenade.

Which was what I had done right before sliding the weapons over to Joshua.

At the same time, I opened my hand, palm out, showing Catherine and Erica the pin.

While I could shield this from Joshua, Dane, and Ashley, I couldn't hide it from Warren, who was still standing behind me with a gun to my head. I just had to hope Warren wouldn't notice.

He did, though.

"The grenade is live!" he exclaimed, right in my ear.

Joshua stopped talking and looked at the pile of weaponry at his feet. His eyes went wide in terror.

Dane and Ashley, who were right nearby, looked awfully scared themselves.

The three of them dove for safety.

Warren was far enough from the grenade that he probably could have protected himself by simply ducking behind me, but Warren was a chicken by nature, so he just ran.

Which allowed Catherine, Erica, and me to run away too.

The grenade detonated, setting off the ammunition under it as well, resulting in a blast that sent Joshua cartwheeling backward—and shattered the glass floor we had all been standing on.

Unlike the glass floor of the Tower Bridge, which had been above water, this floor was above concrete, which would have been far deadlier to smack into from a great height.

Catherine, Erica, and I reached the safety of the metal platform at the edge of the glass floor just in time. So did Ashley, Dane, and Warren—although Joshua didn't. The blast had thrown him quite a distance, but he had landed back on the glass floor—and now, without two fully functional legs, he didn't have the speed the rest of us did.

Instead, he found himself stranded in the midst of a floor that was rapidly disintegrating beneath him. In the split second before it gave way, he glared at me and snarled, "I *really* hate you."

And then he was gone, screaming in terror as he dropped.

I averted my eyes to avoid seeing what happened to him—and was immediately punched in the stomach.

Warren had gone on the attack.

I stumbled backward, managing to catch my balance a second before I would've toppled through the brand-new hole in the floor, and then launched myself back at Warren.

Meanwhile, Dane and Ashley joined the battle. Both of them had dropped their weapons in their scramble for safety, but they were formidable opponents anyhow.

Erica and Catherine met them head-on, Erica taking on Ashley while Catherine fought Dane.

I squared off against Warren. Normally, it wouldn't have been that much of a fight. Warren had been the worst person in our class at combat. Professor Simon had once said that he fought like a sick butterfly. But I was exhausted and aching from fighting Ms. E earlier—as well as everything else I had been through lately. I felt like I had already tumbled down several dozen flights of stairs. But I dug down, finding strength in the deep reserve of hatred I had for Warren. He had betrayed me. He had betrayed my friends. And I wasn't going to let him get away with it.

I lowered my shoulder and slammed into Warren, driving

him backward into a rack of souvenirs, which collapsed. Cheap Eiffel Tower key chains and snow globes rained down on us while I rained punches down on Warren. But before I could finish him off, he bashed me over the head with a commemorative souvenir beer mug, sending me sprawling into a pile of teddy bears wearing jaunty French berets.

Nearby, Catherine and Erica were fighting valiantly against their opponents. Erica and Ashley had gone crashing through a café, while Catherine was using Dane's own bulk against him. When he charged her outside the patisserie, she gracefully sidestepped him, then tripped him as he barreled past, sending him flying face-first into a case full of éclairs and napoleons.

The problem was, we didn't just have to win our fights. We had to win them before SPYDER's agents arrived on the scene, which wasn't going to be much longer.

Warren came at me again, trying to spear me with a large model of the Eiffel Tower. I grabbed my own model and deflected his attack with it, and then we battled with the towers like they were swords, clanging them off each other as we leapt around the racks of T-shirts and souvenir shot glasses.

"I . . . hate . . . you!" Warren panted as he tried to stab me. "Zoe was *my* girl until you showed up and stole her away!"

"I didn't steal Zoe from you!" I yelled back. "You never had her! She wasn't interested in you!"

"That's . . . not . . . true! She was . . . falling . . . for my . . . charms."

"You'd need to have some charms for that to be the case. Face it, Warren, she never liked you."

"She did so! We probably would have ended up married! But then you ruined everything!" Warren screamed in delusional rage and charged me with his model tower, intending to drive it straight through my spleen.

I simply cocked mine back like a baseball bat and then whacked him in the face with it.

Warren sailed backward, smashing through a rack of souvenir plates, and collapsed unconscious to the floor.

I hustled out of the store with the proprietor screaming after me, and found Erica in the café next door, having just laid Ashley flat with a crepe pan.

"We have to go!" I told Erica. "SPYDER will be here any second!"

"Almost finished." Erica gave Ashley a final whack on the head to make sure she was out for good. "Have you seen my mom?"

"I'm here!" Catherine said, racing into the café. She was covered from head to toe with cream filling and icing and had a macaron stuck to her forehead, but she was still standing, which I took as a good sign.

"Where's Dane?" I asked.

"He won't be bothering us anymore. Let's move." Catherine dashed from the café. Erica and I followed her, leaving a gaggle of startled tourists behind.

We all bolted for the stairs at the northeastern leg of the tower, passing the patisserie. Or what remained of it. It had been destroyed by Catherine and Dane's battle. Every chair was broken. The walls were splattered with red.

"Is that . . . ?" I said, on the verge of nausea again.

"It's not blood," Catherine said. "It's raspberry jam. I had to throw Dane through a case of tarts. Speaking of which . . ." She pulled two éclairs from her pocket. "I thought you two might be hungry. I know it's generally frowned upon to eat dessert before lunch, but when you defeat a horde of enemy agents, you deserve a special treat."

"Thanks!" I snatched the éclair from her hand and crammed it into my mouth as we ran. It was probably decent to begin with, but in my famished state, it was the most delicious thing I had ever tasted.

Behind us, in the southeastern stairwell, SPYDER's agents had just reached the platform, coming up from the ground. At the same time, the French police, having finally reversed the elevator, were streaming down to the platform from the stairwell above.

Some of the agents and the police recognized one

another and started fighting. Others came after us.

We ducked into the northeastern stairwell and raced down it as quickly as we could, switchbacking through the iron struts of the tower. Lots of other tourists were heading down too, while a few hardy souls were climbing up. We had no choice but to rudely shove them aside in our haste.

Erica hadn't accepted the éclair from her mother.

"You're sure you don't want this?" Catherine asked. "I know you don't like carbohydrates and refined sugars, but you could really use the energy boost right now. And it tastes divine."

There was a scream of rage behind us, coupled with several screams of terror.

I spun around to see that Dane Brammage was coming after us, clutching a large kitchen cleaver. He was even more coated in icing than Catherine, and a large dollop of raspberry cream on his face made it look as though he had suffered a nasty head wound. The sight of him scared the pants off many unfortunate tourists.

Erica shot her mother an annoyed look. "I thought you said he wouldn't be bothering us anymore."

"I thought I'd taken care of him," Catherine said apologetically. "That man is bloody hard to stop."

"Tell me about it." I groaned.

Dane charged down the stairs toward us, the cleaver

raised over his head like a battle-ax. With his enormous bulk, it was as though a train were bearing down on us.

Catherine took the remaining éclair and squeezed it as hard as she could, firing a stream of cream filling onto the stairs. Either Dane didn't see it due to the raspberry jam dripping into his eyes, or he did see it and simply couldn't stop himself in time. He stepped right in the slick cream, and his feet went out from under him. We leapt aside as he tumbled past us and smashed right through the protective grating at the next landing. He passed from our sight after that, but we heard a few *clang*s and Danish curses as he bounced off the iron struts and then the distinct sound of a very large cream-slathered thug crashing through the roof of the ticket office.

This was followed by a great number of screams. Probably the people in line for tickets.

"We've ruined the vacations of a whole lot of people today," Erica observed as we started running back down the stairs.

"We *did* save the world again," I pointed out.

"True," Erica admitted. "But none of them know that."

Above us, we could hear more people charging down the stairs after us. Whether they were police or SPYDER agents, I couldn't tell.

We arrived at the base of the stairs, reaching the great plaza in front of the tower. The plaza was teeming with souvenir sellers, caricaturists, mimes, and tourists, although everyone seemed to be distracted by the various bodies that had fallen from the tower. I was thrilled to finally be back on solid ground, but there was no time to celebrate.

A dozen police cars were coming toward us, lights flashing and sirens wailing. They swerved off the road along the bank of the Seine and raced across the plaza.

Despite the éclair I'd wolfed down, I had almost no energy left. It was taking almost every ounce of strength I still had to remain standing. There was simply no way I could keep running—and from the looks of it, Catherine and Erica weren't in much better shape.

Just as I was about to give in to despair, however, salvation arrived.

With a roar, our helicopter came zooming in from the other direction, almost at ground level. Alexander piloted it right under the tower and directly over our heads. The wash from the rotors upended the cheap souvenir shacks in the plaza and sent a flurry of caricatures flying toward the police cars, which had to slam on their brakes.

The helicopter dropped to the ground in the gap between us and the police. The door swung open, revealing Zoe and Mike, who waved for us to climb aboard.

We clambered inside as quickly as we could.

Orion was in one of the jump seats, still in his pajamas.

Ms. E was bound and gagged with duct tape in the seat next to him.

"Alexander shook the other copter and came back to get us!" Mike explained.

"We brought SPYDER's computer!" Zoe added. "We've got the list of double agents and a ton of other evidence. They're going down for good. . . ."

She didn't get to finish the statement, as her eyes suddenly went wide in terror.

Jenny Lake was standing only a few feet away from us. Unlike the rest of SPYDER's agents, she had remained on the ground, perhaps waiting for a moment just like this to ambush us.

There was a gun clutched in her hand, and it seemed to be aimed directly at me.

But before she could fire it, she gasped in pain, then pitched forward and face-planted in the plaza. A sedation dart was sticking out of her neck.

We slammed the door shut, and Alexander lifted the helicopter into the air.

"Which of you fired that dart?" I asked.

No one answered.

"None of us did?" I asked.

"Guess not." Erica sank into a jump seat, exhausted, then looked to her father. "Nice timing, Dad."

"Nice work taking care of that EMP!" Alexander replied. He gave Erica a proud grin and, to my surprise, she returned it. Which was the first time I could recall Erica smiling at her father.

I wanted nothing more than to sit down, but I stayed pressed against the window, looking at the ground as it dropped away below us, wondering who had come to my rescue and taken out Jenny Lake.

The police were pouring out of their cars and shaking their fists in rage at us. The souvenir salespeople and caricaturists and mimes all looked annoyed too. Hundreds of tourists were watching the show.

Although one person in particular caught my eye.

It was the one person who wasn't watching us. Instead, he was walking away from the plaza where Jenny Lake was sprawled, unconscious—and away from the police as well, heading for the cover of the trees at the edge of the plaza.

The person had a very distinct, shambling gait.

The police helicopter that had been hovering around the tower all along now dropped in beside us.

Catherine slid into the seat next to Alexander, beaming at him. "Think you can lose these guys too?"

"Sure," Alexander said. "This is all coming back to me. It's just like Karachi all over again. Although I don't have enough fuel to get us back to England."

"Then get us to the French countryside," Catherine said. "I'm sure we can find a safe place to lie low and keep a close eye on Ms. E until all this bother gets straightened out. It might take a few days, but I think we could all use a nice vacation."

Everyone else chimed in enthusiastically.

"Hey!" Orion exclaimed. "I think I own a château in the French countryside. Or maybe it's in Switzerland. Anyhow, you're all welcome to lie low there for a few weeks."

"Really?" Zoe asked.

"Sure," Orion said. "I know you broke into my house and threw my life out of whack and all, but honestly, my life was *boring*. Being forced to lie low because I was working for criminals was lame. I only want to work for the good guys now. You guys are awesome!" He paused a moment, then added, "Er . . . you're not planning to arrest me for working with the bad guys, are you?"

"I suppose we could keep you out of jail in return for helping us take down SPYDER," Catherine said.

The helicopter was now quite high above the ground.

The person I was watching was just a dot down below us, although right before he stepped into the trees, he looked up toward me. And even though I couldn't possibly see his face from that height, I had the distinct sense that he'd winked at me. And maybe even grinned.

Murray Hill.

I wasn't sure what Murray was up to. Maybe he was plotting something devious once again. Or maybe he was just slinking off to lie low himself for a while. Knowing Murray, it was probably something devious, but there was nothing I could do about it at the moment, seeing as we were all fugitives from justice ourselves.

Alexander suddenly banked the helicopter to the left, making an evasive maneuver.

We all had to grab on to the sides of the helicopter to keep from falling over.

Ms. E tumbled out of her seat, rolled across the floor, and banged painfully into the wall.

We raced above the city of Paris with the police in pursuit.

I grabbed a jump seat in between Erica and Zoe. Mike strapped in across the helicopter next to Orion.

Orion was right. My friends *were* awesome. We might have had our issues on occasion, but overall we were an incredible team. We had tracked down and captured Ms. E, and we now had the evidence to bring down SPYDER once and for all as well. Which was something the entire CIA had failed to do.

I was still bothered that Murray Hill was on the loose, wondering how he had managed that and what he might be plotting now.

But I had something much more important to focus on first.

I sat back against the wall of the helicopter, placed my head against Zoe's shoulder . . .

And fell fast asleep.

April 4

, France

Dear Cyrus,

I hear that you are recovering from your concussion and no longer believe that you're in the Revolutionary War. Or that you are a giant chicken. (I'm not sure if you ever believed that last part, to be honest. Erica told me that and she might have been joking. Anyhow, I'm glad you're feeling better.)

I hear you have been in touch with Alexander about the success of Operation Screaming Vengeance, but I wanted to bring up a few things with you:

1) I am still worried about my parents' safety. I know that, thanks to the evidence we recovered on Ms. E's computer, we have revealed who all the double agents are in the CIA, the FBI, MI6, and lots of other spy agencies—as well as governments all over the world—and that those people have all been arrested. And I know that SPYDER has been destroyed once and for all, and that Ms. E is in jail, and that all the other leaders of the organization are being hunted down and captured. But I fear that not everyone will be caught, and even if they are, there are plenty of other bad guys out there in the world. If SPYDER can threaten my parents, so can they.

Jawaharlal O'Shea and Chip Schacter might not be able to protect my family next time someone wants to use them to get to me. So is there any way we can protect them? And while you're at it, can we get word to them that I'm safe and sound and that anything they might have heard about me being wanted for breaking into the British Museum and destroying artifacts was a case of mistaken identity . . . again?

2) While I'm at it, it'd be nice if I—and everyone else on Operation Screaming Vengeance—could be cleared of the charges against us. I know we destroyed parts of several museums and monuments, but that was all done in the name of bringing SPYDER down. Catherine tells me that people are working to clear our names, but that it's bogged down because the English and French are still really annoyed about the trouble we caused. So as a respected spy with government connections, anything you could do to expedite the process would be greatly appreciated. We are having fun here in ▌▌▌▌▌▌▌▌ for the time being, but it'd still be nice to not be wanted criminals.

3) Murray Hill seems to be on the loose again. The more I think about it, the more I am sure that it was Murray himself who tipped the French police off that we were coming to Paris. Yes, it grabbed the attention of the police when we parachuted onto a national museum in broad

daylight, but there are some things about their response that now seem suspicious to me. They seemed to be looking for *us*, rather than some random parachutists, as they recognized us when they saw us. There is no way that could have happened without them knowing we were coming—and almost no one knew we were coming to Paris. Also, I know Murray Hill. There is no way he would ever sacrifice himself for other people unless he had something to gain from it.

I am guessing that he got ahold of Alexander's phone at some point on our flight, alerted the police, and then possibly made some sort of deal with them for his freedom in return for the information. I'm aware that I don't have any facts or evidence to back this up, but I'm positive I saw Murray going free just as we were leaving the Eiffel Tower.

Well, I'm 95 percent positive it was him.

4) This isn't exactly official CIA business, but since you're still down in Mexico recovering, do you think you could get me another T-shirt from Aquarius? The one I wore on my mission got all torn up and still smells like sewage. Boys medium. I'll pay you back. It'd just be nice to have something to remember the mission by.

Thanks,
Agent Benjamin Ripley

acknowledgments

This book, like *Spy School Goes South*, started with a vacation. My family and I went to England and France, where we visited many of the locations in this book, and quite often my kids would tell me, "This would be a great place for an action sequence." Since my children are both very smart, I listened to them. We even spent quite a bit of time working out that final sequence on the Eiffel Tower. (They were not so pleased when I took them down to explore the Paris sewers, however.)

So thank you to my children, Dashiell and Violet, for your great ideas, and to my in-laws, Barry and Carole Patmore, for accompanying us, and to Sir David and Lady Gillian John for hosting us at their home in the Cotswolds, which was not quite as big as the palace in the book, but was still quite magnificent and incredibly fun to play hide-and-seek in. (By the way, I did not make up most of those names of towns in the Cotswolds. They really exist. Even Upper and Lower Slaughter.) Finally, thanks are due to my wife, Suzanne, who passed away tragically last year, but who accompanied me on several trips to London and Paris, all of which provided inspiration for this book.

In the wake of Suzanne's death last year, I foolishly omitted thanking a few dear friends in the acknowledgments of *Spy School Goes South*, so I wanted to make up for that here. I am so thankful to Jenny Grin, Sheryl Gibbs, Tom and Brooke Krasnoff, Danna Young, Marti Noxon, Jeff Bynum, Meeghan Holloway, Carey and Greg Lesser, Barbara Raymond, Deb and Beny Levy, Jeff Still—and, of course, Georgia Simon, who has always been an incredibly loyal and trusted friend (although many people consider her my third child). And thanks to my main support crew throughout the year: Alan Patmore and Sarah Cradeur, David and Tara Stern, Ken Parker and Carol Normandin, Garrett Reisman and Simone Francis, Christopher Heisen and Laura Diamond, Cheryl Bosnak and David Bosnak, Rachel BenDavid and Jon Steinberg, HJ Paik and Bill Johnson, Adam Zarembok, and Kevin Maynard.

Thanks are also due to a few fellow authors and members of the writing community who have continued to provide friendship and support over the last year: Christina Soontornvat, Varian Johnson, Ally Carter, Karina Yan Glasser, James Ponti, Rose Brock, and Sarah Mlynowski. And I simply couldn't have made it through this last year without the help of my parents, Ronald and Jane Gibbs; my sister, Suz; her husband, Darragh; and my niece, Ciara; and our amazing family helper, Andrea Lee Gomez.

My intern, Kelly Heinzerling, did some fantastic research for this book. Plus, I am deeply indebted to everyone on my team at Simon & Schuster: Liz Kossnar, Justin Chanda, Anne Zafian, Lucy Ruth Cummins, Milena Giunco, Audrey Gibbons, Lisa Moraleda, Jenica Nasworthy, Chrissy Noh, Anna Jarzab, Nicole Benevento, Devin MacDonald, Christina Pecorale, Victor Iannone, Emily Hutton, Caitlin Nalven, and Theresa Pang. And as usual, I must give massive props to my incredible agent, Jennifer Joel, for making all this possible.

Finally, I would like to thank the hundreds of readers (and parents of readers) who wrote to me offering support over the last year. When I wrote in the acknowledgments of *Spy School Goes South* about my wife's death, it never occurred to me that I would hear from so many of you. (I guess more of you read the acknowledgments than I realized.) Thanks so much for taking the time to write to me. Every single message means a great deal.

A Reading Group Guide to
Spy School British Invasion
by Stuart Gibbs

Discussion Questions

1. In a classified document, the Operation Screaming Vengeance team learned that they might finally be able to take down SPYDER. While all their efforts to end SPYDER have involved dangerous tasks, what is it about this particular mission that implies this could be the most dangerous mission yet? Do you think the team is afraid? How might they handle fear? Explain your answers.

2. Members of Operation Screaming Vengeance are offered a chance not to accept this mission because the CIA might disavow their statuses as agents-in-training; for those who do choose to move forward, do you think they are making the right decision? Why do you think they choose to participate? Explain your answers. What are possible consequences of accepting this mission? If you were in this position, what would you do?

3. As the novel opens, readers learn that "the key to defeating SPYDER, the MOST dangerous consortium of evildoers on earth, sat in the middle of the dining room table of the penthouse suite." How does it make you feel to learn that an old-fashioned silver key is the key to possibly defeating this evil organization? Do you agree that the key is the answer? Does it surprise you? How does Ben and his team feel about it? What is it about this small key that still feels problematic?

4. Ben stated, "Unfortunately, Murray wasn't the slightest bit trustworthy. Despite how upset he was at SPYDER for double-crossing him, he had double-crossed me plenty of times." Consider what you've learned about Murray throughout the Spy School novels, and specifically in *Spy School British Invasion*. Why do you think Murray continues to behave the way he does? Do you think there is any real hope for him to change his ways? Has his relationship with Ben remained consistent, or has it evolved? Explain your answers.

5. After standing close to her, Ben realized that Zoe was "much more attractive" than he realized. Can you think of any ways in which this feeling presents a problem for Ben? Would you describe their relationship as complicated? Explain your answers.

6. Murray told Ben and his team, "'As I'm sure you know, SPYDER is a tricky organization to work for. There's no honor among thieves, and everyone is always worried someone else is stabbing them in the back. Literally.'" Besides being willing to execute evil plots, what makes working for and with such a group so problematic? How important is trust within a group, and how might you know if you can trust someone?

7. Why did learning Joshua and Dane got the better of Cyrus put the team at such unease? Up to this point, what role has Cyrus played for these spies in training? Now that he's out of commission, predict how they will do without his leadership. What qualities make for a good leader?

8. In what ways does Mike's cleverness help Operation Screaming Vengeance's mission? How does this prove challenging for Ben? Do you believe Ben has a reason to feel this way? Explain your answers.

9. While trying to solve the key's mystery, Zoe told the group, "'The number isn't important. At the moment, I mean. But what is important is that it's in Tottenham font.'" What does this attention to detail indicate about Zoe's potential as a spy-in-training? In what ways does Mike and Zoe's shared passion for typography possibly change their friendship?

10. Ben said, "Until only a few months before, I hadn't even been on an airplane due to the costs." How has Ben's life changed since the CIA recruited him for spy school? Do you believe he's made the right choice by attending the school? Explain your answers.

11. How is learning that Operation Screaming Vengeance is being hunted by MI6 because of the unfortunate destruction at the British Museum problematic? Do you think the group was wise not to reach out to the CIA or MI6 for assistance for the rest of this mission? Explain your position. What might have happened if they had reached out?

12. What are your first impressions of Orion? Given his occupation and income, what did you find most interesting about his home and hobbies? He stated, "'I've always dreamed about having a place like this, ever since I was a kid. But there are some serious problems with it.'" What were these serious problems? Did you get the sense that Orion was happy in his home? Explain your answers.

13. While describing Erica's legacy as a spy-to-be, Ben stated, "'I would have already died several times over had Erica not been my partner on multiple missions.'" Based on what you've learned in *Spy School British Invasion* and other books in the

Spy School series, what makes Erica so gifted in this regard?

14. After Erica asked Zoe about her feelings on the parachute jump, Zoe angrily replied, "'Oh. Now you want to know how I'm feeling?'" Why did Zoe react poorly when she witnessed Ben helping Erica? In what ways does Ben's friendship with Erica complicate his relationship with Zoe? Why do you think Ben didn't just tell Zoe that Erica temporarily lost some of her vision? Do you believe he made the right decision to keep Erica's secret? Explain your answers.

15. Before leaping out of the helicopter, Erica responded to Alexander by saying, "'Thanks, Daddy. See you soon.'" What makes Erica's comment to her father so unusual? Given what you know from the previous Spy School adventures, do Alexander's actions in *Spy School British Invasion* surprise you? If so, in what ways?

16. As the team passed through the Musée d'Orsay, they discovered that hiding in plain sight was actually not particularly challenging. Why is that so? In what ways do they use their age to their advantage?

17. Consider what you've learned about Mr. E, the head of SPYDER, in previous Spy School novels. Do the revelations about Mr. E's identity in *Spy School British Invasion* surprise you? If so, in what ways? How do they change your opinion of SPYDER, if at all?

18. Thinking back to events in *Spy School British Invasion* and the Spy School series as a whole, name your favorite mission that Ben and his team have undertaken. Why has this mission stuck with you? What did the characters learn from it? How did it impact their relationships, or their fight against SPYDER?

Turn the page for a
sneak peek of
spy school
revolution!

DECLASSIFICATION

CIA headquarters
Langley, Virginia
April 16
1000 hours

"I'm afraid we have lied to you," said Alexander Hale. "A lot."

My parents looked at him with surprise for what might have been the twentieth time that morning. They had been surprised when Alexander and I had arrived at their house just as they were about to head to work; they had been surprised to learn that their bosses had already given them the day off so that we could have an emergency meeting; and they had been *really* surprised when Alexander had driven us to CIA headquarters and been allowed through the imposing gates with nothing more than a grin and a cursory examination of his ID. Their eyes had been wide and their jaws agape almost nonstop.

"What exactly have you lied to us about?" my mother asked.

"Er . . . Just about everything," Alexander replied.

The four of us were sitting in a conference room on the top floor of the main building at headquarters. For security reasons, there were no windows and the door had a coded keypad entry lock. There were no pictures on the walls, and every piece of furniture was a bland beige-like color. It was the most nondescript room ever built.

The building we were in didn't even have a name. Everyone simply called it "the main building." It sat in the middle of the CIA campus, a sprawling tract of land in suburban Virginia, about thirty minutes from Washington, DC. There were a few smaller buildings arrayed around the main building, and all of that was ringed by acres of woods.

A box of doughnuts sat in the center of the conference table. An assortment of glazed, chocolate, coconut, jelly, and ones with pink icing and sprinkles. My parents had each taken a doughnut, but barely touched it. I had eaten two already; they were fantastic.

My parents were still dressed for their day jobs; Dad had his butcher's clothes on for work at the grocery store, while Mom was dressed for a day of accounting. I was in my usual school uniform, shorts and a polo shirt. Meanwhile, Alexander wore a custom-made three-piece suit and shoes so polished they were almost blinding.

I said, "Remember, back in February, when I got that medal for saving the president's life?"

"How could we ever forget?" Dad asked. "That was one of the proudest days of our lives."

"Well, I wasn't at the White House that day to hang out with the president's son," I said. "I was there on a mission."

"A mission?" Dad repeated, confused. "What do you mean?"

"Perhaps we should start at the beginning," Alexander suggested. "As I'm sure you recall, around fifteen months ago, I came to your home and told you that Benjamin here had received an all-expenses paid scholarship to St. Smithen's Science Academy for Boys and Girls."

"That wasn't true?" asked my mother.

"Not a single word," Alexander admitted. "In fact, there *is* no St. Smithen's Science Academy for Boys and Girls. And I am not a professor of astrophysics there. Instead, I am a spy for the Central Intelligence Agency—and Benjamin was recruited to our top secret Academy of Espionage, where he has been training to be a field agent."

My parents' eyes grew even wider. Their jaws dropped even farther. Finally, my father managed to formulate a response, although he was so stunned, it took him a while to get each word out. "That . . . is . . . amazing."

My mother turned to him. "You think it's amazing that this man lied to us and that our son has been training to be a spy?"

"Yes!" Dad exclaimed. "In fact, it might be the most amazing thing I've ever heard in my life!" He turned to me, beaming. "We thought you were just going to some boring science school! But you're training to be a spy! My son, a spy!"

Alexander heaved a sigh of relief, pleased that things were going well with at least one of my parents.

Mom, on the other hand, wasn't as easy a sell. She fixed Alexander with a stern look and said, "Benjamin is only thirteen! What gives you the authority to recruit him without our permission?"

"The government of the United States of America," Alexander replied. "Mrs. Ripley, I understand your concerns about this. But there is simply no way that we could have asked for your consent. The whole point of being a secret agent is that it's . . . well, a secret. No one at the Agency can tell their family what they do."

"Even you?" Dad asked.

"I'm sort of a special case," Alexander said. "My father is an agent. And so was his father. And his and his and his and so on, going all the way back to Nathan Hale."

"That's incredible," Dad said. "So it's like your family business?"

"Yes. My daughter is also training to be a spy—along with young Benjamin here. And my ex-wife is a spy as well, but being British, she works for MI6. Although, to be honest, Catherine even kept that a secret from *me*. I only found out the truth a few weeks ago."

"Wow," Dad said. "She sounds a lot more interesting than *my* wife." The moment the words were out of his mouth, he realized they had been a mistake, and he turned to Mom apologetically. "Which isn't to say that you aren't interesting, darling . . ."

"You should probably just stop talking," Mom told him. Then she shifted her attention to Alexander. "So what changed?"

Alexander looked at her blankly. "Excuse me?"

"For the past fifteen months you've been keeping all this a secret. And now it's not secret anymore. What changed? Does it have something to do with the events at the White House?"

"In part," Alexander said. "You see, Benjamin's experience at the academy hasn't exactly been . . . traditional. Normally, our students study and train at the school for seven years before moving on to work at the CIA. But Ben has already been activated for several missions."

"*Several* missions?" Dad swiveled toward me in his chair, glowing with excitement. "You've done more than just save the president? What else? Have you faced any bad guys?"

"A few," I admitted.

"A few?!" Alexander crowed. "Mr. and Mrs. Ripley, your son is being humble. He has faced a great number of miscreants. In fact, he recently helped defeat SPYDER, the most nefarious organization of evildoers on earth!"

"Wow!" Dad exclaimed again. He was grinning from ear to ear.

Meanwhile, my mother wasn't happy to hear this at all. She glared bullets across the table at Alexander. "You let my son confront the *evilest* organization on earth before he even finished his training?"

Alexander shrank under her gaze. "It wasn't like this was standard CIA policy," he explained. "Benjamin kind of got roped up in all this by accident."

I winced, knowing this was only going to make things worse. Alexander wasn't a very good spy, and he was prone to making mistakes. But he *looked* like a good spy, and since he had been the one who had recruited me in the first place, the CIA had felt it made sense for him to deliver the bad news to my parents. Plus, no one else at the Agency wanted to do it.

Ordinarily, my mother wasn't so prone to anger. She was merely being protective, like a mother bear who had just learned that her cub had been recruited by a shadowy organization and sent out on covert missions against hunters. She was gripping the arms of her swivel chair so tightly that her knuckles were white. "Are you telling me that this agency is so incompetent that you *accidentally* allowed my son to confront evil enemy operatives?"

"Yes and no." Alexander took a silk handkerchief from the breast pocket of his suit and mopped his brow with it. "It's complicated. But I assure you, Mrs. Ripley, that young Benjamin here was rarely without adult supervision in the field . . ."

"Rarely?" Mom echoed crossly.

". . . and he has proven to be an extremely adept young agent!" Alexander said quickly. "In fact, if not for his keen intellect and quick thinking, we wouldn't have thwarted SPYDER's evil plans on multiple occasions."

Dad riveted his gaze on me. "Like what? Let's have some details!"

"Well," I said, "remember how, a few weeks ago, you thought I stayed at school over spring break to work on a science project? I was actually in Mexico, preventing SPYDER from melting Antarctica and flooding the Earth. And then I went to England and France to help defeat SPYDER once and for all."

After all that, my friends and I had been forced to lie low in France for a while until the CIA said it was safe to come home. We had only returned to Washington a few days before. I had thought my life was going to go back to normal—or at least, as normal as spy school got—until receiving a coded message from Alexander the previous afternoon, detailing how the time had come to reveal the truth to my parents.

"Benjamin also saved Camp David from being blown up in a missile attack," Alexander added proudly. "And prevented the nuclear annihilation of Colorado."

"Oh right," I said. "I forgot about that."

"You *forgot* about preventing Colorado from being nuked?" Dad asked, stunned.

"It's been a busy year," I said.

Finally being able to tell my parents the truth was a massive relief. Having to lie to them had been one of the worst things about being a spy. (It wasn't as bad as having people try to kill me on a regular basis, but still, I didn't enjoy it.) But it was also satisfying to let them know about everything I had accomplished, and the pride in my father's eyes made me feel wonderful.

Conversely, my mother was giving me the same skeptical look she'd given me when I was six and had claimed burglars had broken into the house and eaten all the chocolate cookies. She was obviously having a hard time believing the stories Alexander and I were telling. "*You* did all that?" she asked doubtfully. "No offense, Benjamin, but you're not the most coordinated person in the world. When you played Little League, you had a negative batting average."

"I wasn't the one who handled the physical stuff," I explained. "Alexander's daughter, Erica, did most of that. She's really good at beating people up and defusing bombs and that sort of thing. I do more of the figuring out what the bad guys are up to."

"He's extremely good at it," Alexander said. "Which is why the bad guys want all of you dead."

The suspicion instantly vanished from Mom's face and was replaced by fear. "What?!"

Alexander paled as he realized he had made yet another mistake. "Er . . . You asked what had forced us to admit the truth about Benjamin being a spy-in-training. Well, this is it. Regrettably, Benjamin's identity has been compromised. Which means that *your* identities have been compromised as well. And thus, any of Ben's enemies can potentially get to you."

To my relief, Alexander did not tell my parents that this had already happened. When I was in France, SPYDER had posted operatives outside our house, threatening to harm them unless we aborted the mission. Thankfully, my friends from spy school had captured the killers without my parents ever knowing they had been in danger.

However, my parents were still shaken by the idea that this *could* happen.

"So . . . ," Dad said, getting his head around the idea.

"We're potential targets for assassination?"

"Yes," Alexander replied.

"Can we tell our friends?" Dad asked.

"No!" Alexander exclaimed. "This is highly classified."

"I wouldn't have to tell *everyone*," Dad said. "Just a few people. Like the Petersons."

Mom looked at him, confused. "The *Petersons*? Why would you tell them?"

"They think they're *so* much better than us," Dad said. "Bob's always going on about his fancy golf club and how they went to Hawaii for vacation. I bet no one's ever targeted *him* for assassination."

"You can't tell anyone, Dad," I said.

"All right," Dad agreed, though he sounded almost as upset about this as he had about finding out his life was in danger.

"The bigger issue here is your safety," Alexander said. "I'm afraid the only way to protect you is to place you both in the Federal Witness Protection Program."

Mom, who had finally taken a bite of a doughnut, spit it right back out again in shock. "You mean, we would have to give up our lives here, move to a different place, and pretend to be entirely different people?"

"Yes," Alexander said gravely.

Mom considered that a moment, then shrugged and said, "I'm cool with that."

The news that my parents would have to go into the Witness Protection Program had not been news to me. I had suggested it myself, after their lives had been threatened. But my mother's response threw me—and Dad, too.

"You are?" Dad asked her.

"Don't take this the wrong way," Mom told him, "but our lives could use a little shaking up." She turned to Alexander. "Is there any chance we could be relocated to Florida?"

"That's definitely a possibility," Alexander replied. "From what I understand, there are entire communities down there that are nothing but relocated federal witnesses."

"I've always wanted to live in Florida," Mom said dreamily.

Dad looked at her curiously. "You do realize that we'd have to give up our jobs?"

"We don't like our jobs," Mom told him.

"And you would never speak to your family again?"

"That just might be the best part of all this," Mom said.

I had always known that my mother didn't get along with her parents or like her job, but even so, her response to all this surprised me. Just as my father's response to learning that I was a spy-in-training had surprised me. I wondered if my parents were thinking clearly. It was possible they were in shock. I tried to imagine how I would have reacted if I had suddenly discovered that *they* were covert operatives; I probably would have been dumbfounded.

Two CIA agents suddenly entered the room. They were women I had never met before. Both wore suits and clutched coffee cups from the CIA Starbucks. One was stick-thin with severe features, while the other was heavyset and round. Next to each other, they sort of looked like the human version of the number 10.

"Good morning!" the rounder one said cheerfully. "I'm Heather Durkee, the CIA liaison to the Witness Protection Program."

"We were just discussing that," Alexander said. "Mrs. Ripley here is very open to relocating to Florida."

"Also," Mom said, "I'd like to work with animals, if possible. Maybe at a veterinarian's office?"

"Ooh!" Agent Durkee exclaimed. "That sounds fun!" She turned to my father. "And what would you like to do?"

"I still can't believe we have to move," Dad said. "Is it really necessary?"

"I'm afraid so," said the extremely thin woman. She spoke in a tone as sharp as her features, like she was perpetually annoyed. "My name is Agent Nora Taco. I'm in charge of—"

"Did you say 'Nora Taco'?" Dad interrupted.

Agent Taco gave him a severe look. "Yes."

"That's a pretty unusual name," Dad observed.

"So I've been told." Agent Taco spoke as though she had gone through this every day of her life and was sick of it.

My father didn't pick up on this. "Is it weird, being named after a food?"

"My family is not named after a food," Agent Taco said curtly. "The food is named after my family. My ancestors invented it."

"Your family invented the taco?" Mom asked, astonished. "I had always thought . . ."

"Tacos always existed?" Agent Taco said. "They didn't. The same way that sandwiches didn't exist until the Earl of Sandwich invented them. There were no tacos until Don Diego Taco came along."

"Wow," Dad said, impressed. "You learn something new every day."

"As I was trying to say," Agent Taco went on, "I'm in charge of internal investigations concerning double agents here." She grabbed one of the neon pink doughnuts with sprinkles and then shoved the box toward Agent Durkee.

"None for me, thanks," Agent Durkee said. "I don't eat gluten. Or refined sugars. Or anything that's a color that doesn't exist in nature."

"More for me, then," Agent Taco said, grabbing a second pink doughnut.

"Unfortunately, we've had a bit of a mole problem here at the CIA," Alexander explained to my parents. "SPYDER, the evil organization that Benjamin was instrumental in bringing down, had corrupted a great number of our agents. That's how Benjamin's identity—and yours—were leaked. Thankfully, Benjamin managed to not only thwart SPYDER but also recover a list of the moles . . ."

"Which I'm currently using to root out corruption throughout the Agency," Agent Taco concluded. There was now a tiny fringe of frosting on her upper lip that made it look like she had a thin pink mustache.

"How could the CIA have let so many agents get corrupted?" Mom asked accusingly.

"Obviously, mistakes were made," said Agent Taco, then added, "By other people. Not me. That's why *I* have been tasked with cleaning up this mess. And, to ensure that nothing like this ever happens again, I am creating a new division at the CIA with the sole purpose of policing the Agency. I'm calling it the Double Agent Detection Division."

"DADD?" I said.

"Yes?" my father asked.

"Sorry," I said. "I wasn't talking to you. I was referring to the acronym of the division: DADD."

"Yes?" my father asked again.

Agent Taco sighed. "I might have to rethink the division name."

"Ooh!" Agent Durkee said excitedly. "You could call it the Mole Patrol!"

"I will do no such thing," Agent Taco said flatly. "Anyhow, I'm assembling an elite team to track down and neutralize any agents who have been corrupted."

"But the damage has already been done where you're concerned," Agent Durkee told my parents. "The best we can do now is to relocate you. I apologize for the inconvenience."

"Inconvenience?" Dad echoed. "It's a bit more than that. You're asking us to give up everything!"

"I know," Agent Durkee said. "But I promise we are going to do everything possible to protect you from now on. That's why we decided to have this meeting here, at CIA headquarters, rather than at your home. This building is the most secure facility in America. You're as safe as—"

The air was suddenly split by the scream of something moving very fast, after which came the sound of an explosion extremely close by. The entire room shook. A lighting fixture fell out of the ceiling and landed on the doughnuts with such force that all the jelly-filled ones exploded.

"Take cover!" Alexander Hale shouted. "We're under attack!"

Apparently, we weren't nearly as safe as the CIA had hoped.

Looking for another great book?
Find it
IN THE MIDDLE.

Fun, fantastic books for kids
in the in-be**TWEEN** age.

IntheMiddleBooks.com

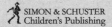